Date: 5/11/21

GRA ISUKARI
Isukari, Yuba,
Yokohama Station SF /

PALM BEACH COUNTY
LIBRARY SYSTEM
3650 SUMMIT BLVD.
WEST PALM BEACH, FL 33406

YOKOHAMA STATION SF

YUBA ISUKARI

Illustration by
Tatsuyuki Tanaka

YEN
ON
NEW YORK

Yuba Isukari

Translation by Stephen Paul
Cover art by Tatsuyuki Tanaka

This book is a work of fiction. Names, characters, places, and incidents are the product of
the author's imagination or are used fictitiously. Any resemblance to actual events, locales, or
persons, living or dead, is coincidental.

YOKOHAMA EKI SF
©Yuba Isukari, Tatsuyuki Tanaka 2016
First published in Japan in 2016 by KADOKAWA CORPORATION, Tokyo.
English translation rights arranged with KADOKAWA CORPORATION, Tokyo, through
TUTTLE-MORI AGENCY, INC., Tokyo.

English translation © 2021 by Yen Press, LLC

Yen Press, LLC supports the right to free expression and the value of copyright.
The purpose of copyright is to encourage writers and artists to produce the creative
works that enrich our culture.

The scanning, uploading, and distribution of this book without permission is a theft of the
author's intellectual property. If you would like permission to use material from the book (other
than for review purposes), please contact the publisher. Thank you for your support of the
author's rights.

Yen On
150 West 30th Street, 19th Floor
New York, NY 10001

Visit us at yenpress.com ❖ facebook.com/yenpress ❖ twitter.com/yenpress
yenpress.tumblr.com ❖ instagram.com/yenpress

First Yen On Edition: March 2021

Yen On is an imprint of Yen Press, LLC.
The Yen On name and logo are trademarks of Yen Press, LLC.

The publisher is not responsible for websites (or their content) that are not owned
by the publisher.

Library of Congress Cataloging-in-Publication Data
Names: Isukari, Yuba, author. | Tanaka, Tatsuyuki, illustrator. | Paul, Stephen (Translator),
    translator.
Title: Yokohama Station SF / Yuba Isukari ; illustration by Tatsuyuki Tanaka ; translation by
    Stephen Paul.
Other titles: Yokohama-eki SF. English
Description: First Yen On edition. | New York : Yen On, 2021. | Audience: Ages 13+
Identifiers: LCCN 2020056569 | ISBN 9781975319519 (hardcover) | ISBN 9781975319526 (ebook)
Subjects: CYAC: Science fiction.
Classification: LCC PZ7.1.I896 Yo 2021 | DDC [Fic]—dc23
LC record available at https://lccn.loc.gov/2020056569

ISBNs: 978-1-9753-1951-9 (hardcover)
       978-1-9753-1952-6 (ebook)

10 9 8 7 6 5 4 3 2 1

LSC-C

Printed in the United States of America

YOKOHAMA STATION SF **CONTENTS** :::

YUBA ISUKARI PRESENTS

1. A Clockwork Ticket

Mt. Fuji was black that morning.

Yesterday, it had been white, covered in concrete, but the mountain's surface had turned escalator black overnight. It was a sign that the long rainy season was over and summer had arrived.

"It's affected by the incline," said the professor, who looked in the mountain's direction as he sat on the shore. "The structural genetic field is written to form escalators where the incline passes a certain angle. At the same time, it deploys concrete roofing during periods of continual rain. Because of weather discrepancies between the peak and base of Mt. Fuji, you'll see layers of escalator and concrete across its slope, like a piecrust. This is the principle behind White Fuji and Black Fuji."

"Uh-huh," grunted Hiroto Mishima. He understood almost nothing of what the professor had said, but he replied anyway. Keeping the lonely old man company was one of his jobs.

The partly senile man they called the "professor" had shown up in Ninety-Nine Steps about twenty years ago. Hiroto had been very young when he'd found the man crumpled up like a rag at the foot of the escalator, though he didn't remember that anymore.

Back then, the professor had sported black hair and a crisp mind, but they'd barely been able to understand each other. On the Inside, he must have lived in a region quite far from the cape.

About the only thing Hiroto could understand was that the man had been a "professor" at a place Inside called the "Lab." If he'd gotten kicked out of Yokohama Station, it must've been for a fraudulent Suika credential. Every now and then, the station would spit out unauthorized users like him, along with the waste goods, at the cape.

Hiroto didn't know for sure what the professor had done to get kicked out, however, and by the time the old man had grown accustomed to the language of the cape, his mind had started to slip.

After delivering his speech about the layers of Mt. Fuji and the principles behind Yokohama Station's expansion, the professor looked over to gauge his audience's response. Only then did he recognize that it was Hiroto to whom he was lecturing.

"You were leaving today," he said.

"Yeah. Thanks for everything."

"Same to you."

The cape where Hiroto lived was located at the foot of a long, long escalator—two lanes, both descending—coming from Yokohama Station Exit 1415, which is how it got the name Ninety-Nine Steps. The escalator actually had many, many more steps than that. If you stopped to rest while climbing against the escalator's descending rotation, it would send you back down in no time. Climbing all the way to the top of the Ninety-Nine Steps was a test of courage for the children of the cape—proof you'd finally come of age.

At the top of the escalator was a dump they called the flower field. After walking across it for a while, you would reach the ticket gates of Yokohama Station, the entrance to the Inside. To Hiroto and the other children, that was the extent of the world. They were born outside of the station and didn't have Suika memberships, so they couldn't get Inside. Aside from sailing a boat to trade with one of the other colonies dotting the shoreline, they were destined to spend their entire lives clinging to the cape.

"Hey. You going?"

Yosuke was at the top of the escalator. He was a cleaner here at the flower field, making use of the garbage dumped out of Yokohama

Station. Every day, things like expired food and mechanical parts came flowing out of the station. The cleaners sifted through it for anything that could be used and sent whatever was salvageable down the escalator, tossing everything else into the dust chute near the entrance gates. Nobody knew where the dust chute went.

"Signal's strong today. A new tower must have grown nearby. Weather's good, too. The right kind of day to leave on a trip," Yosuke remarked, banging away on a terminal keyboard. The towers for Yokohama Station's internal network, Suikanet, were only found Inside. If you were somewhere very close, though, like the flower field, sometimes you could pick up stray signal waves. Unfortunately, the tower locations changed from moment to moment, making the signal volatile and inconsistent.

"Check it out. I got this picture from the net. A climber must've taken it," Yosuke said, pointing at an image of a sign. It was one of the common internal guideposts. It read: YOKOHAMA STATION, HIGHEST ELEVATION - 4,012 METERS ABOVE THE SEA.

"At the peak of Mt. Fuji?" Hiroto asked.

"Yeah. The natural peak is only about 3,800 meters, I hear. The station keeps piling up higher, though, and now it's over 4,000," Yosuke replied.

Black Fuji was visible from the windows of the flower field. The mountain had once been a volcano with snow, soil, and all the rest. In the two hundred years since Yokohama Station had started expanding, however, there were virtually no natural mountains left on the island of Honshu.

"So did you find what I asked you for? Detailed maps of the station and stuff?" Hiroto inquired.

"I tried but had no luck. All this system does is trawl for packets coming off the Suikanet, so I can't tell it to look for specific information. If I had proper Suika authorization, I'm sure I could do a lot more," Yosuke answered longingly, switching the image on the screen. It displayed a diagram. "This is the latest map I've found. Just a partial layout from twenty years ago. Based on the location names, I think it's around the Oshika Peninsula in Miyagi. Want to take it?"

Hiroto only grimaced.

"Yeah, you'll have better luck looking for one in there. I'm sure the information for Inside residents is much better than out here," remarked Yosuke.

"That's true," Hiroto said, scratching his cheek. Yosuke took a slug of flat cola. "Yosuke, you should go back down sometime. Your mom's worried."

"No way. All I do is eat and sleep these days; my legs have gone soft. I'll never get back up the escalator if I go down now."

Yosuke's body was much rounder than it had been the previous time Hiroto had seen him, at the end of last year. It was impossible to recognize the boy he'd once raced to see who could get to the top of the escalator first.

"What about you?" Yosuke asked. "You're just going to leave Maki behind? You could have asked her to come with you."

"An 18 Ticket lasts five days for one person. If I split it two ways, the time is halved. That's what Higashiyama told me."

"Uh-huh. Well, if you never come back, I'll take care of her for you."

"How about you take care of yourself first. Find something else to do with your life aside from eating what comes out of here," Hiroto said.

"Nah, it's fine. We're the ones supporting life in Ninety-Nine Steps. The people below get it," Yosuke insisted, cackling.

Those living on the cape farmed what little land they had and sent out boats for fishing and trade. Like Yosuke, some also cleaned the garbage, but there wasn't nearly enough work to go around. For one thing, the amount of food dumped from Yokohama Station was far more than needed to support the number of people on the tiny spit of land. Hiroto didn't have a steady job there, so he typically spent his days staring out at the sea and keeping the professor company.

One constant concern was the relative uncertainty around the food that Yokohama Station dumped. If the flow of garbage changed due to some whim of the station, it could mean the end of the food supply in Ninety-Nine Steps. Stories told of more than a few colonies that had died out this way.

"A life independent of the station," the village elder liked to urge, but in reality, the food they produced on their own was just a pittance, a way to pass the time. Several of the villagers sardonically called themselves "Yokohama Station livestock." Hiroto thought livestock were supposed to serve a purpose for the station in that case, but he couldn't begin to imagine what would be considered meaningful to the megastructure.

Hiroto left Yosuke's side and headed for the entrance. The automated turnstiles threw up their arms to block his way in.

"suika not recognized. please present your suika credentials or a valid entrance ticket," demanded the six turnstiles in unison. The feminine voice did not match their stark, metallic bodies.

"I've got this." Hiroto removed a small box-shaped device from his pocket.

"18 ticket detected. it will be valid for five days from this point on, once activated. when the five days are over, you will be removed from the station. please touch the screen to indicate that you agree to these terms."

A button reading, I AGREE TO THESE TERMS AND CONDITIONS, appeared on the turnstile's face panel. Hiroto tapped it.

"welcome to yokohama station," it said. "thank you for your visit."

The arms of the turnstiles slowly, heavily lowered. Hiroto squeezed through and went Inside. It was his first time entering Yokohama Station and the first visit for any Ninety-Nine Steps resident in decades.

◆

The man from the Dodger Alliance showed up at Ninety-Nine Steps about a year before Hiroto left. The fishermen had rescued the thirty-year-old man and brought him to the cape. He was small and pale—traits shared by many Insiders—with narrow eyes that made him look like a fox. He called himself Higashiyama.

Yokohama Station pushed up against the coast everywhere around the cape, but there was enough space to walk along it during low tide. Despite being tagged for Suika violation, the outcast had managed to evade the automated turnstiles, until they'd eventually caught him near Kamakura and spit him out at the shore. He'd walked all the way to Ninety-Nine Steps from there, in search of civilization.

"I'm one of the lucky ones. The rest of my alliance got caught by the turnstiles inland. I managed to escape all the way to the coast."

"What happens if you get caught inland?" Hiroto had asked.

Higashiyama's expression had twisted in disbelief at Hiroto's ignorance as he answered, "The turnstiles don't just kill you for unauthorized use. They'll knock you out with tranquilizers or tie you up with ropes, then toss you into the nearest spot outside of the station. That's what makes it so bad if you get caught inland."

Even now, when Yokohama Station covered nearly all of Honshu, there were places inland where the ground gave way into holes unoccupied by the structure. These were known as "station hollows."

When automated turnstiles caught unauthorized visitors, they mechanically transported and ejected them into the nearest hollow. In most cases, these were barren, mountainous regions with nothing to eat. Once stuck there, one's only option was to wait to die from cold and hunger.

If you were exiled at the coast, however, you stood a chance of happening upon a human settlement by walking along the shoreline. That was why this man had snuck past the automated turnstiles and fled for his life toward the coast.

"My crime was rebellion against Yokohama Station," Higashiyama had boasted. He seemed to think he was better than your average violator.

It wasn't rare for Suika exiles to wash up at Ninety-Nine Steps. The most common reason for getting kicked out was "causing trouble for employees or fellow guests" by harming or killing other people. The second-most common crime was "destruction of property."

Many of these exiles were from the bottom rung of Inside society, and while people like the professor—who couldn't even speak the same language—were rare, most of them didn't want to talk about their stories once they were at the cape. Consequently, the people of Ninety-Nine Steps barely knew anything about what went on Inside.

Higashiyama was a rare exception, as he was exceedingly chatty. Plenty of people, including Hiroto, had gathered to hear him talk at first. He informed them that he was a member of a group called the Dodger Alliance.

"So what's the point of that alliance?" someone had asked.

"What's the point? What else would it be? To free humanity from Yokohama Station's control," Higashiyama replied. Hiroto didn't understand why that was so obvious, but he was willing to take the man's word for it.

"What does that mean, 'free humanity'? You're not talking about just going outside of the station? You had a Suika, so you could come and go as you please."

"You might find it difficult to understand," Higashiyama began, "But originally, humanity controlled the station. Our leader always said, 'Let's put an end to this life of being dominated by the station.' You've got to move past this miserable existence of sifting through the refuse it dumps on you."

Higashiyama always talked down to the people of Ninety-Nine Steps like this, and those who'd initially been fascinated by his stories eventually lost interest. After a few months, only Hiroto would go to listen to him.

Eventually, winter arrived, and Higashiyama's health deteriorated. It was common for people who came from Inside to have trouble bearing the outside environment. The professor gave some complicated explanation involving the term "immune system," but all Hiroto really took away from it was that the people who grew up in the ideal Inside environment had weak constitutions.

"I need to ask you to do something." Higashiyama made a request of Hiroto when things really took a turn for the worse. "I want you to save our leader, who's still in Yokohama Station, hiding from the turnstiles. Everyone else has been caught. You're the only one I can ask."

"Help? What do you mean?" Hiroto prompted.

Higashiyama pressed a little palm-sized box device into Hiroto's hand. "That's an 18 Ticket. We found it on one of the older floors Inside. With this, even someone without a Suika implant has free access to the station."

Hiroto took it. The 18 Ticket was hefty for its size. The little screen read, *Valid period: Five days after activation.*

"Our leader's a genius. If anyone can find a way to free the Inside and this village from Yokohama Station, it's them."

That was the last thing Higashiyama said before he died.

The first person Hiroto told about the 18 Ticket was the cape's elder. He thought that if the valid period was five days for one person, perhaps they should find someone better suited for it than he was.

However, the elder had insisted, "You've always talked about wanting to see the Inside world, ever since you were a child. You should go."

No one else argued for the ticket, either. If any of them were curious about Inside, the thought of the terrifying faces of the turnstiles caused them to shrink from the idea.

The only person who expressed displeasure at the notion of Hiroto's journey was the elder's niece, Maki. When he told her about the scheme at his house, she'd asked, "Why would you do something so dangerous? You don't owe Higashiyama any favors." She was furious that Hiroto had decided to go off on his own without her input.

"It's not out of obligation. I just want to go. Helping his group's leader or whatever is just the cost of admission. I don't even know where this 'leader' is," Hiroto admitted.

"I see. You always hated this cape. You were just waiting for an opportunity to escape, and here it is."

"…I'll come back. I mean, I can only be Inside for five days."

"You should find some other exit, then, and spend the rest of your life over there. It's what you've always wanted," Maki had spat. Then, she stormed out of the house. Not a moment later, Hiroto's neighbor, the professor, appeared. The shouting had roused him. Hiroto told him about the 18 Ticket and his decision to go Inside.

"Oooh. So you're going on a journey Inside," the professor had remarked. Typically, his mind was distant and his eyes stared far away, but in that instant, he was sharp and present.

"Yeah."

"Will you be back for dinner?"

"That's the plan. I just don't know which dinner."

"When are you going?"

"Once I'm ready for it."

"Where are you going?"

"I haven't decided yet. I'm supposed to search for someone, but I don't know where they are."

"Go to Exit 42."

"…42."

"You'll find the answers to everything there."

Hiroto didn't know what it was the professor was talking about. His mind was very soft these days, and he often spoke nonsense. There were moments like these, when his words carried great certainty, however, as though delivering a prophecy.

"Exit 42. Where is that?" Hiroto asked.

"Yokohama Station."

"Yokohama Station is everywhere."

"That's right. It's everywhere. It's there, too," the professor replied, pointing at the escalator. Following his finger led the eye to a sign for YOKOHAMA STATION EXIT 1415.

Hiroto gathered up his belongings—which didn't take very long. He looked for anything that could be used as a weapon, but he owned nothing that would help him against the automated turnstiles. Even the fishermen's harpoons wouldn't do him much good if they alarmed the Insiders. Ultimately, he just took enough food and water for the trip, a few personal items, and his favorite shoulder bag.

"You wanna use the elevator, it's five hundred milliyen," said the annoyed, fat, middle-aged woman before the door. These were the first words Hiroto heard uttered by a human being Inside.

"Eight hundred for a round trip. That's a deal—it'll take you two hours to walk all the way to Kurihama."

Hiroto had been walking north for thirty minutes, up Yokohama Station Corridor 5772156, which led away from Ninety-Nine Steps. He'd imagined Inside being a bustling, active place, but nothing could've been further from the truth. The only things wandering around besides him were the automated turnstiles. He was starting to get worried when he finally came across a living person: this elevator manager.

"Elevator?" Hiroto asked her. He was looking at a metal door with a glass window, through which he could see a small coffin-like room, about one meter tall and three meters wide. The door opened up and down, apparently. A placard read, OCCUPANCY: 6, but it was sideways, for some reason.

"It's a vehicle?" Hiroto asked.

"That's right. You never been on an elevator before? Get in this, and it'll take you twenty minutes to get to Kurihama. Less than ten years since it grew, so it's an easy ride, not much shaking."

Hiroto had heard of the place called Kurihama. It was on the coast if you sailed east from Ninety-Nine Steps by boat, but Yokohama Station cramped the land tightly to the water thereabouts, and no one would dare settle there. There was only a shed where the cape's fishers stored some tools, and in the summer, residents from Inside sometimes came out to swim.

"No, I don't want to go there. I'm looking for directions. Do you know where Exit 42 is?"

"Forty-two? I've never even heard of a number that low. If you want directions, you should use that terminal there," the woman explained, pointing down the corridor. There was a machine there, like one of the automated turnstiles without arms. Its legs were attached to the wall, so this was not one of the mobile types.

"There's plenty of people in Yokosuka, so you could try asking there, too."

"Yokosuka. Is there an elevator to get there?"

"Not that I've ever seen. Elevators never grow where you really need them, and if they do, the big companies and yakuza fight over them." The large woman sighed. "My husband was the first person to find this one, but hardly anyone comes here. It's an easy job, but we get almost nothing from it. My husband was a station explorer, and he was so excited about finding treasure buried under here. Now I wish he'd found himself a better job, because this elevator was about the only useful thing he discovered."

The woman had probably been guarding this elevator all on her own and was dying for someone to talk to again.

"You shouldn't wander around too much, dressed all strange like that. The staff is all on edge lately, what with the saboteurs from the north around."

"Staff? What's that?" Hiroto asked, much to the woman's surprise.

"You don't know what staff are? They're the ones who capture people who do bad things," she explained with a tone one would've used with a child.

"You mean the automated turnstiles?"

"What? What are you talking about? Why would the automated turnstiles be staff?"

"Oh, of course. I get it now. Thanks." Hiroto ended the conversation there. He didn't want to expose too much of his ignorance and reveal that he was from outside, without a Suika. Perhaps an update in wardrobe was in order as well. His outfit was a patchwork of clothes dumped from Yokohama Station, so it was probably old-fashioned by Inside standards.

The fixed terminal had grown a long time ago. The paint was peeling from its cabinet, and the metal parts were rusting here and there. When Hiroto touched the screen, it came to life and displayed a colorful menu title that read, YOKOHAMA STATION SUIKANET ☆ KIOSK TERMINAL. Below this were two touch-screen buttons.

USE AS A PAID MEMBER (SUIKA MEMBERSHIP REQUIRED)

USE FOR FREE (AD VIDEO WILL PLAY)

Hiroto hit the free option. Bright, happy music began blaring loudly from the speakers on the side of the screen. On the display itself was a video of the familiar sight of Black Fuji. The escalator steps were clearly visible. The footage had been taken from somewhere much closer to the mountain than Ninety-Nine Steps.

"This summer, why not take the whole family to Mt. Fuji? Its elevation rises year after year and it currently stands at 4,050 meters. If you've climbed it before, why not set a new record? Escalators along all routes make it easy for children and seniors! We offer plans with food and lodging included, starting at 35,000 milliyen per person. For more details, reach out to Suika-net #0120-XXX-XXX."

With obnoxious fanfare, the commercial ended abruptly, and the screen switched back to the menu.

"How can we help? (1) Looking for an object (2) Looking for a person (3) Looking for a place (4) Looking for work (5) Keyword search (6) Return to the home screen."

Hiroto mulled over the idea of searching for Higashiyama's leader with the second option, but if that person was on the run from the automated turnstiles, Suikanet probably wouldn't find them, and doing so might put Hiroto himself in danger. Instead, he chose *Looking for a place.*

"Tell me where Exit 42 is," Hiroto spoke into the mic.

"searching for exit 42..."

An hourglass icon spun on the screen for ten seconds before the results showed up.

"1 hit found."

The map it displayed was straightforward. It seemed to be a topo-graphic chart of a mountainous area covered with dense, contoured lines. Right in the middle was a dot marked Exit 42. There were no other facilities or points of interest around it.

Pressing the EXPAND button until it zoomed out as much as possible only made the details harder to discern and provided no help in deduc-ing Exit 42's general location. It seemed that the station map's guid-ance system could only display up to one kilometer in each direction at the most.

Hiroto considered his options and said, "How do I get there? Tell me the route and travel time."

"Searching for a route from your present location to Exit 42..." the screen replied. Within a second, it changed to, *"Route does not exist."*

"What does that mean? Is it too far?"

The terminal did not answer. Hiroto hit the START OVER button to go back to the menu, and another loud video ad played. Hiroto repeated the process several times in different ways but never arrived at any information about how to get to Exit 42. Over time, the ads became more attractive to him than what he actually sought. After thirty min-utes of grappling with the machine, he had gleaned the following:

- Exit 42 was in a distant mountain range somewhere.
- The primary tourist spots for Yokohama Station were Mt. Fuji, the colossal sea wall in Iwate, Ise Grand Shrine in Mie, and the ruins of the ancient city of Nagoya, among others.
- The famous traditional dish of the Yokosuka area was curry rice. A new restaurant called Kaiji had just opened last week, with an unbeatable grand opening special on its extra-large plate for only 400 milliyen, a total steal.
- Yokohama Station's popular animated series, *Mr. Shyumai*, would be getting a new feature film next week titled *Mr. Shyumai Goes to Space*.
- Mr. Shyumai was a shumai dumpling–shaped robot (foodroid)

from the future. After children abandoned him, he died and became a ghost. Whenever he spotted a child being a picky eater and leaving food behind, he blasted them with a million-volt shock of lethal electricity.

The important thing was that Yokosuka was the central city in this area. According to the sign overhead, it was 12,000 meters to Yokosuka (150 minutes). Hiroto was used to walking on the craggy ground of the cape, so a distance like that, over flat pavement, was an easy task for him.

The corridor heading north from Ninety-Nine Steps was piled high with dust. The braille blocks had fallen off the walls, and the ceiling lights flickered constantly. Eventually, the sunlight filtering in would grow scarce, and Hiroto wouldn't be able to see without a flashlight. Like the guard at the elevator had said, there was no one walking this hall.

"I thought Inside would be cleaner," Hiroto muttered. He'd imagined the entirety of the station would look like what Yosuke had pulled off the Suikanet—a major city with people coming and going. In a metropolis like that, new corridors were continually growing and grouping into thick bunches like overworked muscles.

But the area around Ninety-Nine Steps held nothing of interest for the people Inside. It was like the appendix of Yokohama Station. The only ones who ever emerged here were swimmers on their way to Kurihama and railroad geeks. The latter would look at the signs and advertisements the station walls grew and bask in the historic atmosphere they created.

I guess I should go to Yokosuka. I'm sure I'll find something there, thought Hiroto.

◆

"Now then, let's hear your explanation for this," said the staff member in the long-sleeved uniform to his two subordinates. It was two o'clock in the afternoon. The temperature outside had reached eighty-six degrees, but the Yokosuka security station was as cool as an underground basement. In the busier, urban parts of the station, the growth of new corridors stacked the structure in layers, but the sun's heat didn't reach the lower areas.

"Yes, sir. This man just ordered a curry rice plate at the recently opened Kaiji in the restaurant district on the third floor," replied a thin staffer. SATO, NINTH-CLASS EMPLOYEE, was written on the name tag on his chest.

"Uh-huh. And?"

"This dish is a popular item at Kaiji. It's intended to conjure images of the era when curry first made its way from India to Yokohama Station," offered the heavier ninth-class staffer. His name was Shio.

"That's hardly pertinent."

"Yes, sir. Sorry, sir."

Hiroto was at their mercy. He looked at the thick, heavy uniforms of the employees and thought they'd suffer heat exhaustion if they wore them outside. There was a machine that looked like an air conditioner in the room, but the plug and pipes were removed. It obviously hadn't been used for a long time.

"The price of the curry rice, including food sanitation tax, consumer tax, and station heat use tax, is 400 milliyen," Sato continued.

"Uh-huh. And?"

"The food sanitation tax the station management agency collects represents the minimum cost needed to support a secure and healthy food system Inside," Shio, the other subordinate staffer, explained.

"Again, hardly pertinent."

"Yes, sir. Sorry, sir."

"Consequently, when the waiter presented this man with a bill for 400 milliyen after his meal, he handed back this metallic token," elaborated Sato.

"Uh-huh. And what is it?" asked Sixth-Class Employee Motosu as he peered at the item in question. It fit into the palm of his hand and had the number *500* stamped on it. "Ah, I know what this is. It's called a coin. They used to settle payments with pieces of metal like this in the days before Suika. I didn't know they still existed."

"I am impressed by your erudition and the generosity of your knowledge, Mr. Motosu," said Sato.

From Hiroto's location, he had a glimpse of Motosu's device screen in the mirror. The man seemed to be distributing points to Sato and Shio for each of their comments. That last one had earned Sato five points.

"So based on his physical currency and clothing, I can only assume this fellow has time-traveled here from the past. I'll call him Samurai Man," Motosu concluded.

"Yes, sir. Very good, sir," chimed the subordinates.

"That was a joke. You were supposed to laugh."

"Aha-ha-ha-ha-ha!" they roared. Motosu took ten points away from them both.

"Anyway. There's nothing wrong with presenting an antique like this at an eating establishment. It doesn't violate the law. So what's the problem?" Motosu inquired.

Shio answered, "Well, sir, according to the employee at Kaiji, after presenting this currency, the man fled the restaurant. I caught him later, but there was an error with his Suika payment device, and the transaction couldn't be completed."

"In other words, he ate without paying due to lack of funds," Motosu reasoned.

"Well—" Shio started to say, but Sato eagerly cut him off.

"That's right, sir."

Hiroto was unaware that physical currency wasn't used Inside. He knew from talking to exiles that transactions were conducted through Suika, but he mistakenly assumed the money used outside the station would also be valid Inside. He'd brought five days of rations just in case, but his desire to eat curry in Yokosuka had been his undoing.

About an hour earlier, Hiroto had just finished his curry and handed the waitress his coin. She gave him a confused look, but said, "Thank you," and slipped it into her pocket. After that, another employee brought Hiroto a Suika terminal and stated, "Here is your bill, sir." Hiroto, thinking he'd already paid, didn't want to submit to a Suika scan and tried to flee the restaurant.

Shio happened to be nearby and caught him. When he pressed the Suika reader to the back of Hiroto's head, the device gave an error: *Suika brain waves not detected.* Neither the waiters nor Shio had ever seen that error before, so Shio called Sato at the station for help, and they'd brought in Hiroto together.

"The crime of eating without payment means that we must confirm this man's identity," Sato stated.

"Uh-huh. And?" Motosu said.

"But to use Suika's personal information cross-reference function, we must submit a cross-reference approval form, stamped by a station employee of fourth-class or above," Sato continued.

"Uh-huh. And?"

"Because today is Saturday, no fourth-class or higher staffers are working at the management agency, so we cannot request the form," Shio finally finished.

"You are the very model of a station employee for reporting to work on the weekend, Mr. Motosu," praised Sato. Hiroto was impressed by their ability to talk so promptly on demand while saying so little of importance.

"Uh-huh. And?"

"Therefore, I believe we will need to keep him in the holding area until his treatment can be determined. That will require the permission of a seventh-class or higher employee, which is why we have called upon you, sir," said Sato.

"Uh-huh. Well, go ahead and do that. Carry on," Motosu responded as he pressed the Send button on his device. On the screen were the words, *Employee Ninth-Class Sato: 520 pts remaining until promotion to Eighth Class. Employee Ninth-Class Shio: 143 pts remaining until termination.*

"As for you, Samurai Man, you're going into the holding cell for eating without payment," Sato declared, pulling Hiroto up by the cuffs. Only the chain linking the cuffs was metal. The parts around his wrists were made of hardened rubber.

"You're lucky," Shio whispered into his ear. "Last year, an employee hurt a prisoner with the all-metal cuffs, and he got arrested by the turnstiles. That's why we have these now."

The two employees escorted Hiroto to the holding cell. While Shio was the larger of the two, he was still more compact than Hiroto. From walking around Yokosuka, Hiroto had observed that the people Inside were just smaller in general. It made him wonder if living in cramped interior environments had made their bodies shrink naturally.

According to the staffers, Hiroto wasn't going to be released for at least another two days. Given it would take that long just to get his personal information verified by Suika, he couldn't begin to guess how long they would keep him locked up once they learned he didn't have a Suika at all. It was only the afternoon of Hiroto's first day Inside, but his journey was already in danger of ending.

The holding cell was a space about the size of a bedroom. It was also already inhabited.

"Yo. Look at this young fella! What'd you do to get thrown in here?" asked the man, who looked to be around fifty. Like all Inside residents, his skin was pale, but his hands were dark and dirty like he was used to doing hard labor.

"Just eating without paying," Hiroto replied.

"Ahh. That's unfortunate. You a student?"

"You could say that."

Hiroto didn't know what a student was, but going along with the other inmate's assumption seemed for the best.

He could see that Shio was standing outside the door. He didn't want to talk too much and give away information that might identify himself.

The room held four beds and one toilet. The metal door bore a sign that read, EMERGENCY EXIT. It was the kind that locked from the inside, but they'd stuck a padlock on the outside. It must have been a generic room the station had generated that the staff had turned into a holding cell. There was one light on the ceiling, and the walls and floor were concrete.

"Well, they won't do too much to ya for an eat-and-run. If you need work, I can help you with that," the man offered.

"What kind of work?"

"Sellin' cigarettes."

He explained how his job worked. First, the spelunkers found the vending machines that grew here and there in Yokohama Station. They were station property, of course, so if you destroyed them, the automated turnstiles would come. You could, however, buy their wares legitimately with your Suika and then sell them to the right customers for several times the machines' base price.

Smoking was against the law Inside as a general rule and could get you arrested by the automated turnstiles, but not if you went to the designated smoking areas. Separate from the turnstiles, however, the staffers also forbade smoking—including at the smoking areas—and would levy fines on you.

"They just wanna make rules and boss you around, whatever it takes to do that. 'Oh, we're upholding the safety by following the code of Yokohama Station and the automated turnstiles,' they say, but they'll make up rules the turnstiles don't care about so they have somethin' to do. And they demand taxes for every little thing. They're the worst," the man grumbled.

While he was talking, Hiroto worked on formulating an escape plan. They were in a concrete room without windows. The door was locked from the exterior, but the padlock itself probably wasn't station property, so the automated turnstiles wouldn't care if someone broke it. How could Hiroto break a padlock without damaging the door, though?

"Believe it or not, I'm a well-known cigarette carrier. Pretty much any vending machine spelunker in the Yokosuka area works for me," the middle-aged man bragged.

"But you got caught. What are you going to do now?" asked Hiroto.

"Not a problem for a guy with connections like mine. The second-class staffer here is a real heavy smoker, you see, and we got a nice arrangement goin'. One of my boys brings him a carton tomorrow, and he'll see that I'm released."

Then that would be his opportunity to escape, Hiroto decided. Sato was thin and small. Alone, he could easily be overpowered. If it was

Shio, who was larger, or both of them at once, though, it would be more difficult. It didn't seem like the staffers carried weapons, but there was still the chance that someone with an 18 Ticket was subject to the same laws against violence that the automated turnstiles enforced.

In any case, if there were a chance to escape, it would be tomorrow. For now, Hiroto would rest and conserve his strength. He got into one of the beds and pulled up the blanket, which smelled of tobacco.

Surprisingly, the chance for a jailbreak came sooner than expected.

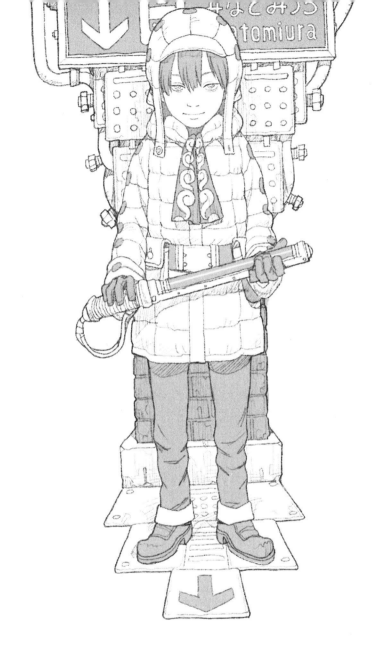

Hiroto dreamed of his childhood.

Even in the drab, unchanging world of life on the cape, his boyhood memories were fresh. The most vivid among them was from when he was eight. That was when he'd first climbed all the way up the escalators of Ninety-Nine Steps, which only went down.

All the blood in his body had been boiling as he raced up the mercilessly descending stairs. It'd felt like he'd been climbing for an hour. Of course, no child was capable of such a feat, so it'd likely been closer to five or ten minutes.

When a cleaner at the time saw the boy leap onto the silver landing, he looked startled and asked, "You the Mishima boy?" Then, he reached out and pulled Hiroto to the boundary of the Inside. The six automated turnstiles set up there looked at the two of them and declared, "ѕuiꜧa nоt rесоgniᴢеd. ɪ'm ѕоrry, bu you may nоt еntеr." They put up their arms to form a wall, blocking the way into the station.

It was Hiroto's first time seeing the turnstiles, but he remembered not feeling much of anything. They were just part of the scenery to him.

When he went back down to report in, his parents were delighted. Climbing to the top of the escalator at Ninety-Nine Steps was a sign that a child was a full-fledged person. As far as anyone knew, eight years old was the youngest it had ever been done.

The other kids had marveled over Hiroto's feat, and he became a bit of a hero around the village. They held a celebration at the house and had invited the professor from next door. At the time, they could barely understand a word the strange man said, but he seemed to comprehend that it was a special occasion and gave something that sounded like a celebratory speech. To Hiroto, they sounded like magic words that transformed a child into an adult.

As his body grew, climbing the escalator got easier. At age ten, Maki was able to do it, too. At eleven, so could Yosuke. All the kids around Hiroto's age eventually gathered in the space at the top and played in the mounds of trash, looking for useful items. At that point, Hiroto was no longer the hero.

One time, he, Yosuke, and Maki set up empty plastic bottles in the space at the top of the escalators and played bowling. Hiroto hurled the soccer ball too wildly, though, and it went past the automated turnstiles. They blocked the children from getting the ball back, even though it was just sitting there, a few meters away.

The soccer ball was never retrieved.

That was when Hiroto learned that reaching the top of the escalator and becoming a full-fledged adult had only expanded his world by a few dozen meters.

No matter how much they grew, their possibilities ended right there.

A small tapping noise roused Hiroto from sleep. There was a child wearing an unfamiliar outfit standing in front of him.

The child's waist was at Hiroto's eye level. Several tools Hiroto had never seen before were stuck under a belt. This curious visitor's face was hard to make out; it was backlit by the one, constant light source in the ceiling.

Why is it so dark? Is it still night? Hiroto looked past the child and saw the cigarette seller sleeping. *Oh, right, I'm in Yokohama Station. The staffers caught me and put me in a holding cell.* The memory caused the taste of the curry from earlier in the day to flood into his mouth.

Hiroto turned his attention back to the child. Why was a kid here? The young visitor didn't bear a resemblance to any of the staffers.

Suddenly, Hiroto's vision went red, bringing all his thoughts to a halt. It took several seconds for him to grasp that it was caused by a long, narrow, electronic sign the child was holding.

"♦Sorry for waking you up."

A string of words ran across the sign.

"I'm only passing through, so I'd appreciate it if you didn't make noise.♦"

"Wait. Who are you? How'd you get in here?" Hiroto asked in a low whisper, to avoid waking his cellmate. After pulling the blanket off himself and sitting up, Hiroto was eye level with the kid.

"♦I'm just passing through. I apologize for making a hole in the room, but it will close up over time, so don't worry. This doesn't seem to be your home, though.♦"

With that, he—Hiroto assumed it was a boy—pointed at the ceiling. An aperture, smaller than a sewer manhole, had been gouged into it. It was just large enough for a person to fit through.

"You opened that hole?"

"♦I did. I was going through the passage above, but there was no exit, so I had no choice."

The reply message scrolled by. The strange thing was that the child wasn't doing anything to type or create the on-screen letters. There was no visible control panel or anything like that.

"By the way, while you were sleeping, I took a look at your characteristic brain waves. You don't have a Suika installed. How did you get here?♦"

Hiroto hesitated but decided that it would be unwise to lie, given the child's technological prowess. He pulled his bag out from under the blanket and removed the small box-shaped device.

"I used this," he said. "It lets me go in and out of the Inside for a limited time."

"♦That's an 18 Ticket. I heard about them from Yukie recently, but I've never seen one in person.♦"

"Yeah. I got my hands on this one and decided to take a little vacation into the station. I don't know the ways here, so I got caught by the staff. I'm going to be stuck here until my time's up, and then the automated turnstiles will come to toss me out."

The cigarette seller groaned in his sleep and rolled over. Hiroto continued, quieter than before, "I want to get out of here. Can you help me?"

The boy thought it over.

"**♦All right. But in exchange, I want you to give me that 18 Ticket after it expires. Our company would like to examine it to see how it works. ♦**"

"Sure, if you don't mind it being pre-used."

"**♦You've got yourself a deal. I'm getting out of here now, so could you please use that blanket to cover this? There, just like that. Let's go. ♦**"

Then the boy took something like a flashlight off his belt, pointed it at the floor, and hit the switch. The light that emerged was surprisingly powerful, and the cigarette seller grumbled again. Hiroto hurriedly stripped another blanket off the bed next to him and held it up with his own to dampen the glow. That darkened things enough that the middle-aged man offered no further complaints.

After half an hour of digging through the floor, the two emerged into a passage beneath the holding area. It was much brighter than it had been under the cell's solitary ceiling light, but the mustiness made it plain that this was an old road that had fallen into disuse. Like in Yokosuka, this station grew more tunnels to support increased foot traffic, but because the newer corridors were piled on top, the lower you went, the older the shafts were.

"It's a good thing there was a passage close by. We should get away from Yokosuka, though. If we get to a different city, the staffers will be from a different agency, and you won't have to worry about getting caught," the child explained, speaking aloud for the first time. His voice was neutral in nature, neither juvenile nor mature. The foggy glass on the sign couldn't completely hide the message inside: 125 Minutes on Foot to Kamakura. They began to walk.

The boy was only half as tall as Hiroto. He looked much smaller than Hiroto had been when he'd first climbed the escalator at

Ninety-Nine Steps. Perhaps the kid was six or seven. Then again, everyone Hiroto had seen Inside was smaller than he was.

"I've got a lot of questions…but first, what is that? It looks like a flashlight," Hiroto inquired, pointing at the device that had opened the hole in the holding cell.

"It's a structural genetic field canceler. Our company developed it."

"Structural jenn…?"

Hiroto thought he'd heard the professor say something like that before, but he hadn't been listening very intently and couldn't remember.

"To put it simply," the boy stated, "when you shine this on something, that part of Yokohama Station goes away. It's easy to dismantle it that way, and the automated turnstiles don't react."

He might as well have been saying, *If you press this button, the sun will rise in the west.* To Hiroto, it was merely a fact of life that once a part of Yokohama Station had formed, it could not be destroyed by human hands.

"Well, I feel a bit bad about putting a hole in the station management agency's cell. In a few days, the surrounding concrete will fill in the hole, though, so it won't be a big problem."

"What's the management agency? Are there people managing Yokohama Station? I didn't think it was something human beings could manage," admitted Hiroto.

"It's just a group of people around here who call themselves that. I've seen several such organizations in my time," the boy revealed. "Depending on the area, they call themselves the police, or train crews, or the government, but most of the time, they're just called staffers. They're usually narrow-minded by nature, so in my line of work, they spell trouble."

Hiroto gave the boy a piercing look. *Depending on the area? In my line of work?*

"…By any chance, are you with the Dodger Alliance?" he asked.

"Dodger Alliance?"

"The people who gave me the 18 Ticket. I'm supposed to rescue their leader. He said the leader's going to free humanity from Yokohama Station."

"Hmm." The boy was silent for a while. "We're aware of such a group, but they're not capable of building tools like these, as far as we know."

That made sense to Hiroto. His mental image of the man who'd made his way to Ninety-Nine Steps after being exiled by the turnstiles did not fit with the advanced technology this child possessed.

"Those guys are mostly concerned with controlling Suikanet. They seem to be attempting to free humanity from Yokohama Station by taking over the network that manages the automated turnstiles. Physical defense isn't something they require."

This was news to Hiroto. Higashiyama had always spoken passionately about the concept of liberation, but Hiroto couldn't remember him sharing any real details about what his organization truly did.

"Physical defense," Hiroto repeated. It was then that he understood just who this boy was. "You must have come from beyond Honshu."

"That's right. Oh, I haven't introduced myself yet. I am Nepshamai. I was dispatched here from JR North Japan."

"It took me a year to get this far."

Nepshamai, the field agent from JR North Japan, told his story as he and Hiroto traveled from Yokosuka to Kamakura. They'd been walking for an hour now and were halfway there. Despite his smaller size, Nepshamai moved faster than Hiroto but didn't seem to be rushing. He had a very precise and effortless gait.

"I meet all kinds of people on the way. The people of the Inside have a variety of feelings about Yokohama Station, I've noticed. Around the Iwate area, for example, they have that famous sea wall. People there worship the station like it's holy. They say Yokohama Station was born during the Winter War to protect the country."

"Hey, Shamai. If you're some kind of secret operative, why are you telling me all about your background?" Hiroto asked.

The little agent laughed. "I think you're mistaken. I'm not an enemy of the people of Yokohama Station. Our purpose is only to prevent Yokohama Station from reaching Hokkaido. My mission is to collect intel, so talking with people from Honshu is part of my job. You never know where you might find the information you need."

Hiroto decided this made sense. His mental image of an operative came from war movies grabbed off Suikanet. They were from an era when human governments—like Japan and America—were in charge and fought each other over territory.

"That reminds me. When I was a kid, I heard a story that Hokkaido's line of defense had been breached. Was that false?" Hiroto inquired.

"No. It happened. The station got through one time. They said the structural genetic field reached all the way to Hakodate," Nepshamai related. He pulled out the small tube that'd made the hole in the cell earlier, the one he'd called a structural genetic field canceler. "We used these to push it back across the straits. Yukie did that. Once she was made chief of JR North Japan's engineers, she became the first person in history to succeed at pushing back Yokohama Station."

Nepshamai sounded very proud of this.

It was known from the very beginning of Yokohama Station's expansion that it could not cross the sea.

The station had started out with a view of Tokyo Bay, expanding north and west at about the same speed. In a few years, it had swallowed up surrounding airports and used the Aqua-Line Tunnel to cross the bay to the Boso Peninsula to the east. By that point, virtually all trade to Tokyo had been cut off, and it ceased functioning altogether as the capital city. The Japanese government moved farther and farther north, fleeing the ever-approaching Yokohama Station. Like a boulder rolling down a mountain, the state cracked and lost mass along the way. History did not say where it had actually died out for good.

The replicating structure reached the northern tip of Honshu about a century and a half after it'd started expanding. The station could extend connecting hallways over rivers, but it couldn't span the Tsugaru

Strait's nearly twenty kilometers to Hokkaido. Many times, the locals had witnessed Yokohama Station at Cape Omazaki extending its corridors and attempting to reach Hokkaido, only for them to collapse under their own weight long before reaching land.

The biggest concern for JR North Japan in its mission to stop Yokohama Station from making landfall on Hokkaido was the Seikan Tunnel. This underground passage was the primary method across the strait. Filling the tunnel wouldn't help—the structural genetic field could pass right through iron and concrete—and removing the already constructed tunnel from the earth was not something humanity had the means to do at this time.

"Yokohama Station is slowly evolving. Or, to be more accurate, it is made up of a combination of slightly differing waveforms. With each major battle, the station loses the weaker elements, making it stronger than before, on average. We held the line at the Seikan Tunnel for over four decades, and that was how the station broke through."

"I see. So you can't rest easy, even with that weapon at your disposal."

"That's right. Our job is to develop new countermeasures faster than the station can evolve and to find new weaknesses," Nepshamai said, tapping his foot on the ground.

"Hey, what kind of a place is Hokkaido?" Hiroto asked.

"It's big. Natural ground, as far as the eye can see. So big, you can practically see the curvature of the Earth. It's beautiful."

"That's amazing. I hope I get to see it someday."

Hiroto tried to imagine seeing the ground everywhere, but the picture just wouldn't come to mind. To him, the "ground" was just a scrawny patch of brown and green, clinging to the boundary between Yokohama Station and the sea below.

"Before I passed through that holding cell, I was up on the roof of the station, observing the landscape. I could see Mt. Fuji. It was black."

That's because it's Black Fuji season, thought Hiroto.

"Hokkaido has a mountain called Mt. Yotei. Some people also call it 'Ezo Fuji,' or 'Hokkaido Fuji,' because they say it looks like Mt. Fuji used to, but it's much more beautiful than Fuji is now. We have to do whatever it takes to keep Yokohama Station from growing into Hokkaido," Nepshamai declared forcefully.

The more Nepshamai talked, the worse Hiroto felt. The cape at Ninety-Nine Steps was a small place. It only took an hour to circle. He lived off the goods that came out of the station, and he'd been lucky enough to wind up with an 18 Ticket, which he'd used to go Inside to see what it was like. He'd never had a mission or a calling, like this boy from Hokkaido. There was nothing in Hiroto's life that he cherished enough to want to protect.

"Hey, Shamai, does JR North Japan have any information on the leader of this Dodger Alliance? That's my mission—to find that guy."

"Well, of course. That group is one of the big targets we want to make contact with."

"But I bet it must be hard to find someone who's been evading the turnstiles for years," Hiroto said.

Nepshamai stopped walking for a moment to think. "That might actually be a hint. There's no place in Yokohama Station where you can hide from the turnstiles for long. The only possibility is outside."

"...In a station hollow, then," Hiroto deduced.

After he'd been exiled to Ninety-Nine Steps, Higashiyama had described places here and there where the landscape or other factors left the station unable to grow over an empty space.

"But there's got to be tons of those pockets. I heard there were several just around Yokosuka."

"Hiroto, you said the person who gave you that 18 Ticket fled to Kamakura. That tells me this Dodger Alliance can't be far from the Kanto region around Tokyo. If that's true…"

Nepshamai took another device off his belt. This one was shaped like a card. He turned it on and pointed it toward the wall. It projected a map onto the surface.

Map of Capital Area Hollows was written at the top of the image.

"That's a very convenient thing to have," Hiroto remarked.

"Actually, I borrowed it from that man sleeping back in the cell. After all, you might as well steal from someone who knows what he's doing," Nepshamai quipped with a little smirk.

"How did you know he'd have that map?"

"A lot of the station hollows get used as smoking spots. The automated turnstiles don't have jurisdiction over them, so you can do anything there," explained Nepshamai.

The two examined the map.

"There are several hollows, but nothing big enough for a person to hide out in for a long time. Flat land has less of them, because it's easier for Yokohama Station to grow across smooth ground. Based on this, it seems like anyone trying to reach the sea would do well to aim for Kamakura."

Nepshamai pointed to a spot in the west marked KOFU. Red dots indicating hollows littered the vicinity around a wide basin.

"Let's try this area first," the young boy decided.

"Can we even walk that far? My 18 Ticket is only valid for four more days," said Hiroto. Based on the map, it was at least a hundred kilometers to Kofu. He'd never even imagined such a distance before.

"There's a good way to get to Kofu. I can explain when we arrive in Kamakura," assured Nepshamai. They continued onward.

"Wait up, Shamai," called Hiroto, before Nepshamai could get farther ahead. "I feel like we're just walking in circles. I saw this sign earlier, and that weird placement of tiles and pipes is exactly the same, too."

"Oh, no. We're moving forward. I can get our locational data from Suikanet. Look," Nepshamai said, displaying a map on the electronic scrolling sign. It was recording the paths they'd taken so far. Despite winding like a snake, their route was steadily taking them west.

"This is called a repeated sequence. The station is repeating the same structure one after the other. It's a common feature in the earlier sections."

Hiroto visualized the segments of a centipede's body.

"In the first stages of Yokohama Station's expansion, it still had little information about buildings, so it often recreated the same structural patterns. As it grew, the structural genetic field absorbed information from around the country, and the diversity of its newer constructs grew. We call this the Station Divergence Process." The boy looked at the pipes around them and continued happily, "We're close to Yoko-hama City. The structure of the earliest parts of the station is still preserved here. It's valuable information."

"What's Yokohama City?" Hiroto asked.

"The name of the settlement that was the starting point of Yoko-hama Station. It was a city created by humans, though, so most of it was out in the open air. Before the Winter War, it was a major port city with a population of ten million, I hear."

"The entire city was outdoors?"

"Sapporo's still like that."

"Sapporo?"

"It's a city in Hokkaido. That's where our headquarters are."

An entire outdoor city. Hiroto tried to imagine the sight of it, but the only visual he could conjure was a magnified version of Ninety-Nine Steps. An outdoor town that was home to ten million humans seemed impossible.

He'd lived on the tiny cape all his life, but it was always clear from the sight of Yokohama Station looming over them that this little piece of "outside" was just a fluke, a thing pushed to the margins of the world.

"That reminds me," Hiroto remarked as he and Nepshamai marched onward. "Do you know anything about an Exit 42?"

"42?"

"Yeah. It's my other destination. I looked it up on a net machine, but all I know is that it's in the mountains. I don't even know where."

"That's strange. I would've figured any double-digit exit had to be around the Yokohama City area. The numbers of the exits go up as they're created, after all. Yokohama was a port city; there are no tall mountains there," answered Nepshamai.

"Oh, okay. I guess I was looking it up the wrong way."

"There's a phenomenon called transgating, where an exit that's already been created moves locations, but that's a very spontaneous event, and our analysis indicates it doesn't involve very long distances."

The pair kept walking until they'd left the repeating sequence and the sign visuals and layout of pipes began to change. Hiroto peered at a wall in the distance and saw a half-open shutter.

Beyond it was an automated turnstile, seated on the ground. It had a slightly different design than the ones with which Hiroto was familiar, and it clearly hadn't moved in a long time. Something wet and gleaming covered the turnstile's metal exterior. It was dark beyond the shutter, but Hiroto could still see many brown cardboard boxes there.

"What is this?" he asked.

"It looks like a storehouse of some kind. Let's go see."

"Okay."

The shutter was rusted to the point of being immobile, and Hiroto had to duck down to slip through the one-meter gap. Nepshamai just walked straight through.

Inside, there was a low mechanical humming but no sign of automated turnstiles. The cardboard boxes were piled as tall as Hiroto's head, but they weren't dusty. They'd been placed here recently.

Hiroto grabbed one of the containers on top and set it down on the floor. It was lighter than he'd expected. It contained no mechanical components, after all. Instead, it was packed with shirts. A quick inspection suggested they were all the same size and design.

"I guess this is a commercial route for apparel," said Nepshamai.

"They're new?"

"Yes. That's what it means when there are so many of the same thing together."

"And they're *all* new?" Hiroto asked, pointing at the warehouse as a whole.

"That would be the assumption." Nepshamai turned on his electric sign and used it to examine the walls of the room. "There's a moving walkway over there. I'm guessing the clothing production facility is that way."

A steady flow of cardboard boxes was traveling along a black conveyor belt toward them. Hiroto glanced at a few of the cartons, then started pulling some down from the moving pile and opened them. "We only get the scrapped items where I live," he explained. "Ripped clothes, used outfits, expired food, stuff like that."

He tried to consider how he might take at least one box back to Ninety-Nine Steps. The attire was a little small for him, but the people at the cape would be delighted. Hiroto was depressed he couldn't do any shopping without a Suika, but surely taking one box would be all right if they had this much Inside.

"Hey, who's there?" called a thick voice from the back of the warehouse. Heavy footsteps approached. Nepshamai quickly strode in that direction.

"What the hell are you doing, slacking off over here?" chided the man. "Get back to stacking."

Hiroto tried to put the box back where he'd found it, but in his haste, he knocked another one off the stack instead. It hit the floor with a loud thump.

A light turned on outside the shutter. The automated turnstile's display had activated, and it was looking their way. Thankfully, it wasn't getting up to move. Perhaps its mechanical system was somehow broken.

"Excuse me; I'm not an employee here. Do you have the wrong person?" Hiroto heard Nepshamai say.

"Huh? Ah, yeah—that's true. We might be hard up for labor, but we don't hire pip-squeaks like you. A thief, then? Is that your boss over there?" demanded the other voice. Through the collapsed stack of containers, Hiroto saw a man in his thirties, glaring back with beady eyes. The position of his face was a head and a half below Hiroto's, but only because the man had a terrible hunch, not because he was short.

"Wait, you're making a mistake. We're not thieves. We're just traveling," Hiroto explained. It wasn't very convincing, given the mess of opened boxes around him and the fact that he'd just been trying to take one of them.

"Is this your warehouse?" asked an undeterred Nepshamai.

"Yeah. I found it. There's a spot above where the clothes always pop out, so I followed the trail and reached this place," replied the hunchback. He took a small device from his pocket, pulled something up on its screen, and showed it to Hiroto. "That's the certificate."

The picture said, *Station Facility Excavation Certificate.* It also listed the warehouse's coordinates, the name and Suika ID of the discoverer, and a statement of ownership that was valid for twenty years. Last came a stamp that said, *Yokosuka Station Management Agency.*

That's when the hunchback noticed that boxes had been opened. "Hey! Don't muck up the product. Pay me for those!" he shouted, spraying spittle. Hiroto didn't understand why just opening the box would be "mucking up" the contents. Maybe that's just how new clothes worked.

"I don't have any money," Hiroto admitted.

The man stared at Hiroto's outfit and decided that he fully believed this excuse. "Well, fine. If you do some work for me, I'll let you off the hook."

"Work?"

"Yeah. Take the product here to the store up above. You see the stairs over there?" The man pointed to the far side of the warehouse where the light was on. There were metal handrails there with signs that said ASCENDING on the left side and DESCENDING on the right, with arrows to match. Unlike the escalators, these steps did not move.

"And you want me to move the stuff around here?"

"At the top of the stairs, there's a hallway that leads to an old elevator. Just put them down next to it. I'll let you go for thirty boxes. Do it in three hours."

"All right," Hiroto agreed, crouching in front of a box. "Shamai, hold my stuff," he added, handing his bag to Nepshamai, who took two unsteady steps backward from the weight of it.

However, before he went anywhere, Hiroto made sure to remove the 18 Ticket and put it in his pants pocket. That way, he wouldn't have to worry about the automated turnstiles. Then, he lifted two stacks of five boxes, pressing them together, and started walking toward the stairs.

"Whoa, these are heavier than I thought," he muttered. Not only were the stack weights different on each side, but they were also taller than he was once he lifted them. He couldn't see where he was going.

"You've got the right direction, just keep going straight. The steps will be right ahead when you reach the braille blocks," Hiroto heard

Nepshamai say. Bit by bit, he slid his feet forward until, eventually, the sensation turned to a stubbled pattern.

The left side of the handrails was marked as the ascending side, but it was narrow, and he wouldn't be able to go up with two stacks of boxes. Hiroto came to a stop.

"Is everything all right?" asked Nepshamai from a distance.

"Can I go up the descending side, too?"

"Yes. No problem."

Why would they write that, then? Hiroto wondered on his way up the stairs. They were longer than he'd expected, and there were several landings along the way. At each, he had to set the boxes down on the floor first to verify he hadn't reached the hallway yet.

Once Hiroto had placed the boxes in the hallway and returned to the warehouse, he received a surprised reaction from the man. Insiders were weaker on average, so the hunchback clearly hadn't expected Hiroto to have the muscle to lift ten boxes at once.

"Twenty more," said Hiroto, rotating his shoulders and going after another set of ten. "It's hard without being able to see ahead, though. Shamai, come with me."

"All right," agreed Nepshamai. He walked along with Hiroto, offering precise guidance, warning when a landing was ahead, instructing to turn left in five steps, and so on. The second trip was much easier than the first.

"The elevation difference is fourteen meters. That's about five stories," observed Nepshamai, when Hiroto put the cardboard boxes down. "Normally, the station generates elevators or escalators in such a situation, but since the bottom is along the old road, most likely nobody uses it. So the only option was stairs, which is why no one discovered it until that man came along."

"Even though it's a totally normal path?" Hiroto asked.

"To Insiders, stairs that go on and on to an unknown end are an object of fear," explained Nepshamai.

Hiroto had no idea why that would be the case. He'd raced up the down-only escalator at Ninety-Nine Steps so many times in his life that he couldn't fathom why a set of plain old stationary steps would be scary.

When they returned after the second trip, the man said, "Hey, buddy, you're impressive. You wanna work for me? I can give you a monthly salary."

"No, I'm just passing through. I don't have time to hang around here," Hiroto replied. He only had four more days Inside in the first place and no Suika with which to accept a salary.

Hiroto took ten more cardboard boxes and headed back up the stairs. On this third trip, the hunchback joined them, perhaps to observe his work. He'd given Hiroto a limit of three hours, and it had taken less than fifteen minutes.

"There, that's the job. We're going now," said Hiroto at the elevator, thirty boxes resting nearby.

"All right. Nice work," accepted the hunched man.

Just then, the old elevator in the hallway clanked open. Three children emerged: two boys and a girl. They were around twelve or so and even smaller than Nepshamai.

"Hey, you got no work for today," explained the man. "I've already had today's shipment hauled up."

"You already carried it here?" the kids inquired, looking up at Hiroto.

"Are you youngsters employees at this warehouse?" Nepshamai asked them. The children seemed unsure of him—a boy who looked younger than they were but spoke like an adult.

"We can't pay back our money now," one stated.

"Do you owe that man money?"

"Yeah. Still got three hundred and eighty thousand milliyen left."

"Four hundred and ten for me."

"I owe three hundred and sixty thousand," said the girl.

Hiroto had been arrested for not paying for a meal that cost 400 milliyen, so it was clear these were vast sums of money.

"So you're hauling the boxes to pay back your loan?"

"Yep. One hundred milliyen a day."

"We've been doing it for three years."

"But now we can't do it today," they complained, staring at Hiroto with enmity.

"Kyu found that warehouse. Then *he* stole it."

"Who's Kyu?" Hiroto asked.

"Kyu's gone now."

"He got taken away by the turnstiles after he turned six," the kids explained. Their affectation was flat and emotionless. Or at least, if they *were* expressing an emotion, Hiroto didn't know what it was.

After a while, the elevator door opened again. The children got on without a word and took it back up.

It was quiet. Hiroto and Nepshamai started walking toward the signs that marked the direction to the Kamakura area.

"Hey, Shamai, if there's so much stuff Inside, how come people are arguing over ownership and rights and all that?" Hiroto asked. "Where I'm from, we only get trash that's dumped out, but even that's enough for us. We all share what shows up, and we don't force the kids to work like that."

"I'm guessing those children don't have parents, for one reason or another. And that man was shouldering their Suika initiation costs and put them to work for him to pay it off," Nepshamai reasoned. He was still holding Hiroto's bag.

Unlike with the old path along the warehouse, the pair were now traveling a corridor that people routinely used. There was practically no traffic, however, because of the late hour.

Signs indicated that this older shaft was soon going to merge with a new route to Kamakura. Suddenly, Hiroto became aware that he was very hungry. He hadn't eaten a thing since the curry in Yokosuka for lunch the day before. The physical labor from earlier had left him feeling very fatigued.

Hiroto's bag was full of food he'd brought from Ninety-Nine Steps, but since they were coming up on the town, he preferred to wait and eat something good and fresh. Due to not having a Suika, he couldn't purchase anything, but he thought his companion might be able to help with that. The idea prompted Hiroto to ask something.

"Hey, Shamai," he said to the agent. Nepshamai stopped walking and turned to look at him. "How did you get your Suika?"

At that moment, there was a loud popping sound, like a huge balloon bursting. The corridor was empty, so the sound echoed without anything to absorb it.

Nepshamai collapsed to the ground. Immediately, there was another pop, then another. With each, Nepshamai's torso jolted twice. Sparks burst, and a fine, white smoke began billowing from him.

Without changing his expression one iota, Nepshamai silently flopped his arms, rubbed around his neck, and then stopped moving.

"Wait, don't shoot the big one," instructed a deep voice. The door for the new route to Kamakura opened, flooding the dim hallway with bright light. Hiroto squeezed his eyes shut.

"The man there is a human. Shoot him, and the turnstiles will come."

Hiroto slowly reopened his eyes and saw the green EMERGENCY EXIT sign on the door and, below it, two station staffers dressed in uniforms. There was a man with a beard and a woman holding a long gun.

"Hey, you," barked the bearded man, approaching. The badge on his chest bore the phrase, KATAKURI, SECOND-CLASS EMPLOYEE. "What do you think you're doing, escorting a northern saboteur around? Are you a staffer from the north?"

"Wait, wait, no. I'm just a tourist," explained Hiroto. The man rolled Nepshamai over with his foot, and a massive gust of steam billowed upward. There were three fist-sized holes in the boy's body. Ripped cables and pipes could be seen along the edges.

"This isn't your friend?"

"We just happened to be going in the same direction."

"You saying you don't know him?"

"I didn't know he was a saboteur," Hiroto lied. "Or that he wasn't human."

That part was the truth. Nepshamai had seemed strange; that was undeniable. Why would JR North Japan have used someone so young as a field agent, and why was a small child so wise? Seeing those three box-carrying children had only further stoked Hiroto's curiosity.

"Ah, well, I can't blame ya. This is the latest android out of JR North Japan. It's called the Corpocker-3. The second model looked more like the automated turnstiles, but these ones they built just like human beings. It's basically a spy. Since it's not human, it can get in without a Suika, and Suikanet can't track its location. Big problem, these guys."

"Sir, I'm not picking up any Suika brain waves from him. He's dangerous," stated the woman with the gun, pointing her sights in Hiroto's direction.

The bearded man looked suspicious at first, then gave Hiroto a once-over, scratched his beard, and said, "No Suika? Ah, I get it. You're one o' them. What are they called, again? Hollow orphans."

"Hallorfins…?"

"You got tossed out of the station by your parents as a kid, right? Well, you made it. You survived."

"No. I was born and raised outside of Yokohama Station."

"Oh, so you don't know? Well, it's been many generations, then," the man reasoned, scratching his head with his other hand. He seemed very fidgety. "Listen, I'll explain. People born in Yokohama Station don't need a Suika when they're toddlers. Once they reach six and become a child, though, they have to install a Suika. There's a deposit to be paid to Suikanet for that. It costs 500,000 milliyen. That's too much for a laborer living in poverty. If you have a kid, that's one thing, but if you can't raise the deposit cost within six years…"

The bearded man made his way behind Hiroto as he explained, approaching Nepshamai's prone body.

"Then the kid gets nabbed by the turnstiles and tossed out of the station. Usually into the nearest hollow, of course. In most cases, there's nothing you can do on your own down there. You won't survive long. But if it happens to be a place with open space, water, and food, then the abandoned kids come together, grow up, and breed. I hear there are places with little villages in them."

"…?"

"You're probably the descendant of someone like that. How'd you get Inside?"

Hiroto had no answer. He started to lift his arms, for lack of a better option, but the bearded man quickly put his hands on Hiroto's shoulders and backed him against the wall.

"Now let's just calm down. I feel sorry for you, so I'll let you in on the rules here. Violence is against the law in Yokohama Station. If you snap and hit one of us, the automated turnstiles will fly over and toss you out. The result might be the same for you, but that would be a big problem for us Inside folks."

Up close, the man's breath stank of tobacco. Hiroto recalled that in the cell yesterday, the cigarette seller had said there was a station employee who was a heavy smoker.

"So what do you do if someone Inside really rubs you the wrong way? The quickest method is for a big group to seize them and toss them into a locked room without hurting them. Then, you just leave them there for a week without giving them anything, and your problem is solved. When the station started expanding, people did that all the time. That's why we staffers manage all the sealable rooms now. Basically, we cover all the spots the automated turnstiles can't get to," the bearded man elaborated.

"Sir, the recovery team is here," said the woman with the gun.

"Oh, right. Send them in to do their job," the bearded man replied. Three young staffers entered the area at once. One opened a black bag, and another shoved Nepshamai's body into it. The third collected his bits of equipment scattered on the ground.

"Is this bag yours?"

"It is," Hiroto answered. The bearded man tossed it to him.

"Well, the big point is, these northern agents destroy station construction, abduct children with Suikas, and take them back to Hokkaido. Everyone's sick of the havoc these foxy tricksters cause. Since they're not human, the turnstiles are no help. That leaves it up to us to maintain order," declared the bearded man as he finally released

Hiroto. "You don't seem to have any connection to JR North Japan, so I'll let you go. But you'd better follow Inside rules while you're here."

He joined the other staffers carrying the plastic bag and left the old corridor. The door closed as loudly and heavily as it had opened, and then everything went quiet. Hiroto just stood there.

"Hollow orphans," the bearded man had said. The words echoed in Hiroto's head.

Descendants of the children thrown out of the station for being unable to pay their Suika deposit.

Until now, Hiroto had never given much thought to why the people of Ninety-Nine Steps lived on the narrow cape, rather than having a Suika implant like the residents of Yokohama Station.

"No. That's wrong," he said to himself. The station employee had no idea what went on outside. The people living on the islands of Hokkaido and Shikoku and Kyushu had never been residents of Yokohama Station, either. It was possible that places like that remained on Honshu in tiny spots, and maybe Ninety-Nine Steps was one of them.

"Hey, Shamai. How did you get your Suika?"

That was the last thing Hiroto had asked Nepshamai. The boy had turned back to look at Hiroto, and that was when the woman had shot him. The visual was burned into his retinas now. *If I hadn't said something at that exact moment, maybe he would've had the means or the technology to avoid it...*

Thinking about it wasn't going to change anything, though. The important thing now was to keep moving. Unfortunately, Hiroto was too hungry for that. He hadn't eaten a bite since lunch yesterday. Hiroto opened his bag and reached inside. After groping around for a moment, his hand found something hard.

He pulled out the object. It was the long, thin electronic sign Nepshamai had used to communicate with Hiroto when they met in the holding cell. Its length spanned the same distance as Hiroto's shoulders, but it was surprisingly light.

Instantly, the sign vibrated in Hiroto's grip. Apparently, he must have flipped the power button. A JR North Japan logo appeared, followed by white letters.

"Returning from ultra-low-power mode. Because of improper removal from main body, device will be checked for errors. Two minutes remaining…"

"One minute remaining…"

"Fifteen seconds remaining…"

It took about three minutes in total.

"Error check complete."

It was silent again for a few moments.

"♦Gosh, I'm very sorry about all that excitement.♦"

The letters turned red. It was the same display Hiroto had seen the first time at the holding cell.

"…Shamai?"

"♦Yes. I am Nepshamai. I was sent here by JR North Japan.♦"

"You're alive?"

"♦Yes, you could say that, although my body was destroyed, it seems. That really took me by surprise. I'd heard that the Kanto region staffers were hostile, but I didn't think they had anti-personnel weapons. That was an electric pump gun, the kind they used in the Winter War. They used it a lot at the end of the war because it can turn any piece of shrapnel into a bullet. They're not manufacturing weapons in Yokohama Station, obviously, so they must be building them in Shikoku or Kyushu.♦"

The letters were scrolling twice as fast as before, and Hiroto could just barely follow them with his eyes before they trailed off the other end of the screen. Apparently, it had been tough for Nepshamai, having no means to speak after the employee shot him.

"So is this sign your main body, then?"

"♦Not exactly. But my body's battery and main memory device were abruptly cut off, so I transferred my main memory to this electronic sign, my backup power source. It's programmed to do that in emergencies automatically, but my supplemental memory device was in my body. I hate to ask this, but—"

The subtitles froze briefly.

"Who are you, again? I must know you, right?♦"
Somehow, the letters on the scrolling sign *looked* apologetic.

"The wall is thinnest here. Let's make that hole," instructed Nepshamai, the JR North Japan agent, who was now just an electronic sign. This display was his entire body. Hiroto took the structural genetic field canceler out of the bag. Before his body's death, Nepshamai had made sure to slip the sign and the weapon into Hiroto's bag.

Hiroto was surprised to see how simple the canceler looked. It was a tube, like a flashlight, with a knob for adjusting power, an activation switch, and a small LCD panel to show the remaining battery charge. On the base of the device was a fox silhouette that was the logo of JR North Japan.

It was hard to believe that all humanity needed to push back Yokohama Station's centuries of expansion was something so simple.

"So I just press this switch, huh?"

"Yes. It's harmless to the human body, so don't worry. Set the output on low, though, so you don't waste energy."

Hiroto pointed the device at the wall and turned it on. The wall began melting like ice cream touched by a heated spoon.

"The concrete and beams around here have been reinforced by the structural genetic field and by fusing with Yokohama Station, but if you remove them, the crystalline structure instantly breaks down, and they just fall apart. It's like pouring cold water into a hot oil drum," Nepshamai explained.

After a while, the hole in the wall penetrated through, giving Hiroto a view of the space on the far side. It was pitch black, with no illumination. Chilly air flowed out, but unlike the musty air in the old tunnel they had used in the morning, there was no smell.

"And this hole goes all the way to Kofu?"

"Yes. Hiroto, what is taking you to Kofu, by the way?"

"I'm searching for the leader of a group called the Dodger Alliance. Since he's been on the run from the automated turnstiles for a long time, there's a high chance he's somewhere beyond the reach of Suika-net. There are lots of station hollows in Kofu, so that's probably it."

"I see. That's fascinating logic."

"…It was your idea."

Since losing his body, Nepshamai's short-term memory had taken a significant hit. The supplemental memory storage that had archived everything he'd seen and heard had been in his body. Now the only thing in his brain was the small main memory stuck to the electronic sign's back. The result was that Hiroto had to repeat everything he'd seen and heard back to Nepshamai, over and over.

"Yukie designed it, so I don't really know how the tech works," Nepshamai prefaced, the letters cramming the small scrolling screen. "My main memory device on the screen is constructed to be similar to the human brain. It's a plethora of nano-units linked into a network, and when you send data through it, the network structure changes, bit by bit. Normally, the supplemental memory device is consulted numerous times to fix the contents into place."

"And the stuff that happened since you met me is gone because you didn't have time to memorize what you saw?" asked Hiroto.

"That's right. I spend about three hours of every day shutting out external information collection in order to compile. That would be what you consider 'sleep'," Nepshamai explained.

So beyond his appearance, the humanoid from Hokkaido was very different in various ways from the automated turnstiles with their twenty-four-hour activity cycles.

After thirty minutes of excavation, there was enough of a hole in the wall for a person to squeeze through. Eighty-two percent of the structural genetic field canceler's battery remained.

"The recharging function was in my body, so at this point, this electronic screen's battery is all I've got. I don't think we anticipated this scenario arising during the design phase. Why did just my body have to get destroyed? Shikoku is one thing, but there shouldn't have been such an immediate physical danger inside of Yokohama Station," said Nepshamai.

Hiroto didn't answer the question. He crawled into the hole. "So what is this place?"

Based on the acoustics, it seemed to be an incredibly long and narrow tube. The only illumination was Nepshamai's electronic screen, so the area got lighter and darker in time with his words.

"This is the remnant of a railway."

"Railway? What's that?"

"A form of transportation. They connected station to station."

"Station to station? Hang on; I don't understand what you mean. So there used to be more than one Yokohama Station in the past? And tunnels like this were what connected them?"

"Not at all, but I think you're getting the idea."

"So it's basically...like an elevator," Hiroto concluded. He recalled the woman guarding the elevator right after he came Inside. It was only yesterday, but it felt like it'd happened a very long time ago.

"Elevators move vertically," Nepshamai stated.

"The first elevator I saw went sideways," Hiroto answered.

"You come across those every now and then. They tend to grow on peninsula tips and such. Because Yokohama Station is extending itself in a long and narrow way, the structural genetic field tends to mutate. Errors arise in its phototropism and gravitropism, and you wind up with elevators that go sideways and escalators that only descend."

"Okay. So this is like an elevator that goes sideways."

"What is 'this'?"

"I was talking about the railway."

"A railway. Correct. But it's much swifter than an elevator. At their peak, you could get from Tokyo to Osaka in forty minutes," explained Nepshamai.

Hiroto didn't know where Osaka was, but he got the general gist: It was really, really fast.

"So Yokohama Station had vehicles like that, huh? I've never even seen pictures of such things on Suikanet."

"This isn't part of Yokohama Station. Humans built this."

"Humans? Don't be stupid. How could humans dig a huge hole like this?" Hiroto wondered aloud. His understanding of construction was limited entirely to the lodgings erected at Ninety-Nine Steps. Their houses were assembled from wood cut down from what little land there was on the cape and materials dumped out of Yokohama Station. The town hall, the biggest building they had, was only forty meters wide. It was impossible to believe that people had built something that spanned entire kilometers.

"Besides, why would there be something people built inside of Yokohama Station?"

"This is a superconductive-type railway. Yokohama Station's structural genetic field is repelled by superconductive material, so it doesn't incorporate the space around the railway. It just covers it up with concrete."

They walked through the darkness in the direction of Kofu for a while. Eventually, Hiroto's eyes began to adapt to the sea of black, and he was able to make out faint details around them.

"So this tunnel really goes for hundreds of kilometers?"

"The entire length of the superconductive railway is about seven hundred kilometers if I recall. If you include the Shinkansen and older lines, Yokohama Station contains about twenty thousand kilometers of railroad inside its boundaries."

Hiroto was unable to envision anything that long. You could walk a lap around the entirety of Ninety-Nine Steps in an hour, and that was probably only about five kilometers.

"Here we are. This is a train car," said Nepshamai. There was a metal plate roughly the size of a tatami mat at Hiroto's feet. The top was completely flat without any protruding features, just anchors for attaching it to something else on each of its corners.

"This is the small kind, used for transporting goods. You place a container on top and send it off. I was hoping for a passenger car, but this will work, too. Sit on top, if you don't mind," instructed Nepshamai.

Hiroto got onto the piece of metal as he was asked, and it sank a few millimeters. Apparently, the plate was floating a little bit off the ground.

"Wait…are we going to ride on this?" Hiroto inquired.

"Don't worry. It can't go fast enough to affect the human body. First, open the cover on the front and bring up the port. Yes, like that. Ah, good, it's an AAT*. I can control that. There's a cable on the back of me; hook that up to the port."

Hiroto followed the instructions on the scrolling screen. Once he hooked up the cable, Nepshamai went silent. The letters on the screen that had been the only illumination vanished, leaving the tunnel completely dark. The only sensation was the sound of the heat exhaust fans spinning on either end of his device. It seemed to be a rather laborious task.

"I have broken in." The display turned on again a minute later. "Let's get moving. We can go in the direction of Tokyo or of Kofu. Which way shall we go?"

"Kofu."

"Very well. I'll start the car. Hold on tight."

The problem was that there was nothing to *hold on* to, period. Hiroto had to get down on his stomach and place his hands over the front edge of the metal plate. It rose about a centimeter into the air, then silently began to accelerate forward.

"I did not anticipate this. I have less power than I thought," the screen declared, its display dim.

"Are we not going to make it to Kofu?"

"Oh, no, not that. This railway is probably connected to Yokohama Station's power systems somewhere. That is not a problem."

"Then what's the problem?"

"It's me. Not having a body is rather—"

The electronic screen abruptly went out. The sole source of light was gone, plunging the tunnel into darkness.

The metal plate continued to accelerate. The air buffeted Hiroto's face tremendously and howled in his ears. The edge of the plate bit into his palms. Despite the incredible stress on his body, his mind was remarkably calm as he thought, *I wonder if Nepshamai forgot about his guarantee that this wouldn't have any effect on me.*

*AAT: Almost All Terminals.

3. Do Androids Dream of Electric Rails?

Kofu was one of the major cities of Yokohama Station. The station had filled the vast Kofu Basin, an inverted triangle, like water filling a bowl several hundred meters deep. As a matter of fact, over ten percent of Honshu's population lived inside this many-layered city structure.

When large-scale sea shipping died out with the expansion of Yokohama Station, it became easier for inland cities to grow and become significant hubs within the station's city network, rather than coastal cities like Tokyo. And because human needs prevented Inside cities from expanding farther outward, it was easier for the structure to support larger cities in capacious, three-dimensional spaces like basins, rather than on the flat plains of the Kanto area.

In layered cities like this one, people congregated toward the top tiers, where space was more valuable because of easy access to the outside. Once people gathered at the top, it stimulated the station to grow a higher floor above. This was a large part of how Yokohama Station had become so massive in basins and valleys.

On the other hand, the lower levels quickly fell into disuse. Similarly, no one recalled that right next to the deepest layers were tunnels where superconductive railways once ran.

It was in an open space on this lowest tier where six automated turnstiles gathered by themselves, encircling a vacant spot. They extended their metal arms, as if trying to catch something in the empty air at the center of their congregation.

"unauthorized suika detected. expelling target from station."

"If anything is unclear, please consult with the nearest station employee."

"unauthorized suika detected. expelling target from station."

"If anything is unclear, please consult with the nearest station employee."

"unauthorized suika detected. expelling target from station."

"If anything is unclear, please consult with the nearest station employee."

At that moment, the concrete wall in the corner of the open concourse crumbled loudly, and Hiroto emerged. The turnstiles sent each other commands via glances, and two of the six approached him.

"welcome to yokohama station. I'm sorry, but I don't detect your suika. please present your suika credentials or a valid entrance ticket."

Hiroto took the box-shaped device from his bag and showed it to the turnstiles. He recalled that he'd agreed to give the 18 Ticket to Nepshamai after it expired. It was hard to tell what to do about that now.

"18 Ticket detected. valid time remaining is three days and sixteen hours. Thank you for visiting yokohama station."

The two turnstiles bowed obsequiously, then returned to the others and resumed swinging their arms at nothing while chanting, "unauthorized suika detected. expelling target from station."

Slipping past them, Hiroto decided they must have busted their sensors. In the opposite corner of the area stood a series of huge statues of ancient, armored warriors holding fans. They were all identical.

There was an escalator behind them, which Hiroto used to head for a higher level.

So many people. So many things.

By Hiroto's standards, Yokosuka and Kamakura were already big cities, but Kofu was on a different scale entirely. On either side of the main corridor were apparel stores, teahouses, fresh food shops, optical stores, restaurants, and bookstores. Hiroto kept an eye out for a place that handled electronic appliances, careful not to bump shoulders with the people passing by.

Nakayama Bioelectronics, said a sign. Purchase your child's Suika here before they turn six! We offer the cheapest middleman fees in Kofu for Suika registration. If you find better, let us know.

A middle-aged man who seemed to be the manager called out to Hiroto. "Welcome. Are you looking for something?"

"Is this a store where you can get a Suika?"

"Yes, we provide Suika intermediation. Do you need to make your child's Suika deposit? We can handle the entire process for 570,000 milliyen."

"No, I don't need that now," replied Hiroto. "I was wondering if a child didn't get a Suika before age six and got dumped outside, is there a way they could get a Suika as an adult?"

"That's hard to say. For one thing, abandoned children rarely reach adulthood, and you'd need the deposit for the Suika registration, plus you can't pay without a Suika, of course. It only works if you have someone to sponsor you and pay the fee," the man explained.

"But there's no technical problem with it?" Hiroto pressed.

"None as far as I'm aware, but we've never had such a case here," prefaced the man, before looking around and lowering his voice. Then, he started to relate a story he'd heard, one of those urban legends that got traded around between bioelectronics vendors.

Long ago, there was once a rich man. One day, he found a nine-year-old girl who'd been abandoned outside of the station near Kofu. She'd been tossed out for not paying the Suika deposit—because her parents were poor or for some other family reason—and survived by foraging for food. The man pitied her, so he called a vendor to perform the Suika process on the girl and then took her in as a foster child. Everyone praised him for his benevolence.

But the sad truth was that the man was a pedophile and used the situation to take advantage of the girl. She obeyed him at first, but one day, while he was sleeping, she attempted to escape from his home. His residence was on the top floor of Kofu at the time and was very spacious.

The pedophile woke up, realized that the girl had fled, and chased after her. She threw a flower vase she found in the hallway at him, injuring him. Then, she made her escape far away from his home. Unfortunately, the automated turnstiles found her and deauthorized her Suika for committing violence. For the second time, she was ejected from the station. This time, it was in a place with no food. Eventually, she succumbed to starvation.

"And in the end, fearing that the situation would get out of hand, the man claimed she'd died of sickness," the bioelectronics vendor concluded.

"That's a terrible story."

"Yes. The poor child had lived outside for so long. She probably didn't understand Inside laws. Poor thing."

"…I have another question. Are there any tools that can recharge this?" Hiroto asked, pulling Nepshamai's electronic sign from his bag. The sign's talkative red screen had been silent since the railway tunnel.

"Hmm. Never seen a device like this before. Who makes it?" the middle-aged man inquired.

Hiroto didn't answer. If he said it was from JR North Japan, it risked causing trouble.

"Well, whenever folks have something they can't identify, I send them along to a place called the Trinket Shop on the 117th floor. They'll take any weird thing there. You can get to the higher levels from that elevator." The man pointed.

"All right."

"But the proprietor's a bit of a kook, so the hours tend to be unpredictable."

Hiroto thanked the man and left.

Most likely, he wasn't going to get anywhere without reviving Nepshamai's battery. It was pathetic to think that it had been Nepshamai who'd had the idea to go to Kofu, found the superconductive railway that would take them there, and operated the train car—and now that Hiroto was on his own, he was utterly helpless.

There was no conveyor direct to the 117th floor. Elevators in the metropolis areas of the station grew through the structure about thirty tiers at a time when there was an appropriate vertical space for it. The station seemed to intentionally add elevators to levels with lots of human activity, but it was rarely anywhere convenient because the available space was so limited. To get from Nakayama Bioelectronics on the 59th floor to the 117th, Hiroto had to take many separate trips.

He found lots of automated turnstiles on every tier he visited, but all of them were seated and immobile. Two brothers, around eight years old, were climbing all over one. Their mother exclaimed, "Come, we need to hurry before the store closes!"

When the younger of the two said, "Shyumai Punch! Shyumai Punch!" and began battering the turnstile's rear, the mother went pale. "Don't punch the station equipment!" she shouted, drawing the attention of the crowd around them.

A station staffer rushed over and asked, "What's the matter?" The mother explained the situation, and he kindly assured, "Don't worry, the turnstiles won't react to a child hitting them. But you there, you should listen to your parent!" The mother and her children bowed to the staffer gratefully. The automated turnstile's face display stayed dark the entire time.

Security Inside was upheld by cameras and other devices connected to Suikanet; the turnstiles were just the enforcers. They were often found stationed where they might be called upon at a moment's notice if trouble started. In perpetually crowded places like Kofu, they could be seen sitting against the walls to charge. The uniformed station staffers were busy hustling around instead.

As he walked around Kofu, Hiroto took notice of something odd. There were slight differences between the staffers and the turnstiles here from those he'd witnessed in Yokosuka and Kamakura.

The station employees were, according to Nepshamai, more like unofficial citizen groups formed by humans from the various Inside regions, so it made sense that their uniforms changed. But why weren't the turnstiles all the same?

The Trinket Shop on the 117th floor had a sign in a dated font and was very ostentatious about its old-fashioned Japanese taste. Everything seemed to have come out of a samurai movie. If not for another sign that read, WE DEAL IN ALL MANNER OF ELECTRONICS, you wouldn't have known they handled appliances at all.

"Welcome," said a woman sitting in the middle of the shop when she saw Hiroto enter. She was wearing an apron over an athletic jacket. Her long hair was tied in the back, and she wore silver-rimmed glasses. She looked a little bit older than Hiroto.

"I want to recharge this. Do you have a tool for that?" Hiroto asked, holding out Nepshamai's screen.

She took a quick look at the back of the device and said, "Wait, this is AAT compatible. Where did you dig up something like this? They haven't used that standard in Yokohama Station in ages." Hiroto decided that she was already going to be much more helpful than the last place.

"It's hard to explain, but I really need to get it running again. If you can't help me, I need to take it somewhere else."

"If *I* can't help you, no one in Kofu will. Just sit down there and wait a minute," the woman instructed, pointing to a chair in front of the store counter. She went into a back room and began rummaging through an old, traditional cabinet. It was stuffed full of cables of all kinds that leaped out from the pressure when she opened the drawers. It seemed like a lot of work to get each closed again after it had been opened.

"AAT compatible machines were used a lot before the war because they were so efficient, but it's a lost technology now since Yokohama Station never generated the means of production. I hear they do make them in Hokkaido, but you still need an adaptor to link up to Suika-net, so there are problems…"

The woman babbled on while she scrounged through the cables. It seemed more like she was talking to herself than to him. It reminded Hiroto of someone.

He murmured in reply at appropriate times as he glanced around the shop. A plethora of baffling mechanical gadgets and parts were on display. Yosuke would've probably enjoyed examining all of them.

There was a photo frame on a writing desk in the corner of the room. Contained within wasn't a digital image but a physical print. There were about ten young men and women in the picture. The woman from the shop was in the middle. She looked roughly ten years younger, still a minor, and there was a familiar face next to her.

"Hang on," Hiroto said. The shopkeeper stopped rummaging and looked at him. "Do you know this man?" He picked up the picture and pointed at the face he recognized.

"…You know Higashiyama?" the woman asked.

"Yeah. He showed up in my hometown about a year ago. He was part of a group called the Dodger Alliance but had to flee from the automated turnstiles. I'm here because I'm looking for the leader of his group."

"Looking for the leader," the woman repeated. She tossed a hunk of cables onto the tatami covering the floor and returned to the counter.

"Yeah. The leader must be hiding from the turnstiles, and I'm supposed to help him."

"Where is your town?"

"East of here. A place called Ninety-Nine Steps, on the Miura Peninsula."

The woman tapped the keyboard of a laptop. It pulled up a diagram of Yokohama Station. The Miura Peninsula was illuminated in red, but there was no hit for the name "Ninety-Nine Steps." It was a name invented by cape dwellers, after all.

"Here," Hiroto said, pointing at the screen. It was right where the Suikanet map had a label that read, YOKOHAMA STATION EXIT 1415.

"So Higashiyama asked you to come all this way, just to search for *me*," the woman stated, taking the photograph out of the frame. On the back was a handwritten message: *Original members of the Dodger Alliance.*

Hiroto stared at the words. "That's...what I was supposed to do," he managed. He then looked out the entrance of the store. Just a few dozen meters away, the turnstiles sat silent and menacing. "But it seems like that's not the situation. I heard you were on the run from the turnstiles."

"Yes, I am. Very much so," the woman admitted. "I've got lots of questions for you, but some introductions are in order. I'm Keiha Nijo. I was the leader of the Dodger Alliance. Nice to meet you," she said, giving Hiroto a quick nod of the head.

"Hiroto Mishima," answered Hiroto, taken aback. He had plenty of questions of his own.

ICoCar System (Coordinate Obfuscation System)

Human beings with a Suika implant were continuously transmitting their locational data to Suikanet. If a user's Suika credentials were revoked, automated turnstiles would descend upon those coordinates to apprehend the violator. Lateral and vertical positioning were sent separately. (This was said to be a holdover from the era when GPS satellites were still functional.)

The former leader of the Dodger Alliance, Keiha Nijo, had developed a method of falsifying vertical coordinates. Her home and business in Kofu, the Trinket Shop, transmitted it from its home server. So despite being present on the 117th floor of Kofu, she was believed by Suikanet to be located on the very bottom floor, and Suikanet had dispatched automated turnstiles to that location. Keiha was currently hard at work devising a method to falsify lateral values too. The combination of these two misdirections was to be known as the ICoCar (Imitation of Coordinates in Cartesian Space) System.

"So basically, I can't leave Kofu," Keiha explained. If she tried to move to a different city, it would inevitably lead through places with a very shallow vertical structure. Because she could only falsify vertical coordinates contained within the physical limits of Yokohama Station, once it was flat enough, the automated turnstiles would find her.

"I'm sorry to say that Higashiyama died half a year ago. People who come out from Inside often die pretty quickly. The professor said it has something to do with something called an immune system," Hiroto explained.

"...Oh."

Keiha looked at the photo on the desk. It featured the twelve original members of the Dodger Alliance. At its largest, the collective had numbered close to one hundred. But, as often happened with cyber-groups, there were members whose faces Keiha had never seen.

Keiha explained that the alliance had been quite active until four years ago. Most of their activities involved hacking Suikanet.

Suikanet was the network built into Yokohama Station. It had origi-nally served as a means of communication between the various station facilities and features, such as the automated turnstiles. Roughly a century ago, people had deciphered the APIs and learned to use them for information transmission, but the network's actual internal struc-turing was still largely a mystery.

"So what'd you do to get exiled from Yokohama Station?" Hiroto asked. "Higashiyama told me he was exiled for rebellious behavior."

"He said that?"

"Yeah. He told me the alliance aimed to seize command of Suika-net's infrastructure, control the automated turnstiles, and free human-ity from the rule of Yokohama Station. He said the Dodger Alliance bucks the station's authority and follows a great leader's direction. I remember him bragging that the Dodger Alliance was the only group that had successfully gained control of Suikanet. But because too much interference by human hands is seen as an act of destruction against the station, the Suika credentials of all the alliance members were revoked, and the turnstiles went after them. Something like that," Hiroto recalled.

Higashiyama had proudly repeated this story so many times while he was alive that Hiroto could recite it all from memory. He didn't really understand what it meant. It was just a string of fascinating words to him; a connection to an unknown world.

Keiha looked uncomfortable. "I regret what I did to him and the others. It all started as a personal project for me. But I dragged them into something dangerous," she admitted.

The Dodger Alliance had many ways of gaining access to Suikanet and evaded the turnstiles much longer than the average violator, but ultimately, they were all caught and dumped outside of the station somewhere. By the time Keiha managed to set up her ICoCar System in Kofu and settle in, she'd lost track of her compatriots.

"I don't know what all of that means, but it sounds rough," Hiroto said. "Higashiyama really looked up to you. He kept saying, 'Our leader is incredible, our leader's a true genius.'"

It wasn't necessarily the best memory for Hiroto, since those statements were usually accompanied by a healthy dose of ridicule for the people of Ninety-Nine Steps in comparison.

"This is pretty amazing, though," he continued. "There's a guy in my town who can connect to Suikanet and collect some data, but I had no idea it was possible to falsify your location and control the turnstiles and so on."

"Well, I'm more amazed by this thing you brought in. As well as your little friend," Keiha replied, setting down Nepshamai's electronic sign. She was more interested in the canceler. "Something that can erase the structural genetic field? I find it…hard to believe."

"You should try using it."

"Well, there's a place where I'd appreciate having an open hole. Can you help with that?"

"Sure. Though I can't waste it too much, since I'm worried about the battery."

The two walked out of the store. Keiha turned off the lights and put up a sign with the words CLOSED TODAY.

"It's a business in name only. I just put up the electronics store sign so I can tinker all day and not attract suspicion," Keiha clarified.

"The turnstiles get suspicious?" asked Hiroto.

"Them? No, they're not smart enough for that. I mean the staffers. If they want to, they have the tools to check to see that my Suika was revoked. That would be a big problem for me, obviously—especially since the staffers claim to be carrying out the will of Yokohama Station."

They got on an elevator and rode down to the 91st floor. It was denser than the other levels of Kofu. Past the small residential sector near the elevator, there was an enormous fruit factory. Grape and peach planters stretched as far as the eye could see under red lights. Some workers walked around here and there among the rows.

"An Inside farm?" Hiroto murmured. The people of Ninety-Nine Steps lived off the scraps dumped out of the station. They'd heard that there were food production facilities in Yokohama Station, but this was much larger than he'd imagined. Pillars obscured sizable portions of the facility, but it was clearly much larger than Ninety-Nine Steps itself.

Keiha was not heading for the farm, however. She made her way quickly along the moving walkway. There were partitioned rooms here and there that seemed to be lodgings for the workers. Hiroto wondered if living in an utterly red environment like this made your eyes go bad.

Eventually, they reached the end of the factory, which was marked with a glass barrier wall, on the other side of which was another factory space. There were many conveyor belts in there, each ferrying metal arm parts.

"What's that? Are they making machines?"

"Yes. This is an automated turnstile production plant."

Beyond the conveyor belts, other turnstiles were silently assembling various parts.

"It's all automated," Keiha remarked. "There are no humans here. The entire factory is surrounded by glass infused with the structural genetic field. The only openings are the gates for sending in raw materials and sending out the finished product."

Living outside of the station, Hiroto was very familiar with the automated turnstiles that safeguarded the boundary between the outside world and Inside, but he'd never seen where they were made.

"Who built this factory, then?" Hiroto pressed.

"There was probably an automated factory here before Yokohama Station. It was absorbed into the genetic field and replicated here and there. I've seen identical facilities in several other cities," answered Keiha.

"Did the automated turnstiles exist before Yokohama Station?"

"That's the natural assumption. Yokohama Station can't create complex structures on its own."

They walked alongside the glass wall at the edge of the factory. After a while, they were out of the fruit production facility, and the only things to be seen through the glass were the turnstile factory on one side and empty space on the other.

"Can you make a hole here? As inconspicuous as possible," Keiha requested.

"Sure thing," Hiroto responded.

Hiroto shone the structural genetic field canceler along the glass barrier in a shape big enough for a person to get through. Then, he pushed on the wall with his foot, and the spot where the genetic field had vanished cracked cleanly through. Another kick broke the glass, and the circle shattered. According to the readout, Hiroto had put the power at the minimum level, so it didn't have any effect on the battery's charge. He felt like he was getting the hang of the strange little tool.

"…Amazing. It really did erase the genetic field," Keiha observed. She slipped right through the hole and into the factory without much concern for the shards of glass. "There's so much stuff in here I wanted. Will you help me carry it?"

Keiha removed a number of electric bits from a box labeled "surplus parts" and tossed them into a container. Then, she inserted cables into every port she could see and began copying data. The automated turnstiles working the assembly line continued their silent labor, unaware that the most wanted person in Yokohama Station, the one-time leader of a secret criminal society, was openly pilfering in their presence.

"Amazing. It's got the source for the communications client! I've only ever pulled the binary off of scrapped chips," Keiha marveled, staring at the dark screen of her monitor. "No firmware for the turnstiles, though. That seems to have vanished after the war." Her excitement was so palpable that Hiroto felt it was more likely she'd be spotted by a passerby instead.

"If we blew up this factory with a bomb or something, would that fulfill your goals? It would stop production of the turnstiles so you could be free, right?" Hiroto proposed.

Keiha stuffed more objects into the container. "As long as the structural genetic field exists, it will regrow everything. Even if you used that canceler to erase the entire factory, it would just grow another one somewhere else," she replied.

Hiroto suddenly realized he'd asked a stupid question.

Once she was finished copying the data, Keiha pulled the cable out of the port. "There's no point to destructive sabotage. We're not Winter War-era guerilla fighters."

After an hour, Keiha had finally finished everything she'd wanted to do. She'd filled four containers with parts, and she'd slapped stickers on top of them that read, TRINKET SHOP, OFFERING REPAIRS FOR ELECTRONICS OF ALL KINDS. IN BUSINESS ON FLOOR 117, SUIKANET ADDRESS XXXX-XXXX-XXXX. OPERATING HOURS FLUCTUATE.

She gave three of the containers to Hiroto to carry. The electronic parts were much heavier than clothes, but the containers were designed to be stacked, making them much more comfortable to lug around than the cardboard boxes.

The two made their way back to the 117th floor with the containers. Some station staffers eyed them with piercing looks, but Keiha gave them a polite, "Thank you for your service."

"Well, I guess you believe my story now," Hiroto said.

"Yes. I believe that you got here with an 18 Ticket from

Higashiyama, and I believe your story about the electronic screen from JR North Japan…not that I had any reason to doubt you."

Once she'd copied her newly acquired data to her computer, Keiha got back to the business of repairing Nepshamai.

"I'm sorry to say that this one's going to be tricky," she admitted.

"It's that bad?" Hiroto asked.

"The interface uses the AAT standard, but I've never seen hardware like what's on the inside. If I power it the wrong way, I might fry all the data."

"I'm pretty sure he said something about it being similar to human brains. That it was designed by someone named Yukie," explained Hiroto.

That meant the data contained in the device was Shamai's personality itself. Were it to vanish, it would mean the death of the android. That's how Hiroto thought of it, anyway. He wasn't certain how Shamai would've defined it.

"You said that was the person who invented the canceler, too," Keiha recalled.

"Yeah. Must be an incredible engineer," Hiroto responded.

"Listen…I've been collecting and deciphering information from Suikanet for over a decade, and I've seen a fair number of secret correspondences from JR North Japan. Even ten years ago, though, their level of tech was barely any different than Kyushu's. All of a sudden, I stopped finding their messages. Or to be precise, they were all impossible to crack and buried inside other data."

A few years ago, there'd been rumors that the Seikan Tunnel defense line had been breached and that JR North Japan had fallen into ruin. Maybe the lack of messages from up there had played a role in helping to spread that lie.

"I haven't been able to follow the state of Hokkaido's tech since then," Keiha continued. "But there's no way a single excellent engineer could make such a difference in just a few years and over such a wide array. Even with androids indistinguishable from humans and devices that destroy the structural genetic field, it seems unlikely. This is real life, not some comic book."

"So what's your point?" Hiroto asked.

"The first thing that comes to mind is that 'Yukie' isn't the name of a single person but shorthand for a large group of inventors, or perhaps their representative. But even then, it doesn't make sense that such a large coalition would appear so suddenly. A more practical answer is that 'Yukie' didn't develop all of that tech herself but simply happened upon something that already existed."

"Who would do that?"

"Your little electronic screen friend controlled a superconductive railway to get you here, despite never having seen one before, right? That doesn't make sense. There's no information on superconductive railways in Suikanet anywhere. If I haven't been able to find it, it doesn't exist."

Hiroto decided he didn't have much choice but to take her word for that.

"And historically speaking, there were no superconductive railways in Hokkaido, so if there's still info there, I can only envision one possibility," declared Keiha definitively. "The JR Integrated Intelligence. This 'Yukie' has successfully unlocked the integrated intelligence's language."

"Long, long ago," Keiha began, as though launching into a fairy tale.

The JR Integrated Intelligence was a massive artificial intelligence that once existed to run Japan's railway network. From research into the human brain, it was known that a sufficiently complicated system could form the basis of an intelligent mind. This particular project created a massive, sentient structure using the railway network that crossed the entire nation.

Amid the Winter War, various businesses competed to develop the best possible tactical AIs. Many models were proposed, from massive central-server types in Tokyo, to distributed types spread across a network of ordinary consumer computers. Still, to some extent, all were susceptible to bombardment from space or viral cyberattacks.

The most significant benefit of the proposed JR Integrated Intelligence was its resilience. Unless an enemy physically controlled a majority of the plethora of network nodes (stations) littered across the islands of Japan, it could still function in a trustworthy manner. Losing that much of the homeland would've meant forfeiting the war anyway. Surrendering the capital had already been a real possibility. Faced with nothing to lose, the Japanese government approved the plan. The integrated intelligence functioned as the nation's practical force through the chaotic years after the war.

"But at some point, one of the nodes making up the integrated intelligence—Yokohama Station—began replicating itself, and we don't know why. The integrated intelligence was absorbed along with the entire railway network, and it ceased functioning as an artificial intelligence. All that was left was Yokohama Station, spanning all of Honshu, and the AI's nodes, devoid of their original function," Keiha explained.

"So you're saying JR North Japan dug up one of those old stations and extracted a bunch of data about old technology, like the canceler and androids like Shamai?" Hiroto inquired.

"Digging it up wouldn't be that hard, as long as you excavated the site of a former station. That's what the people in Kyushu are doing. But that's the easy part," Keiha replied.

The JR Integrated Intelligence collected data from the Internet, a network that still covered the globe at that point. It utilized that information within its own system to develop unique thought patterns and language structure. However, since Yokohama Station's expansion shut down the JR Integrated Intelligence's sentient functions, no one had been able to decipher that language. It was abandoned binary data.

Once, someone had had the preposterous idea of preserving a genius scientist's brain so that later generations could unlock its secrets. The notion of deciphering the integrated intelligence's code was just as unlikely to succeed as something that hare-brained.

"This 'Yukie' must have done it, though, right?" Hiroto reasoned.

"Yes. It's not realistic, but that's the most likely answer for all of this," Keiha said.

The people of Hiroto's time knew very little about the history of Honshu before Yokohama Station took over. The inhabitants of that bygone era knew much more about technology than those today, but countries had descended into war and fallen to ruin. Perhaps digging up the relics of that age would provide a means to fight back against Yokohama Station.

Hiroto let Keiha finish her story, although at least half of it was beyond his comprehension.

"So basically, it'll be too hard to bring Shamai back if he's composed of really advanced stuff," he concluded.

"I'll do everything I can think of, but don't get your hopes up. This isn't too far off from raising the dead," Keiha replied.

Hiroto nodded. He thought back on his experiences.

Human beings inevitably died, of course, and machines eventually broke down. Something about Nepshamai felt a little too clean, though.

If he'd been built to resemble the human brain, shouldn't he have exhibited more human-like traits, like fear and panic? Did building an android mean eliminating all of those emotions?

While he pondered this, Keiha removed a small plastic case from the drawer of a writing desk. It contained a pair of old eyeglasses with large lenses. She took off her own silver-framed glasses, put the others on, and then headed for a machine in the corner of the room. It was a large black case about the size of an automated turnstile, with the top covered by a clear plastic lid.

From a container filled with pilfered goods from the turnstile factory, she removed a thin needle wrapped in a polymer bag, lifted the plastic lid, and very, very carefully attached the needle to a mechanical arm before closing the top again.

Then, she removed the cover from Nepshamai's scrolling sign. There was a little cube with sides measuring about three centimeters each inside. This had to be the "main memory storage" Nepshamai had mentioned. Keiha removed the cube with a pair of large tweezers and deposited it into the black case.

She hit a few switches, and with a high-pitched beep, the metallic arm under the lid began to move.

Once her task was done, Keiha removed the old glasses, put them back in their case, and then exhaled. She picked the silver-framed glasses off the desk and placed them back on her nose.

The process lasted about five minutes. Hiroto watched in absolute stillness, as though he were witnessing some austere religious ritual.

"So what were you doing?" he asked after a moment.

"I'm scanning the internal structure. Then, I'll check the Suikanet database for similar structures. If there are any comparable devices Inside, I might have some options."

"Will it take time?"

"Depends on the scanning speed. The highest resolution this machine can manage takes about seven or eight hours," Keiha said.

Hiroto was happy to know there was still hope, but it was also a reminder that he was ultimately dependent on other people with superior knowledge and expertise than himself.

"If all of this *does* work out, what will you do next?" Keiha inquired.

"Hmmm." Hiroto mulled that one over. "This all started with Higashiyama asking me to rescue you, so I guess I've fulfilled the duty that got me this 18 Ticket. I suppose I'll spend the next three days however I like."

"Do you have somewhere to go?"

"Actually, yes. I could use your help looking it up. I tried to find it on a kiosk earlier, and it did exist, but I couldn't determine a route."

"All right. What's it called?" Keiha asked, opening an application on her laptop called *Suikamap: A Detailed Station Guide*.

"Exit 42."

Keiha paused and looked at Hiroto.

"...Say that again?"

"Exit 42."

She thought the name over for a bit. She then turned the open laptop toward Hiroto and pushed it forward. "See the magnifying glass icon in the upper left? Put what you're searching for in there, and you can see for yourself."

"Huh? Uh, all right."

Hiroto brought his hands up to start typing on the keyboard, but all the keys were black, with no letters written on them.

"What's wrong with this keyboard?" he asked.

"They wore off. I've been using it for over a decade."

"Where's the E?"

"Second row, fourth from the left."

"And the X?"

"Second row from the bottom, third from the left."

"I?"

"You what?"

"No, the letter I."

"Second row, and it's the...ninth from the left."

"Oops. I hit U."

"Backspace is the farthest on the right of the top row."

With Keiha's instruction, Hiroto input the letters one at a time, wondering why she was having him go through all this trouble. After a full minute, he had entered "Exit 42," and the icon turned to a rotating hourglass for a few moments.

"1 hit found."

It pulled up a red dot labeled *Exit 42* and a map of the surrounding area. This one had more information than the image Hiroto had seen at the kiosk. It was very cluttered. Thick gray lines surrounded the red dot. According to the map scale, the containment area was about a kilometer wide.

"What's this gray stuff?"

"The station walls. This is saying that it's surrounded by walls containing the structural genetic field. There are no doors, so you can't reach it. No wonder you couldn't find any routes there. That tool changes things, though." Keiha glanced at the structural genetic field canceler.

"Where in Yokohama Station is this? Is it far from here?"

"Press control-minus to zoom out."

"What key is that?"

"...See the zoom-out icon in the upper right? Press that. The icon with the magnifying glass and the minus sign."

Hiroto did as instructed, and the gray box got smaller and smaller, revealing more of the surrounding terrain. The red dot appeared to be in the mountains farther west of Kofu, just about in the center of Honshu. It was as if the point was trying to be as far from the coast as possible. Cities in the vicinity had names like Matsumoto, Hida, and Gero.

"Looks like a straight shot would be one hundred kilometers. That would be difficult over flat land, but there are several mountain ranges along the way, so it's no problem."

"It's better to have big elevation ranges?"

"Well, of course. That's where Yokohama Station grows elevators. Give it to me," insisted Keiha. She took the laptop back and entered a command with incredible finger speed. Windows zipped into being on the screen and vanished.

The map displayed a blue dotted line. It seemed to be the shortest possible route.

"First, you'll cross the Southern Japanese Alps, then descend to Ina. From there, you'll climb Mt. Koma and go down to Kiso. It's a straight ascent from that point on. By escalator speed alone, that just fits into three days, but if you're walking the steps, there should be plenty of time. You've got lots of stamina, right?"

"Compared to Insiders, yeah," said Hiroto, with a note of pride.

The laptop displayed the shortest route using escalators and an expected travel time. Hiroto didn't recognize the names of any of the places on the map. The idea of venturing so far inland left him oddly excited.

"It'll still be difficult, though. I might be able to reach Exit 42 in three days, but I won't have time to get back out of the station," he explained.

"What do you mean?"

"My 18 Ticket's only got three and a half days left."

"18 Ticket?"

"It's like a limited-time Suika," Hiroto said, pulling the 18 Ticket out of his bag. The screen showed that his valid time remaining was three days and thirteen hours.

"So when that time is up, the automated turnstiles come after you?"

"Yeah. Supposedly."

After a long moment's thought, Keiha stared at the charted route again. "Hang on. I'll come up with something for that."

"What do you mean?"

"I can tweak it a little bit. As you can see, my Suika was revoked four years ago, but I'm still here. As long as I have a handle on your precise location, I can cover for you until you escape," Keiha replied, displaying a map of all of Japan on the laptop. She entered prompt commands while muttering to herself.

A green stripe appeared on the screen with the label SUIKANET NODE CAPTURE STATUS. It stretched from Kofu to the far west of Honshu. At the western end, there was an icon with the word KYOTO above it. Here and there, Hiroto saw little status updates that read things like, "Turnstile Dummy OK," and "Direct Communication OK."

Hiroto wondered why Keiha was going to such lengths for a mission that wasn't even hers.

"I try to keep this map as current as possible, but escalator placements are always changing. The major routing shouldn't need altering, but you'll want to use your best judgment on the finer points," she warned.

"Uh, sure," answered Hiroto, though he had no idea what kind of judgment he was expected to utilize.

"So that electronic screen of yours said to go to this place, then?" Keiha asked, looking at the black case. The arm inside was moving very slowly, scanning Nepshamai.

"No, that was an old man from my hometown. He used to live Inside. He was a professor at some lab or something. It was hard to understand his language, so I don't know much about it," Hiroto responded.

Keiha looked suspicious. "You couldn't understand him?"

"Yeah. It was like he was speaking Japanese but not really. At first, I thought that was how people talked Inside, but folks around here sound basically the same as people from my hometown, so I think he must have come from farther away."

"That can't be right. Suikanet has mostly unified language

everywhere in the station. I was born in a city far to the west of here, but the only difference was a few idiosyncrasies in vocabulary. It seems unlikely that anyone would speak so differently that you couldn't understand them."

"Then why?"

Keiha was quiet for a moment before saying, "I don't know." After all the time they'd spent together, this was probably the first time she'd admitted something like that. Hiroto could tell as much by her consternated expression.

"What did this professor say you'd find there?"

"I'm not sure. 'The answer to everything' or something. He was usually vague like that. Plus, he was going senile," Hiroto said.

"And what did your little screen friend say about this place?"

"Nothing. I asked him, but he didn't know anything about it."

"Meaning he didn't know personally? Or JR North Japan as a whole doesn't know?"

"I'm not sure."

◆

"We've got some time to kill. Do you want to go out for something to eat?"

"Out of the station?"

Keiha chuckled at that one. "I guess that's what 'out' means to you, huh?"

"Well, yeah. Have you never been outside the station?"

"Nope."

Hiroto's head was starting to hurt. It made sense that those like him, without a Suika, couldn't get Inside, but the Inside people could venture out all they wanted. The only ones who ever came to the cape were exiles, though. Ninety-Nine Steps hardly ever saw a single person with a legitimate Suika.

It was less that the Inside folk avoided the outside and more that they were explicitly shunning those who lived beyond the station. There was a reasonably large beach a short distance from Ninety-Nine Steps.

While nobody lived there because it was ill-suited for that, a few people would venture out from Inside during the summer to swim.

"Hey, do the Inside...er, the citizens around here live their entire lives without seeing the sun?"

"No. You can do that by going up to the higher levels. Lots of folks go outside to see the sunrise on the first day of the year. Some people like sunbathing. I don't, because it hurts my skin."

Keiha put up the CLOSED TODAY sign again. The pair descended on an elevator to the 109th floor. There was an old placard there reading, RESTAURANT DISTRICT. Numerous flyers and notices for specific restaurants were pasted over it.

Humans had created restaurants inside the station structure with boards and fabric for decoration. Makeshift businesses lined both sides of the corridor, advertising their wares.

DIRECT FROM THE 132ND FLOOR—KOSHU BEEF STEAK.

THE ORIGINAL CUCUMBER BOWL.

INSIDE'S SECOND-BEST SOFT SERVE.

TRADITIONAL MINOBU-STYLE TOFU SKIN.

It was after eight o'clock at night, but many people were still wandering the corridor. Automated turnstiles were sitting in place here and there, making it very difficult to avoid them entirely.

Each restaurant was about the same size, but one glance through their windows was enough to tell Hiroto whether one was a fancy restaurant or an everyday eatery. Apparently, it came down to the customers' clothes. In some restaurants, men and women in suits sat quietly with their forks. In others, young laborers raced with their chopsticks to finish eating and get back to fulfilling their work quotas. Hiroto spotted a few people wearing the same outfits as the farmers on the 91st floor.

"Anything you feel like?" Keiha inquired.

"Well, I don't even have a Suika, so I've never properly bought anything Inside. I'll leave that up to you."

"I'm amazed you got this far."

They went into a dingy place built for laborers. Keiha's athletic jacket and Hiroto's old clothes didn't stand out in a place like this. There were bottles lined up on the counter with the words *Katsunuma Wine* on them.

"Katsunuma?"

"It was once a big place for grape production. They say it was the farm on the 91st floor before Yokohama Station absorbed it. Now it's just a brand name," Keiha explained.

Nepshamai had commented on the same thing; Yokohama Station would incorporate the names of places it covered as it expanded.

"Don't things like this trickle out to where you live?" she asked.

"It's usually discarded stuff. We don't get a lot of nonperishable alcohol or food. Now and then, we'll get a few cases of stuff, though. We leave them at the elder's house and use them sparingly for celebrations."

"Maybe the station generated a new fermentation center somewhere. When the shipping routes are slower to generate, the excess product inevitably gets discarded."

Hiroto looked at the menu, but he was more curious about the bottles.

"If you want to drink wine, you can order it. There's no concern about money."

"No concern?"

"None at all. However, I wouldn't overdo it if you're not used to alcohol. It'll make tomorrow much harder," Keiha cautioned.

Unable to overcome his curiosity, Hiroto decided to order a glass. A server poured an old, well-used glass about half-full.

"Well, here's to today," Keiha declared. She clinked her cup of green tea with Hiroto's glass.

"Was today something worth celebrating for you?" Hiroto inquired.

"Yes. I've had hardly a single piece of good news in the three years since coming to Kofu, but today, I've had three, all at once."

"Three?"

"The first was learning what happened to Higashiyama. I'm happy to know that his end was relatively peaceful, at least. I'm sorry you had to come all this way to 'save' me, but I was glad to hear about that. Some of us suffered much worse fates."

Hiroto took a swallow of the wine. It had much more alcohol in it than the bottled beer that showed up at the cape, and it made his brain feel like it was floating a bit.

"The second was learning that there's a way to counteract the structural genetic field."

"That's good news to you?"

"Of course."

Hiroto didn't understand. Keiha herself had stated that destructive sabotage was a meaningless act. So either she was happy about getting to sneak into the factory and steal mechanical parts or just curious about the possibilities as an engineer.

"I don't understand the way smart people think," Hiroto admitted. Drinking alcohol was making it much easier for him to say whatever passed through his mind. "I'm glad that me coming here was good news for you, though."

"I'm not especially smart," Keiha conceded. "I'm just more selfish than anyone else, and therefore, I need more methods to do what I want."

Hiroto took another mouthful of wine.

"So why did you come here, then?" pressed Keiha. "Did something happen back home that made you feel an obligation to Higashiyama?"

"No, I didn't owe him anything. In fact, I basically took care of him. If I'm being honest, he was kind of a patronizing jerk."

"And if *I'm* being honest, I kind of agree with you," chuckled Keiha.

"But I suppose I just wanted to feel like I had a mission or a calling of some kind," Hiroto decided. Normally, he would never have talked about his feelings like this. Katsunuma wine was pretty powerful stuff.

"At the cape where I live, we have pretty much everything we need to survive, just from trash dumped out of the station. There's not a lot of work to go around. Everyone just finds their own way to pass the time. Once in a while, someone gets kicked out of the Inside, like Higashiyama or that professor I mentioned. It was hard to understand them at times, but it always felt like they had their own compass, their own way of navigating things. So when they asked me to do something, it didn't matter what it was. I just felt like going Inside would help me find the version of myself I wanted to be. Whether that was by helping you or going to this Exit 42 place."

Hiroto didn't feel like he was explaining himself very well, but Keiha listened intently, nonetheless.

"Let me be clear, though," she cut in, her expression severe. "While I said there's a way to get you outside of the station, it's not a hundred percent reliable. The place is far from here, and you never know what kind of accidents might occur along the way."

Hiroto nodded to show he understood. If it were that easy, Keiha wouldn't have lost all of her companions after their Suikas were revoked.

"Whether you go there or not depends on how much trust you have in your professor's claim and my tech. If you want to get out of the station safely, I recommend heading south from here, passing Mt. Fuji, and exiting into Suruga Bay. Three days is more than enough time to get there. Following the coast east along Izu Peninsula will take you back home."

The waiter brought bowls to the table. It was a kind of food Hiroto had never seen before—thick udon noodles in pumpkin soup. They ate without talking.

The woman at the register asked if they were paying separately, and Keiha said, "I'm getting both." She put her hand on a small box next to the register. The screen on the device displayed the words *Withdrawing 2,415 milliyen.*

Back at her shop on the 117th floor, the clock on the pillar said it was ten o'clock. Hiroto always got sleepy when he drank, and his eyelids felt very heavy now.

"What time do you wake up?" Keiha inquired.

"Normally...I go to sleep about now and wake up at six."

"Then you should use the room in the back. I normally sleep from seven in the morning until two in the afternoon."

She opened the sliding door. There were a number of machines humming away with their fans in the back room. In their midst was a single set of blankets, neatly folded into thirds.

"Thanks. I had to sleep on the hard bed of a holding cell last night, and then that guy woke me up," Hiroto recounted, pointing to Nepshamai's screen.

"I'll do whatever I can with this one while you're asleep. But don't expect too much."

"All right."

"Get your rest and decide whether you're going or not tomorrow," Keiha instructed, and she shut the sliding door.

It was clear Keiha wanted Hiroto to go to Exit 42. He didn't know what was there, but Keiha *did* know something about it. She just didn't want to say anything. That's why she let him choose how to proceed.

Even with the lights off, the flickering bulbs and buzzing fans of the machines continued. Plus, there were the sounds of Keiha working in the room next door. Thankfully, between the interrupted sleep of the previous night and all of the walking, Hiroto fell unconscious rather quickly.

As Hiroto's mind slipped into dreams, he wondered if the professor was actually part of that JR what's-it-called intelligence. Maybe that was why he'd spoken so oddly. Was it even possible for an AI to go senile, though?

Toshiru Kubo spent all his time thinking about how to steal weapons.

In the interest of conserving energy, JR Fukuoka's employee dorm turned out the lights at ten o'clock. In the dark, Toshiru set his device's screen brightness to the minimum and examined the layout of the company's armory and the military division's personnel travel routes, devising a plan to steal a gun. As always, he concluded that it was virtually impossible. This was simply one of his daily habits after work hours.

Crossing over to the island of Shikoku from Kyushu was going to require a means of defending himself. Shikoku was not the kind of place you could survive without a good weapon. Unfortunately, all Toshiru had was the ordinary pistol afforded to all Kyushu residents for self-defense.

In the armory, however, there were the latest electric pump guns, the N700 line. The company had started developing them shortly after Toshiru had joined, and he'd taken part in their production. In his twenty-four years of life, that'd been the only worthwhile event. Setting aside the question of whether owning an electric pump gun was necessary, he really wanted one.

Electric pump guns were weapons manufactured in Kyushu, but they were utterly useless at stopping Yokohama Station's advance from Honshu. It was an anti-personnel weapon, and anything above a certain level of power was under the sole control of JR Fukuoka, Kyushu's sovereign force. The company produced the armaments, distributed them to its military division, and tightly managed every last one.

Stealing one out of the armory at the Hakata headquarters was impossible. You'd never get out of the building. The warehouse at the Kumamoto branch was a more practical choice. The trouble was, it would be tough to steal from a place where you were unfamiliar with the layout and then flee to Shikoku while avoiding detection.

"Dammit, this is a pain in the ass. I just wish humanity would die out," Toshiru muttered. Closing his eyes, he focused on listening. Sounds from a movie were pumping into his earphones. It was an old sci-fi film extracted from the JR Integrated Intelligence's input layer.

In it, a group of astronauts was on an interplanetary mission when full-scale nuclear war broke out, exterminating humanity on Earth. Driven into a panic, the crew killed one another until only one remained to carry on the mission. It ended when the star Proxima Centauri, four light-years from Earth, came into view.

The story was so devastatingly depressing that the movie had been a commercial failure, but Toshiru had enjoyed it many times over.

"Captain Lewis's heart has stopped beating. By order of succession, you are now in command. Your orders, please, Captain Taylor," requested the spaceship's AI to the protagonist. The dubbed Japanese was ancient, but because Toshiru had watched it with modern subtitles so often, he could tell what they were saying just based on the sound now.

"What's the matter, Captain?"

"It's nothing, HAL. Just realizing that I've got more oxygen to work with now," he said, expressionless. Behind him was the body of a fellow crewmate.

The next shot in the movie was of a red dwarf star. The ship began to slow from sub-light speed to transition to planetary orbit.

Then, there was a *ping*.

Toshiru returned to consciousness. The noise wasn't supposed to happen. He opened his eyes and saw it hadn't come from the movie but an e-mail notification. When he spotted the name of the sender, a vein twitched on his temple. It read, "JR Fukuoka, Intelligence 1st Division, Okuma."

> **Toshiru Kubo, Engineering 4th Division**
> **It's been awhile.**
> **I have an idea of what you're thinking, and I wanted to offer you advice as your senior.**
> **Come to the defense line base next Sunday.**
> **Bring a sponge cake to facilitate discussion.**
> **Okuma**

Okuma was just about the last person Toshiru wanted paying attention to him. Perhaps this unpleasant revelation would offer a way forward, however.

Watching movies from the High Civilization era made it clear that they envisioned any downfall as happening swiftly, whether from nuclear war, meteor strike, or zombie outbreak. It could be that was just a consequence of having to tell a story in two hours, though.

Actual downfall, in fact, was far more stubborn, nasty, and pernicious. After hundreds of years, the Winter War had slowly burned out civilization. All that remained was a human-made structure growing out of control, and the humans across the Straits had been trying desperately to keep it at bay for decades.

The Straits were a narrow stretch of water separating the main island of Honshu from Kyushu. It represented the westmost point of Yokohama Station and the line of defense for JR Fukuoka as it attempted to keep the station at bay. This was the only place that could happen; if the station breached the line, it would cover the rest of Kyushu, except for the smaller islands off the coast.

JR Fukuoka's frontline base on the Kyushu side was covered in a special structural-genetic-field-resistant polymer that gave off a constant chemical smell. Toshiru, carrying a boxed sponge cake, showed his employee badge at the security gate, then made his way to the Intelligence First Division office where he would find Okuma.

The thirty-year-old was sitting in an office chair with his feet up on a table. He had a bird-shaped pastry in one hand and a tablet in the other. He seemed to be reading a book on it.

"Yo! How's it been? You look like you have no interest in life. Same old, I take it?" Okuma greeted, setting the tablet down. He caught sight of the sponge cake box in the bag Toshiru was holding. "Very smart of you. I've been stuck on the front line so long that I haven't had sponge cake in three whole weeks. I was about to launch a DoS attack on the company network."

Okuma pushed forward a box of steamed buns and asked, "Want one? Eight was too many for me."

"No. I don't like sweets," Toshiru replied. He spoke without inflection, like a robot.

Okuma took a sip from the teacup on the table and glanced at the other man. "Toshiru Kubo. I understand that you desire to steal one of our company's weapons," he said. Toshiru didn't react. He stared out the window.

"The intelligence division manages the company network that you use, of course. You might have encoded your actual communication, but just looking at the location of the other end tells us quite a lot," Okuma continued. Again, there was no reaction. It was as if the very concept of acknowledging things was illogical to Toshiru.

"Of course, you're free to think what you like. We have freedom of thought and freedom of speech. However, we are also burdened by an obligation to reveal information. It's going to get reported within the company eventually, so I'll give you a tip. A dozen N700s were stolen from the armory the other day."

Toshiru's hand twitched.

"They were found immediately, of course. The culprits were a trio of soldiers from the military division. They were in charge of armory storage and conspired to make off with the weapons, but as you know, it is all but impossible to steal a gun and escape from our armory.

Kawakami from the military division is questioning them right now. It won't take long."

"How did you find them?" Toshiru asked. Involving the people in charge of weapons management seemed like the most practical means of achieving his goal. He didn't have the charisma or negotiation skill to pull it off, though, so he'd never taken that idea seriously.

"The three of them were going to exchange their guns with traders from Yokohama Station to get themselves Suika credentials and flee Inside. Four weapons per person, the deal was. For *some reason*, though, their communication with Suikanet was easily discovered by our fine intelligence division," Okuma said.

The first thing that Toshiru felt was irritation that those guns had been valued so cheaply. How could it cost four of them just to gain access to that freakish building?

"Now, Toshiru, I've got a little quiz for you. Say you wanted to get some armaments that not even the armory managers could steal. What would be the best way?"

Toshiru gave no reply.

"Here's my answer. When stolen goods have been recovered and returned to their rightful place, vigilance drops, and people relax. Now, most people wouldn't be able to seize upon such an opportunity, but let's say we were talking about someone who daydreamed about stealing guns and escape routes. I think he'd suddenly have a much higher chance of success," Okuma speculated, staring Toshiru in the eyes. Toshiru didn't meet the gaze.

Okuma's phone trilled. "Oops, Kawakami's coming back. I've got to handle this. You just keep your mouth shut," he warned. Then he grinned. "Sorry. That was unnecessary. You never open your mouth, period."

A general from the military division faced three soldiers in a formal, seated position. A dozen long guns were arranged on the floor between them—N700 electric pump guns, manufactured by JR Fukuoka.

Such rifles had begun circulating during the Winter War, when ammunition could no longer reliably be produced. The ability to turn any material into a lethal projectile was highly practical. Many regarded them as the most used weapon in human history after stones. The N700 line was the latest iteration, powerful enough at maximum output to sever a human body in two—but still meaningless against Yokohama Station and its structural genetic field. They were weapons for maintaining peace in Kyushu.

"Now, according to the intelligence division," began Kawakami, the military division general. "The three of you accessed Suikanet with your personal devices to contact traders located in Shimonoseki on Honshu. In exchange for four electric pump guns per person, you asked for Suika registration so you could move into Yokohama Station. An inventory of the armory showed that the expected number of weapons was missing."

Kawakami picked one of the rifles off the floor.

"The guns with the corresponding IDs were found under your beds. If this is all true, you must be punished for the unauthorized removal of armaments and attempted escape. Do you have anything to say for yourselves?"

The general tapped the shoulders of the soldiers with the end of the gun. The three stared at each other. Two of them were looking reproachfully at the third. They were the kind of expressions that said, "This was your idea. You said it would be easy. You dragged us into this."

The third member resigned himself and admitted, "I-I'll explain. W-we think that we should stop this fruitless war and just w-welcome Yokohama Station onto Kyushu."

"So you abandon your responsibility as citizens?"

"We've fought this war for fifty years, and not only have we not defeated Yokohama Station, but it's gotten stronger. The recent bombing attack sacrificed two of our comrades. Perhaps entering Yokohama Station is the peace that Kyushu seeks."

"That's not for us to decide. And do not speak of lofty ideals for the people of Kyushu when you are fleeing to save your own skin," Kawakami glared. The soldiers just stared at the floor and trembled.

Kawakami opened the door to the intelligence division's office, where Okuma was sitting cross-legged. Next to him was a young employee, someone unfamiliar. He was staring out the window, oblivious to the fact that a senior officer from the military division had just entered the room. Engineering 4th Division, Toshiru Kubo was written on the man's badge.

"That was good work. All three of them admitted their guilt," Kawakami said to Okuma.

"Excellent. I'm glad to hear it," Okuma replied, taking a bite of sponge cake. The ace of the intelligence division did not care in the least that Kawakami was far his superior in both age and rank.

"Well, I hate to ask this after reporting them to you, but would you mind taking it easy on them? They joined the company the same year as me. Oh, would you like one?" Okuma inquired, offering the box of steamed buns, but Kawakami held up a hand. It was a wonder Okuma had such an appetite at this chemical plant of a base. One of the man's biggest mysteries was how he acquired so many boxed sweets at the front line.

"Punishments will be meted out fairly, according to company policies. I do not have any sway over the matter," stated Kawakami.

"Listen. You can't blame young folks like us for being fascinated with Yokohama Station. It was a youthful passion! Please don't be too hard on them."

Okuma was here at the strait from the intelligence division because he was responsible for deciphering Suikanet data. His job was to collect and analyze information that traveled through Yokohama Station so it could be used for tactical purposes. Very little of it was actually useful in that sense, though.

Data found on Suikanet was all personal to the people in Yokohama Station—news about a delicious new restaurant in Shimonoseki that served cheap fugu and things of that nature. There was no way to get data about Yokohama Station itself through that structural genetic field yet.

To maintain the illusion that he was producing results, Okuma had found and reported his coworkers when they'd plotted to escape.

Inside the station across the narrow strait from Kyushu were many traders who would offer outsiders a Suika for a price.

These merchants couldn't accept payment in milliyen, the currency of Inside, because there was no way to get it in Kyushu. That left bartering, and unlike Inside, where all necessities were generated left and right, it was challenging to acquire 500,000 milliyen worth of goods produced in Kyushu. One of the few exceptions was the electric pump gun made by JR Fukuoka.

As such, there were constant issues with soldiers seeking to escape Inside. Some of them joined JR specifically as a gateway to that opportunity.

JR Fukuoka's main purpose was to protect the people of Kyushu from Yokohama Station's expansion, so this was a grave situation. If they failed to keep it under control, they might lose the people's support and collapse. Shikoku's JR lost its way after the Great Seto Bridge was breached. Ultimately, it ceased to be after a series of coups over fifty years ago. The island had been in a state of anarchy ever since.

This was why Okuma's ability to accurately find deserters gave him a lot of sway inside the company.

"Why do you suppose those electric pump guns are so valuable to the Yokohama Station people, anyway? Violence is supposed to be outlawed in there."

"There are probably people who need weapons like that for peace of mind, even if they're not supposed to use them. You know, like the nuclear weapons of the past."

That seems illogical, Toshiru thought. It was a mockery of the process of engineering. At the very least, it was a mindset he didn't want to bring into contact with his own life.

Kawakami glanced at the screen on the table. "What sort of writing is that? All those old-fashioned kanji and mathematical formulas."

"A physics textbook from before the war. They excavated the images from the input data layer."

"The folks from Kumamoto, you mean? Anything in there seem useful?"

"Well, it's a pain to parse the Japanese, but it looks like it's explaining the laws of propagation for the quantum field that's the underlying principle of the structural genetic field. It's all human-written documents, though, so I'm sure the engineering division already knows this stuff," replied Okuma, glancing at Toshiru.

"Any hints on a possible way to counteract the genetic field?" asked Kawakami. "If we don't tackle that, we're just perpetually stuck in this showdown with the concrete monstrosity."

"Good question. Maybe if we can get some data from the output layer and the hidden layer. Without being able to decipher the description language, though, there's nothing doing."

"No progress on that, huh?"

"Our excellent decryption team is working around the clock, but basically, the task is about as easy as acquiring an alien's brain soaked in formaldehyde and attempting to figure out its sexual proclivities."

"Still, it's one of the few sources of hope we have. I pray you're able to figure it out."

"If you really feel that way, maybe you could negotiate with the board of directors to increase our budget. Why do they spend all their money on firepower? Are they that stupid? You don't win a battle of material resources against Yokohama Station. We have to pay for our own tea, for goodness' sake."

"Watch your mouth. You might be good at your job, but that only gets you so far," Kawakami cautioned.

The base's sirens abruptly sprang to life.

"The station is launching an emission! Coordinates of four-seven, three-three, one-two-eight. All personnel, report to location at once."

Kawakami grabbed the uniform resting on the chair and headed for the door. "That's me. I'll be back."

"Sure thing. Have fun with your glorious undertaking," drawled Okuma.

Throughout the entirety of the conversation, Toshiru Kubo had remained still at the window, as if to convey that he hadn't an iota of interest in the people talking.

The battle at the Straits, the far west end of Yokohama Station, had been in a stalemate for over half a century. The body of water had originally been less than a kilometer across. Due to Yokohama Station's relentless attempts to send over connecting walkways, however, a long process of coastal reshaping had expanded that gap over threefold. JR Fukuoka, the controlling body of Kyushu and its surrounding islands, literally pared its own fat to stay healthy.

The first generation of the defensive battle had involved concentrated firepower, bombarding the walkways Yokohama Station sent probing over the water like a plant growing vines. At its fastest, Yokohama Station still needed half a day to extend a platform to the far bank. It was easily enough time to focus firepower on any attempts and knock them down.

Unfortunately, after a few decades, Yokohama Station changed tactics. It would complete a connecting hallway of an adequate length within its interior, then attempt to fire it over. That method took less than thirty minutes. It'd forced JR Fukuoka to rapidly expand the strait and give its cannons more mobility. Their current system was equipped to shoot down any station emission within ten minutes, no matter where it was coming from. The problem was that the discharge speed of the walkways was steadily increasing.

In the last few years, the end of the connecting walkways had started exploding and sending shards of concrete out in an attempt to infect the far bank with the structural genetic field. The development of this kamikaze tactic had significant consequences for JR Fukuoka. Previously, they'd always been the attacker inflicting damage on the station; now they were suffering casualties for the first time. This deserter incident was just one of the symptoms of the company's lowered morale.

It was hard to believe that some human or computerized intelligence within the station was coming up with these strategies. The engineering division thought the structural genetic field was simply mutating at random and that some algorithm was preserving whatever most benefited the station's growth.

"This should give us another twenty years to fight," bragged the manager of the science division after they'd developed the structural-genetic-field-resistant polymer. Covering the coastline with that material drastically reduced the chance of infection by the structural genetic field. Once they scaled up to a mass production level, the plan was to ship some of it to Shikoku, too.

It was a once-in-a-century tactical advantage. That was time beyond human understanding, an amount on a mythical scale. Kawakami chuckled as he mused that JR Fukuoka's struggles might someday be regarded as myth.

After Kawakami left the room, only Okuma and Toshiru remained.

As cannons along the strait boomed in the distance, Okuma took his teacup to a sink to rinse it out. After a little while, there was a high-pitched *bweeen* sound from outside. Yokohama Station's walkway attack had begun.

"The level of station activity differs depending on the day of the week. Did you know that?"

"No."

"It's only especially raucous on Sundays and Mondays. Why do you suppose that is?"

Toshiru said nothing.

"It's probably a remnant from the civilized age when it was used for public travel. Apparently, the information is contained within its structural genetic field. The interesting thing is that it's Sunday and Monday, not Saturday and Sunday. After two hundred years of expansion, its circaseptan rhythm seems to have shifted a day."

Toshiru remained silent. It was less that he was uninterested in the topic than that he didn't see the necessity of responding just to show he was listening. Okuma wasn't bothered; he'd known since their training period that Toshiru was like that.

Okuma placed the teacup upside down on the drying rack, then sat on his office chair again. Toshiru Kubo remained standing and gazed out the window. In the distance, the military division was sending up plumes of smoke.

"Let's talk hypotheticals," Okuma started, leaning back in the chair. "If you were, theoretically, to exchange guns for a Suika, what would you do Inside?"

"I've never wanted a Suika."

"Which is why it's hypothetical."

"Hypothetically, if I had enough guns to trade for a Suika, I would take them to Shikoku instead," Toshiru answered.

Okuma made a ridiculous expression. It looked very intentional. "It's a good thing I wasn't taking a big sip of tea right then. I might have spit it out."

"Okuma," Toshiru began to say, then paused and reconsidered. "Hypothetically, if *someone* caught deserters in the military division and aided the escape of an employee from the engineering division, what would they be trying to accomplish?"

"That's a good question," said Okuma. "I would say that this *hypothetical* person wants to see a solution to the problem that keeps arising. Employees of JR Fukuoka, the protector of Kyushu, should not be fleeing into Yokohama Station. It strikes at our very authority. On the other hand, there's a fascinating smaller problem of how someone sneaks past our heavy security to steal guns."

He picked up two of the precut slices of sponge cake. "You see, Toshiru, the secret to enjoying life is ample sugar and mental exercise. Matching the input and output amounts make for a healthy metabolism."

There was another high-pitched *bweeen* from outside.

"Ugh, it's so noisy," grumbled Okuma, closing the curtains. The polymer shades were good at blocking both light and sound, and the room was suddenly quite dark. Toshiru remained as he was, still gazing out the window.

"Sounds like the station's started its kamikaze attack. I hate that sound. It doesn't have any gunpowder in it, so how does it explode like that? I couldn't begin to guess. Does the engineering division have any ideas?"

"No. And I'm only in weapons development."

"Ah. Maybe I could find out if I was in there."

"Hypothetically speaking, Okuma, you might be able to get Inside just by presenting yourself."

"Yes, I hear that from Kawakami, too. 'With your expertise, there will be jobs for you in there. Some Suika trader will take you in.' Usually, he says stuff like that when he's in a foul mood."

Okuma raised his head and sat up straight in an imposing manner. His eye level was ten centimeters higher than the top of Toshiru's head.

"But don't you even joke about that," he warned. "I *am* in a position of responsibility."

"Responsibility, huh?" repeated Toshiru skeptically.

"Indeed. Less than one percent of Kyushu's denizens could arrange to pay the cost of a Suika deposit, and it's our company's duty to prevent the station's infection from reaching our island, for their sake. That's why I've received a salary paid by their taxes for the last ten years. Do you understand what I'm saying, Toshiru Kubo?"

"If Yokohama Station gets past us, then the Inside population grows as Kyushu's shrinks. There are probably more people who stand to gain from that than the other way around."

"Ah, I see. An application of Bentham's greatest happiness principle, then. Perhaps we should end our conversation here. It may prove ethically problematic," Okuma stated. Toshiru turned back and glanced at him for just an instant—long enough to impart a sense of disdain.

Toshiru's eyes shone with a clear question, "Why doesn't he understand something so obvious?"

Okuma wanted to reply, "How much easier my life would be if I could oversimplify things the way you do," but thought better of it. There would be no point.

"I'm disappointed, Toshiru. I thought of you like a little brother."

"I think of you like an older brother, too."

"What does that mean?"

"That blood relations are basically meaningless."

"Ah, yes."

Okuma leaned back in his chair again.

Bweeen! The sound echoed once more. Evidently, today's hallway emissions were especially fierce.

Two days later, Toshiru Kubo was at the military harbor in Oita. There was an N700 electric pump gun in his hands. He was small enough that the gun seemed large by comparison. Its ID tag had already been scrubbed off. If you knew the internal workings, removing the tag without harming the weapon's functionality was easy.

Since Shikoku's JR had collapsed, Fukuoka oversaw ships that would accept refugees fleeing from the anarchy and chaos there. Those vessels sailed in and out of Oita.

It was a military port, so it was off-limits to civilians. Just on the other side of the barbed wire fence surrounding it, though, protest banners hung by the sides of bridges and roads.

No more refugees!

Go back to Shikoku!

See to our own needs first!

The signs exhorted the authorities in JR Fukuoka's Hakata headquarters to prioritize the people of Kyushu rather than take in those displaced from Shikoku. Quality of life in Kyushu was several levels below what was enjoyed Inside, where physical necessities were always available. The main reason was the long, long battle over the strait. The need to materially support a war to beat back a station that could endlessly replicate itself was straining the lives of the islanders bit by bit. More than a few were upset about the idea of taking on more people from Shikoku on top of that.

When the protesters saw Toshiru walk up in his military uniform, they glared at him or openly lamented his presence. Toshiru showed no interest in them. Instead, he spoke to the officer at the security gate.

"I'm Toshiru Kubo. I was dispatched to answer the request for more personnel. I'll be on the refugee ship leaving tomorrow. I've got my own weapon already."

Annoyed, the guard typed at his computer. "I don't see any message to that effect."

"The station's started emitting again, so the command structure's a little chaotic, I assume. Here's the notice. And my badge."

Toshiru held up a sheet of paper. It was a poorly done fake made with a copier, but the guard just glanced at it before saying, "Ask the director for more details. He's on the third floor," and letting Toshiru through. He went there and repeated his story. The white-haired director puffed on a rolled cigarette, then had his secretary print up orders regarding the refugee ship leaving tomorrow.

Just last month, there had been a conflict between the displaced Shikoku denizens and protesters, and several people had been hurt. The director welcomed as much protective manpower as possible, as long as it wasn't suspicious. And Toshiru's badge, at least, was genuine.

Toshiru headed to the pier next. His intention was to get a look at the ship that would be leaving tomorrow. He found the dismantled pieces of the boat, tied to thick ropes and floating in the sea. It was like they were performing some bizarre kind of fishing.

"What's going on here?" he asked a passing engineer at the port. The tanned, middle-aged man looked at Toshiru and his gun and decided he was talking to someone from the military division of headquarters.

"Scattering the genetic field. Ships that come from Shikoku have to spend three days soaking in seawater. It's the regulation," he explained politely.

"Dunking them in seawater scatters it?"

"Well, we know the field is weak in water with electrolytes in it. That's the reason Yokohama Station can't expand over the sea."

"Why break down the ship to pieces?"

"To promote the scattering by increasing surface area. Apparently, the smaller the mass, the harder it is for the structural genetic field to maintain itself. I don't know the details of exactly how it works."

"You tear it down after every trip? Isn't that inefficient? The structural genetic field can't possibly soak into it that much," Toshiru said. According to JR Fukuoka intelligence, Yokohama Station's structure had only proceeded as far as northern Kagawa after passing the Great Seto Bridge. Even if the genetic field was preceding it in spreading across Shikoku, surely it hadn't penetrated as far as Uwajima on the west coast of the Ehime region.

"We have to do it. The citizens won't accept anything less. We're building the boats to be modular, so reassembly only takes half a day now."

So it's all a performance, thought Toshiru. They were doing technically unnecessary things just to satisfy some human pathology. What's more, it went without saying that making the process of accepting refugees less efficient pleased the people of Kyushu.

JR Fukuoka's engineering division was researching the nature of the structural genetic field. It was the quantum state that carried the information of Yokohama Station's structure and transmitted that to its solid state. It transferred exceptionally quickly over metal, which is why the station's initial spread had happened along the railways.

However, it could infect any uniformly solid material, like concrete or plastic. The larger the solid, the easier it was to maintain.

For that reason, despite desperate requests from the Shikoku side for rescue, the process was only carried out by a handful of small boats, which had to be dismantled and rearranged in the military port each time. It was an extremely inefficient method of providing asylum.

Accepting tiny amounts of people at a time proved a successful kind of pressure release for the unhappy people of Shikoku, though. If Kyushu completely refused to take any of them, the population as a whole would rush to invade. JR Fukuoka considered it a much better deal to accept small numbers at a time instead.

The dismantled ship was put back together overnight while Toshiru slept in the port's dorm, and it looked like a proper boat again in the morning. It struck him as being similar to the way the station structure naturally assembled itself.

"The ship will be setting off for Uwajima momentarily. All crew report to your stations," the PA system announced. Toshiru didn't know if he had a proper station, so he just picked a spot to stand and waited there. Several soldiers glanced his way, but he ignored them. The port was perpetually understaffed, so last-minute additions were a regular fact of life.

They arrived in Shikoku in about two hours, where a large crowd of refugees was waiting. It was still spring, and the nights were cold, but there were plenty of children and elderly people wearing nothing but short-sleeved shirts in the crowd. They must have fled from the armed gangs controlling much of the impoverished island to get to the western coast.

While the refugees submitted to searches, Toshiru stood on guard with his gun out to ensure there was no trouble. It was the last job he would perform as an employee of JR Fukuoka.

Many employees had attempted to cross the Straits and earn a Suika on their way Inside. No one would've expected an escapee to flee to Shikoku instead, though. In that sense, Toshiru's getaway was quite easy.

Just before the refugee ship took off for Kyushu again, Toshiru slipped away into the night.

There was nothing but sea to the left.

Shikoku's rainy season ended ten days earlier than in the Kanto region to the east, and summer had arrived. Summer weather along the Seto Inland Sea was generally excellent. It was clear, but it was too far to the opposite bank to see Yokohama Station in the Chugoku region of Honshu. If any land was visible over the water, it was one of the little islands in the inland sea, which were uniformly green.

Being unconnected to Honshu in any way, these islands were likely to remain little pockets of nature, even if Yokohama Station managed to cover all of Shikoku. Perhaps they'd come to serve as an escape for people without a Suika.

Toshiru Kubo rode on a small electric scooter east along the coast of the inland sea. Two months had passed since he'd snuck onto Shikoku in the refugee ship.

The upper limit the scooter's speedometer was ninety kilometers per hour, but on a road with hardly any pavement, the best he could do was thirty. Any faster and the scooter's body would twist like intestines, and it was less energy efficient.

There was hardly a human-made object in sight. Occasionally, he came across a bit of rusted guardrail or a road sign that was virtually illegible—the only clues that this road had once been known as National Route 11, in a city called Shikokuchuo. The name meant "Central Shikoku City." It must have been a bustling metropolis with a title like that, but there was no sign of its pre-Winter War prosperity.

Toshiru was fortunate to have acquired this scooter in his first month in Shikoku. Otherwise, he was prepared to walk all the way across the island to Tokushima. Keeping the meter-long electric pump gun balanced on the scooter was difficult. Breaking it down to smaller parts was easy, but in a place where assailants could strike at any moment, you needed to have a combat-ready weapon at all times.

In the end, Toshiru had laid the gun flat and tied it to the luggage carrier. At the very least, he could fire it that way, and the presence of the weapon would hopefully scare off potential trouble. It made the scooter's profile too wide for some narrow areas, but such situations were rare. There was no oncoming traffic to worry about.

The road here was on higher ground, offering a pleasant view of the clear sky and sea. No matter what happened on land, the sea and sky always had the same color.

Toshiru continued along on the undulating Route 11 for a while, until the pressure of the wind hitting his face began to weaken considerably. The scooter was slowing down.

"Ah, dammit. That's it for today," he muttered. The remaining battery gauge showed that it was almost dead.

Two solar battery panels on the luggage carrier supplied the scooter with power. Age had significantly curbed their efficiency, however. They could provide a single day of riding power only after several days of charging, and it was worse in the rainy season.

The sun was quickly setting, but the scooter's control panel indicated that it was only three o'clock in the afternoon. Toshiru had acquired the vehicle nearly a month ago, and he'd never seen the readout show any time other than three o'clock.

There was a simple wooden sign on the roadside that read, STORE HERE, so Toshiru turned the handlebars left. The lack of power had already taken out the directional display, but he'd never needed that in the first place.

The "store" was a shanty built facing the Seto Inland Sea. A middle-aged man waited inside the dark, wooden building, which didn't even seem like it could keep out the rain.

"Welcome. No guns inside, eh?" he said. Toshiru turned the scooter such that his rifle was pointed away from the establishment.

"You're dressed like a JR person, eh? Hot in those long sleeves, eh?"

Toshiru didn't answer. He glanced at the products on sale. There were plastic boxes placed directly on the ground, with items like mixing implements, shoes, and tools lined up on top of them. There were no listed prices. In contrast to the shabbiness of the structure, many of the wares were new. Perhaps there was a factory making them nearby.

"I want solar battery panels. As big and new as possible," he stated. The man dug through a wooden box and pulled out a few that were roughly twenty centimeters to a side. Toshiru examined one of them; it was virtually untouched. He couldn't believe he'd found these at this dingy old place.

"Do you take JRY?" Toshiru inquired, pulling paper bills out of his pocket. JRY was a currency that'd spread after the fall of the Japanese government, and it used to be a shared tender across Kyushu and Shikoku.

"Haven't seen that in a while, eh? Sorry, but it's just paper now, eh?"

"Will you barter? I've got dried rations."

"I can pick up food that appears on the far bank now and then, eh? Not much worth to me, eh?"

"Far bank?"

"The spot where it washes up is a secret, eh?" the man replied, pointing at a boat right along the shore. He was taking it across the water to the other side and picking up stuff produced Inside.

"Do battery panels show up on the far bank too?"

"They do, eh? They don't get the sun over there, eh? So everyone throws them out, eh?"

Toshiru had to wonder why Yokohama Station would generate something like that, then. He'd heard that its structural genetic field replicated any matter it incorporated. Perhaps Honshu had been covered in solar battery panels during the Winter War.

"Then what *will* you trade for?"

"Got any antibiotics, eh?"

"No."

"Mechanical parts, tools, eh?"

"A few."

Toshiru lifted the scooter's seat and removed a small collection of components he'd collected from abandoned and broken machines during his trip across Shikoku. The pieces themselves would still work, and he figured that, at the very least, he could use them as ammo for the electric pump gun.

"I'll give you four for the whole bunch, eh?"

"Not the whole bunch. I only want two."

"Okay, eh?"

Toshiru picked out half of the parts at random and handed them over. Then, he added the two panels to his scooter and connected the power feed to the batteries. Even as the sun sunk below the horizon, it started recharging the meter.

Toshiru rode on slowly, conserving what little juice he had left and keeping the rear end of the scooter with the solar panels pointed toward the sunset. There was an old concrete structure a short ride off the road up ahead.

The concrete wall was covered in vines, but there was an open space where part of a sign could be seen, reading "ion."

"Is this what I think it is?"

Toshiru used the end of the gun to pull off the vines. To the left of the

"ION" on the sign panel were the letters "STAT." It was a station. There were more panels farther to the left, but they were too worn down to read anymore. The name of the station itself would remain a mystery.

"A JR Integrated Intelligence unit, huh? So there are some left in Shikoku. So strange to see one with the building body intact," he murmured. Toshiru was aware that traveling alone made him talk to himself more. He hadn't realized it after so much time living in a four-man company room, but when he was alone, he could be quite a talker.

He circled around the station on the scooter but couldn't find anything that looked like tracks. In the hundred or so years it had been abandoned, everything metal must have been repurposed. He couldn't even find a railroad tie.

Without a functioning central government for decades, Shikoku's infrastructure had no upkeep. The asphalt had all been torn loose, buried by dirt and covered with grass. The only man-made objects he saw were the occasional building and, every now and then, a gray telephone pole standing amid the trees.

Ironically, this slowed the advance of Yokohama Station. Compared to uniform metal and asphalt surfaces, the station structure's spread was much slower on natural ground. The Great Seto Bridge had been breached over a century ago, yet the station itself only covered part of Kagawa.

According to JR Fukuoka's intelligence, Yokohama Station had already formed a structure over the majority of the north bank of the Yoshino River. The Awaji Island route was being taken very slowly, because there had never been a railway there. The route across the Shimanami Expressway from Hiroshima was going even slower. Because Yokohama Station's permeation of the Hiroshima area was relatively recent in its lifespan, it would be a long time before the station proceeded across the expressway's islands to reach Imabari on the tip of Shikoku.

Spiderwebs were strewn thick across the entrance to the building. No one had been inside in quite a long time. He searched every corner, but all of the electrical power systems had been removed. There wasn't going to be any rapid charging of the scooter's batteries.

But that was no surprise. If such a system were still around and working, someone would be living here already. It was a bonus just to find a structure with walls and a roof here.

He rolled the scooter inside and parked it. There was a one-liter metal bottle inside the seat pocket. He took a swig of the cloudy liquid inside.

The catalytic cellulose-depolymerizing bottle would take any plant matter, whether grass or twigs and, with the addition of water and heat, break it down into glucose. It was developed during the war as an emergency food source while on missions. It was pungent and disgusting if you weren't wholly starving, but Toshiru was uninterested in the flavor of food as a general concept. He thought of the sense of taste as a failure of evolution.

Something was written on the glass that partitioned the rooms inside, but it was done in an older style and had been worn down to the point of illegibility. It seemed likely to be "ticket counter" or "lobby." Toshiru went into the ticket counter area.

Rubble was strewn about inside, the ceiling material falling loose, but at least he wouldn't get woken up in the middle of the night by rain here. Satisfied, Toshiru pulled a folding mat off the scooter, kicked some of the debris out of the way, and laid it out once the floor was flat enough that he could go to sleep.

He awoke to the sound of rustling.

Someone was wading through the deep grass that surrounded the building. It wasn't just one person, more like four or five.

Toshiru sat up, trying to be as quiet as possible, and approached the ticket counter. The men had come into the station building and were tinkering with the scooter, which was sitting next to the bench in the lobby. They were trying to start the motor.

Toshiru fired the gun over the counter. A needle sped through a hand touching the scooter.

"Aaagh!" the man yelped, and his arm jerked upward on reflex. Toshiru had found the needle on the shore. It'd probably been used to fish. It had no lethal capability.

"Don't touch the scooter. It's valuable," Toshiru stated.

The men crowded around the scooter looked in his direction.

"How many? Four. I wonder if I have enough ammo," he muttered as he loaded a pachinko ball. This wasn't the Sakura long gun he'd stolen from JR Fukuoka but the smaller Mizuho pistol that was his personal property. The meter-long N700 series weapons were inconvenient to use in cramped spaces, which is why Toshiru had made sure to keep the short-barreled armament.

The pistol made two unimpressive popping sounds, and a pair of pachinko balls struck two men on the arm. They grunted, and the metal pipes they were carrying fell to the floor.

Electric pump guns could turn any metal into a bullet, but if you wanted accuracy, then spherical objects were best. Air resistance would cause a screw, for example, to follow unpredictable trajectories. This made obtuse ammunition particularly unreliable with more compact weapons.

"I'm aiming for your arms so you can still run away; I suggest you do so. Your dead bodies are only going to get in my way," Toshiru threatened.

It was the middle of the night, and only a bit of moonlight coming from the platform's direction lit the scene. The four men whispered to each other in low voices, then scampered out of the station building.

Toshiru picked up one of the pipes they'd dropped. One of the two new solar battery panels he'd just attached to the scooter had been pried off. He'd screwed them down, but they'd dug it out with a knife or some other edge, leaving just a jagged bit of metal. *What a waste*, he thought.

Toshiru rose at dawn and drove the scooter back to the store he'd visited yesterday, despite the lack of juice.

The shanty along the coastline had been ransacked. There wasn't a single item left—only the storekeeper on the ground, beaten and cold.

"Dang. He's dead," Toshiru murmured. The attackers had taken all of the goods and even torn the man's clothes off his body. It had to have been the group from last night. Perhaps they'd followed the tracks of Toshiru's scooter.

"I should have traded for four. That was a mistake."

Toshiru leaned against the wall of the shack, eating dried rations and watching the morning sun. Did JR Fukuoka's intelligence division know about the integrated intelligence unit here? Idly, Toshiru mused that Okuma would probably be delighted if he were to report that bit of information.

◆

"Yokohama Station's spread across the other side of the river, so you can charge up all you want over there," said the old woman of the village.

"Can you use Yokohama Station's energy without a Suika?"

"There are charging stations here and there, and more pop up all the time. But the places where the most power and food are, you'll find scary people in control."

"That's not a problem," replied Toshiru, glancing at the weapon resting across his scooter.

After several days of travel from the JR Integrated Intelligence unit, he'd reached a small village on the Yoshino River's south bank. They'd built a wall of trees atop a tall hill, and several men with electric pump guns watched the gate. It was an impressive amount of security.

But the armaments were quite old in comparison to Toshiru's state-of-the-art model. They were heavy, weaker, and less accurate.

His request to use the village's electricity was soundly rejected. They had a hydroelectric generator in the river, but it was barely enough to keep the village's lights on. They didn't have a single watt to spare for some unknown wanderer.

The village was guaranteed to end up buried under Yokohama Station in the next five or ten years as it expanded south. Out of the hundreds of locals, not a single one of them had any chance at acquiring a Suika. If any of them did, they wouldn't be here in this dangerous, unstable place; they would've crossed the river for the security of Yokohama Station long ago.

Since their fate was so short-lived, Toshiru wondered why they needed such extreme protection for the village at all.

The solar battery panel was keeping his scooter going, but it would soon reach its end. He needed a proper charging facility to boost it back up to full. If he could get his backup power topped off, he could stay on the move and only stop at the permanent charging stations on the military map. That would put him in a much more secure position.

"Is there a bridge I can use to traverse the river?"

"Not a single one that will carry your vehicle over. There's just a few hanging rope bridges."

"That doesn't help me," he said.

Toshiru considered getting the scooter on a boat to row over, but finding a suitable craft seemed unrealistic. He'd seen a number of ferries on the way here, but they were all tiny, not capable of holding more than a handful of people.

"Any power stations that aren't Inside?"

"There is one, but you don't want to go there," the old woman advised, scowling.

"Why not?"

"Ghosts," she murmured, her head tilting downward.

"Actually, I'd like to see that."

"You like ghosts?"

"I don't know. I've never seen one. Maybe I'll like them more than people," Toshiru replied, and the old woman reluctantly told him the location.

The place was about twelve kilometers south. The Shikoku mountains rose south of the Yoshino River for a while, but eventually, you'd happen upon a little, abandoned power station. If local superstition was to be believed, it was haunted by the ghost of a girl. She and her family had died during the Winter War. She had no legs but would confuse anyone entering the station for her parents, and she'd come crawling on her hands and elbows.

The Winter War ended two hundred years ago. That would be a

very old ghost, indeed. Toshiru imagined it being as ancient as Sugawara no Michizane, the spirit that'd haunted that shrine at Dazaifu in Fukuoka.

Toshiru rode the scooter up into the mountains, following the directions the old woman had given him. The screeching of the cicadas rattled his ears as he climbed the hill, and the trees blocked the sunlight, sending his battery into overdrive, but at last, he reached a sign with POWER STATION crudely written on it in white paint. He wondered who was putting up these wooden signs.

The building was a container-style electric well. It was the kind that a truck drove to a spot with geothermal energy and unloaded. Once the metal rods were stuck into the ground, it would produce electricity. Smaller, locally sourced generators like this had become standard after the bigger power stations were destroyed in the Winter War. Even in Kyushu, aside from JR's large matter furnace, every village had one or two of these portable hydroelectric or geothermal generators.

Toshiru opened the heavy metal door of the container, hoping to get the chance to recharge his scooter. "Anyone in here?"

It was dark inside. There was a light on the ceiling, but it wasn't on. Toshiru could see the machine's light and hear the sound of it working, so he knew there was power. Perhaps someone had turned off that overhead light for a reason.

He sensed a shape moving in the back of the container.

It was too small to be human. The head was only as tall as the back of a chair. There was no bottom half. The top portion was resting on the ground, and a girl's face was glaring right back at him. It kind of looked like a bust from a museum.

"Ghosts are real? I thought they floated," mused Toshiru, pointing his long gun, Sakura, at the strange thing. "Don't move. Oh, but just for clarification, do guns work on you?"

"They don't," answered the girl. For a ghost, her voice was relatively clear. It sounded like an average child's voice, but something was off about it. Maybe it was the echo from the metal container.

"How come?"

"Shoot me and find out."

"Okay," Toshiru accepted, simultaneously pointing Sakura, the electric pump gun, at her and pulling the trigger. The *pomp* sound filled the generator room, sending a coin at the girl at three hundred kilometers an hour.

The girl caught it in her hand. The action produced a metallic noise.

"Is this a one-yen coin? There's still Japanese government money around?" she remarked, looking at her hand. There was a broken circle of aluminum in her palm.

"I've never seen a ghost before, so I don't know how it works. Can you stop bullets? I didn't think spirits had that kind of power," Toshiru said. He was getting used to the darkness and could see her face clearly now. She looked about six or seven years old.

"And I've never seen anyone shoot me when I say, 'shoot me and find out.'"

It was at this point that Toshiru recognized the source of the strangeness he felt. Her voice and mouth weren't quite in sync. It was like watching a ventriloquist dummy.

"Uh-huh. Well, since I did it once, can I do it again?" Toshiru raised the output of the electric pump gun from low to medium.

"Sure, but if you do, I'll attack."

"I'd be curious to see how a ghost attacks."

Toshiru pulled the trigger again. An instant before the projectile was loosed, the girl smashed the floor violently with her arms. It made a tremendous racket and shook the entire container. The girl's upper torso floated upward and landed on top of him. Then, she grabbed the barrel of the gun and used the grip to strike Toshiru on the jaw.

"*Ergh!*"

He grunted and fell backward out of the end of the container. The half-girl landed heavily on top of him, pinning his arms after she'd already inflicted a blow to his head. The weight was entirely beyond anything Toshiru would've imagined, and blood flecked his breath when he wheezed.

He wanted to draw his pistol from his waist, but his arms were completely immobilized. They might as well have been nailed down with industrial restraints.

Stuck though he was, he did get an up-close look at his assailant. Instead of guts and organs hanging from her torso, there were cables and electrical ports.

"Wow. Ghosts these days are robots?" Toshiru observed. The taste of iron was thick in his mouth.

The girl grimaced and said, "This is justified self-defense, but I'd rather not kill if I don't need to. Please leave. And drop your weapons before you go."

"Why?"

"Why what?"

"Why don't you want to kill? Is it the Three Laws of Robotics?"

"There's no rule about it. I can kill you if I want," the girl asserted, putting more pressure in the grip on Toshiru's arms. It increased in a direct, constant fashion, like a robotic vise tightening. It was not at all like the sensation of human strength.

"Wait, wait, I give. I don't want you to kill me, either. I only came here to recharge my scooter."

The girl noticed the electric scooter parked outside of the container for the first time. "If you only want to recharge it, why did you shoot me?"

"I heard there was a ghost. So I shot you."

"I'm not a ghost."

"Yeah, I figured that out. I don't shoot machines."

"What kind of decision process is that?"

"You don't know what'll happen if you shoot a ghost. So I tried it out. When you shoot a machine, it breaks. That's a waste," Toshiru reasoned.

"You're weird."

At last, the girl released him. With one hand, she grabbed his rifle, and with the other, she hurled her body back inside the container by pushing off the ground. Toshiru felt his fingertips burning as the blood flowed through his arms again.

"Why don't you have legs? Were you designed that way? Why

wouldn't a higher-up have complained about that?" Toshiru inquired, once he had caught his breath again and sat up to face the girl.

"I do have legs. Right here."

The automaton used her arms to climb up the container's power generator and pulled down a pair of legs she'd hidden there. The bone structure was metal, with thick wires and plastic-looking parts stuck onto them. One of the legs was torn from the knee, as though having been ripped off with great force.

"Ahh, I see. Your leg got damaged, so you hid in here for shelter."

The mechanical girl nodded. "There just happened to be a generator here. It was easier to get around without my legs after they stopped working, and it's less of a power drain, too."

"Nice," said Toshiru. He examined her closely. The way she'd dragged herself along the ground with her arms was anything but human, but when merely resting on the ground, she looked like any other girl. If anything was off, she didn't quite have the natural sway of a biological human.

"Can you show me your legs? I'm curious how they work."

"Do you know much about machinery?"

"According to my résumé, I do."

Toshiru produced his company badge. The words JR Fukuoka, Engineering 4th Division, Toshiru Kubo, were emblazoned on it.

"You're from JR Fukuoka?"

"Formerly. Left the company. I'm Toshiru Kubo," he introduced. It occurred to him that this was the first time he'd told someone his own name since arriving on Shikoku.

"I'm Haikunterke."

"That's a strange name. Where did you come from?"

The girl said nothing.

"Hokkaido, huh? That's a long way away," Toshiru continued, undaunted.

"How did you—?"

"It's written right here," Toshiru observed, pointing at the girl's legs. JR North Japan's fox logo was stamped near the joint, very small. "So the people up north are making weapons like this? I suppose you'd be strong against people, but I can't imagine robots having much effect on Yokohama Station itself."

"I'm not a weapon. I'm an infiltration agent."

"Agent?"

"Collecting information, capturing Suikanet nodes, things like that."

"…Huh."

Toshiru thought he recalled Okuma saying something about the northern folks being adept with Suikanet. Even a man of his technical expertise could only infiltrate the network from Shimonoseki, right across the Straits, to the city of Iwakuni near Hiroshima. A physical presence like Haikunterke changed things, however. You could acquire nodes much more effectively than just hurling signals across the water.

Toshiru had heard that Suikanet worked similar to old concepts like wartime territory: capturing areas, establishing a presence, and so on. JR North Japan held the most nodes on the eastern side of Yokohama Station. Control on the west side belonged to a mysterious group called the Dodger Alliance. They'd vanished four years ago and hadn't been heard from since, though. Their base of operations had been in the Kansai region around Osaka and Kyoto, but that was about all Toshiru knew.

"It doesn't run off of motors? What's this plastic—artificial muscle? A couple of them are damaged and solidified," Toshiru commented as he examined the legs.

"Can you fix them?" asked Haikunterke. She wore no expression, but the tone of her voice was just a bit lighter than before.

"I can't return them to their original form. I don't have the materials. But I can perform a little emergency work on them. In exchange, will you forget that I shot at you?"

The girl said nothing.

"Well, whatever. I guess it doesn't make a difference."

"What was your plan, hiding in here?" Toshiru asked. He was dismantling Haikunterke's legs. A number of the artificial muscle fibers in her right one were damaged and immobilized. Removing them would help improve mobility. There were synchronizers in both limbs, so when the right leg was injured, the left wouldn't work correctly, either. It seemed like bad design to Toshiru.

"I was securing power and making myself safer. And looking for a way to fix myself."

"Looking? How?"

Haikunterke pointed at the back of her head. "My supplemental memory storage. It's got information on how my body works."

"I see. So you know it, but you don't understand it."

"That's very clever. I wasn't really able to explain it myself."

"Well, I am an engineer," Toshiru said. There were control devices here and there around the artificial muscle that allowed you to program certain simple movements. That must have been the system Haikunterke had used when blocking Toshiru's bullet on reflex. If the process were working correctly, it would allow her to dodge a majority of attacks.

"How did you get hurt?"

"It was an ambush. There were so many of them. I couldn't avoid all the attacks."

"These legs would be faster than my scooter. You couldn't run away?"

"It was in a village a bit south of here, and there were lots of kids," Haikunterke explained.

"What do the kids have to do with it?"

"...I don't think you would understand."

"Okay. Fine, then."

As he worked, Toshiru imagined Haikunterke among the children in the village she mentioned. Then, he pictured an armed gang descending upon the settlement. To the best of his imagining, he couldn't conceive of a reason that would've prevented the robot from escaping.

"Are there lots of people like you at JR Fukuoka?" Haikunterke inquired.

"I don't know. I can definitely say there are none like you. We're all organic," Toshiru answered. He realized it was getting harder to see what his hands were working on. A glance through the skylight told him the sun was already down.

"It's dark. Are there lights in here?"

"Hang on."

Using just her arms, Haikunterke climbed on top of the generator and turned on a light switch. The LED on the ceiling activated. Its glow was faded and weak; it was probably well past the unit's intended shelf life.

"Can't a robot shine lights out of her eyes or something?"

"I don't need to. I have infrared vision."

"Nice. Very logical," Toshiru praised, glancing at a small flashlight-like tube resting next to Haikunterke. He then examined her from top to bottom (a span less than a meter) and asked, "Why a child?"

"It's easier to sneak Inside."

"Why?"

"Kids under six don't get checked for a Suika. Didn't you know that?"

"I've heard it before. When you have a kid, you're supposed to make a deposit before they turn six or whatever."

"Yes. My being built to look like a child grants me a certain amount of leeway when avoiding the automated turnstiles. It's not perfect, though. The station's immune system uses physical shape as its baseline detection process, I hear."

"Ahh. I thought it was just what the designer wanted for you," said Toshiru. Haikunterke glared at him.

"Doesn't the JR in Fukuoka study this kind of thing?"

"No. Our people are only interested in weapons," Toshiru replied. He pulled and pushed on her artificial leg muscles. *Our machinery is more advanced than this*, he thought. The robot's design was trying to make up for inefficient construction by way of superior materials. That was lousy cost performance, however, and made the product harder to maintain. Toshiru decided the difference was probably a reflection of each company's circumstances.

Kyushu's defensive line was a narrow strait of water, so their primary method of fighting was macro-destruction—structurally annihilating the connecting walkways the station tried to shoot in their direction.

However, the feature that separated Hokkaido from Yokohama Station was the Tsugaru Strait, which was much, much wider than the Kanmon Straits. They had no concern about connecting walkways coming over the water. Their problem was the Seikan Tunnel, which was permeated by the structural genetic field and couldn't be destroyed. Their battle was one of micro-evolution, of material science. Something meant to counteract the genetic field itself.

Perhaps that fundamental difference explained why their machine design was so clumsy.

"So they don't know you're a machine inside as long as you look like a human? Maybe we should have tried building one of those."

"You'd find it difficult."

"True. We could whip up a bipedal robot right away, but we can't build humanlike brains like yours. Not that we need to."

Haikunterke glared at Toshiru again. Her expressions were very hard to read as a whole, with the one exception being this grumpy face.

"So about this leg," Toshiru began, showing Haikunterke her own limb. It was about fifty centimeters long, a bit lengthier than his arm from the elbow on. It used a kind of metal he'd never seen before. It must have been a unique product of Hokkaido. "It uses artificial muscle to bend a metal arm that represents the bone. The number of bones and bundles of fibers are exactly the same as a human's."

"What about it?"

"Why is it built so similar?"

"I told you. Making it look human is how you avoid the attention of the automated turnstiles."

"But the materials are different. What's the purpose of making the inner workings so analogous? It would be way more efficient to use motorized actuators for the joints than artificial tendons. That's how the turnstiles work. Especially if you're moving around as nimbly as you do. There's a built-in lag to muscle extension and contraction. When you move that violently, it's going to take a toll on the material," Toshiru explained.

He removed four of the damaged muscle fibers from the right leg. He then took two from the left leg and transferred them to the right.

It meant lower leg power overall, but at least Haikunterke would be able to run.

"This construction seeks to be as close to human as artificially possible. What was your designer thinking?"

After a pause, Haikunterke admitted, "I don't know. I don't know much about machines."

Toshiru stared at her, then covered his nose and mouth with one hand and began making strange noises that sounded like, "Guh! Guh! Guh!" He had to stop working for a few dozen seconds as the noises continued.

"What's so funny?" Haikunterke asked after realizing the man was trying to hold back his laughter.

Toshiru collected himself. "That was the funniest joke I've heard in my entire life."

"Sounds like you've had a very boring life, then."

"I wouldn't know. I haven't had any other lives to compare it to." He wheezed a few more times, then hit a second wave and started to make the "guh" sounds again.

"I've been on this mission for two years now," Haikunterke said. "This is the first time I've felt like I truly hate someone."

"Oh yeah? I've been alive for twenty-four years, and you're the first human-shaped thing I've ever been interested in."

Toshiru bent and stretched the mechanical legs, fine-tuning the tension of the muscles. The newly attached fibers were a little too tense, so he turned the ankle screw to loosen them a little.

The sun had set, but the cicadas continued to drone outside. Toshiru wondered why they all screamed and stopped at the same time.

"I think it's pretty much done. Give it a test to see," Toshiru said, handing the legs back to Haikunterke. The sky was beginning to brighten, and he seemed rather sleepy after his night of work.

"How do I attach them?" he asked her.

"I'll do that myself."

"Can I watch?"

"You should go to sleep."

"That's true. I'm tired."

Toshiru went into the back of the container where the morning sunlight wouldn't reach. There was a cloth sack there, so he used it as a pillow and lay down. His ears caught a metallic clicking and clacking sound coming from the generator motor, but he was so tired that he fell asleep right away.

When he woke, the sun was high overhead. His long gun was resting next to him. Toshiru picked it up and walked outside. He took some dried bread from his scooter, which was now fully charged, and ate a late breakfast. Haikunterke came running down the mountain slope from above.

Even with her legs attached, she was barely a meter tall. She only came up to Toshiru's solar plexus, and he wasn't an especially tall man.

"Feels good?" Toshiru confirmed.

"Yeah. The muscle tension is very different, so it took a little while before I got the hang of it." There was dirt here and there on Haikunterke's clothes. She'd probably fallen on the slope a few times.

"You want to eat?" he asked, offering her a piece of dried bread.

"I don't need it. I run off electricity alone."

"That's inconvenient. You won't find generators all over the place. My scooter runs on solar power, but you must use a lot more energy than that."

"Yes. My mission was intended to take place Inside. There's all the electricity you could want in there," Haikunterke said.

Toshiru considered the system of breaking down organic matter to create power. Since fossil fuel had dried up during the Winter War, Kyushu's JR used vehicles that ran off an organic oxidation system. That wouldn't fit into a body of Haikunterke's size, but Toshiru thought it would be pretty funny if she chewed on twigs and leaves for fuel.

"Now that my legs are fixed, I'm going back Inside."

"To do what?"

"To continue my mission. Reconnaissance of the Shikoku region was part of my assignment, too, but I've been down here too long. I haven't reported back in a whole month. I need to return to a place where I can connect to Suikanet."

"Can I go with you?" requested Toshiru.

"Why?"

"As I said earlier, you're the first human-shaped thing that's ever caught my interest. Plus, your legs need help. Maintenance is part of an engineer's responsibility."

"...If you want."

As the early summer sun warmed Shikoku, the two continued along the Yoshino River's southern side.

Haikunterke's walking gait was very odd. She looked just like an ordinary child, but she kept up with a scooter traveling thirty kilometers an hour.

Following the river east would eventually lead to Tokushima. The plan was to traverse it and turn north to the Great Naruto Bridge. From there, it was just a matter of crossing Awaji Island to get Inside. Finding the roads and keeping your bearings was difficult in Shikoku, but this route was simple enough to follow.

"If you're going back Inside, wouldn't it be faster to cross the river here into Kagawa, where the station's already invading, and take the Great Seto Bridge up to Honshu?" Toshiru proposed.

Haikunterke shook her head as she walked. "That was how I got here in the first place. I was instructed to avoid retracing any of my paths. The point is to capture nodes as widely as possible. I came here along the Sea of Japan route. Next is to move along the Pacific."

"I see."

According to JR Fukuoka's military map, this was where a railway known as the Tokushima Line ran. From what Toshiru could see from the scooter, however, there was nothing that resembled one of the JR Integrated Intelligence's station units. It must have been lost long ago—either during the war or in what followed.

"Incidentally, my destination is close to the Great Naruto Bridge, too. We can go there together," Toshiru stated.

"What are you headed there for?"

"Tourism."

Haikunterke didn't pry any further. Instead, she pointed at the scooter and asked, "Did you bring that from Kyushu?"

"No, I got it here. It was right after crossing into Shikoku. I got lucky."

"From whom?"

"It was a bit south of Matsuyama. I was traveling the mountains in poor visibility. Somehow, I happened to spot someone wearing a helmet riding along on this thing. Suddenly, there was a rope that flew up and tripped the scooter. When the rider fell, about six men jumped out with pipes and wood beams, ready to beat the rider and steal it."

"And?"

"I happened to be just a bit higher than them, so I saw the whole thing happen. I shot all six, and once they stopped moving, I got the scooter."

"What happened to the original rider?"

"Dunno. They got beat pretty bad, but I don't think they were dead. I didn't see the face, but the hair was long, so it was probably a woman."

"...Ah."

Haikunterke looked like she wanted to say something else, but she didn't. They continued for several more minutes in silence.

It was a hot and humid day, but as the breeze while riding the scooter was pleasant, the temperature didn't feel all that bad.

"Why did you flee from Kyushu?" asked Haikunterke, without looking at Toshiru.

"I got sick of weapons development," he answered. "Yokohama Station's attacks evolve year after year. New developments were required to keep fighting it off. JR Fukuoka proposed ideas that basically spent ten times the energy for twice the power."

"So you ran away."

"That's not all. In the planning stages, they told us to exaggerate all the numbers. We were barely getting twice the output, but they told us to say it was three times. And the outreach publication we give the people of Kyushu says it's four times the power."

"That's why you came to Shikoku?"

"That's right. I heard there was anarchy here. I figured that would make everything work logically, so I decided to come and see it for myself."

"Logically."

"Following the laws of nature, I guess you could say. A place where you don't have to consider anything that's unnecessary."

The path along the river undulated here and there. Toshiru busily adjusted the handlebars, steering the scooter over the least bumpy routes. Haikunterke trotted along in tight synchronicity with his path. Her reflexes were much faster than those of a human being.

"Could you run faster before the injury?" Toshiru inquired.

"We're designed for cruising at fifty kilometers an hour, though there's little opportunity to go that fast Inside. I was intended to handle outdoor missions, too. My companions go about twenty kilometers."

"There are others?"

"Yes. Scattered about Inside. They each have their own region they're responsible for. Their body specs are lower than mine, though, so if you shot them with that weapon's maximum power, they probably couldn't withstand it."

"That's good. If the JR up north is mass-producing people like you, that gives us even less of a position to stand on. All we're good at is weapons, after all."

"Does JR Fukuoka make those guns, too?" Haikunterke asked, looking at the electric pump gun resting sideways across the back of the scooter.

"Yeah. That's the N700 line, the latest model. They put that out just after I joined the company, so I only had a minor part in their production."

"How many people have you shot since coming to Shikoku?"

Toshiru thought that one over for a while.

"None without a good reason," he replied.

◆

"That's the village I told you about."

Eventually, their path along the river took them to the town with the hydroelectric generator Toshiru had passed yesterday. It was located higher than most spots along the river, and they'd collected a large number of guardrails and used them to erect a simple defensive wall around the camp. The power-generating device was built into the river.

Haikunterke's watch said it was five in the afternoon. The western sun burned hot on Toshiru's back.

"They told me about the charging station where I found you."

"Uh-huh. And they believed that I was a ghost," Haikunterke recalled, her expression unfazed.

It was only when they got a bit closer that Toshiru realized something was wrong with the village.

"Some strange group over there," he observed. There was a little hill some distance away from the riverside village, and there were unnaturally wriggling mounds moving on its slope. Once they got closer, it became apparent that it was a large number of people.

"They're attackers. Be quiet," Haikunterke commanded softly. It wasn't a hushed whisper like a human being would make but her normal speaking voice played at a quieter volume.

Several dozen men were in formation on the side of the slope. Many of them were holding long sticks. Probably guns.

"Looks like it's a siege. I see one person dead there. A villager, I'm guessing," Toshiru said, pointing at the gate leading into the village. That was the only place where the path continued, and there was no guardrail wall. Someone was collapsed on the ground just outside the village, and the unpaved ground there was dark with blood. It was too far to make out their age, but their clothing suggested they weren't on the attacking side.

"They've got a stable power source, so people have come for it," Haikunterke stated, eyeing the hydroelectric generator.

"Seems like the places I pass by have a tendency to get attacked." Toshiru recalled the man with the shack at the seaside.

"Probably the scooter's fault."

"Yeah."

The wide tires left clear tracks on unpaved ground.

"And this area is especially unstable, even within Shikoku. Yokohama Station's very close by, so you've got people pushed out of their homes and fleeing coming up against people rushing closer for the resources ejected from the station."

"Is it more peaceful on the southern side of the island, like around Kochi? I came from the western side, obviously."

"I saw a bit of it, but there weren't many people, period."

"Ahh."

If the two proceeded along the riverside road, they would pass right through where the villagers and assailants were locked in a faceoff. Even with the scooter (and faster mechanical legs) it would be difficult to slip safely between two armed factions.

"It's hard to see from this distance. What would you say that is, thirty people? That's a lot. Must have a really powerful leader uniting them."

"Thirty-two in all," counted Haikunterke, staring at the slope. "Twelve of them have long guns."

"That's impressive eyesight. Can you tell what type they are?"

"They're not in my database. They look like this."

Haikunterke pulled out a device in her left hand and displayed the attackers' armaments on its screen. This appeared to be an image captured directly through her own eyes.

"That's the DF50 line. Pretty old pump guns. There's no automatic adjustment, so if the bullet has a bad shape, the trajectory will go way off. They're only accurate to about thirty meters," Toshiru explained. *In moments like this, a mechanical person has it pretty easy*, he thought. "The villagers should have a couple of the same, so that won't mean a decisive advantage in battle."

"Of the attackers, twelve have guns. None of the others have weapons that should prove to be a problem. The probability that I can jump out and defeat them all without harm is eighty-seven percent," Haikunterke said.

"Thirteen percent is a pretty high risk for a charitable action," replied Toshiru.

Haikunterke considered this for several seconds. "Yes. Our company forbids taking unnecessary risks."

"Yeah. And you wouldn't want to lose any more of those muscle fibers."

Haikunterke was silent again. Toshiru thought it was strange that, for being a machine, the tempo of her thought and speech were so human. Maybe it was an intentional affectation to make her less awkward in social situations. That would be unfortunate.

"Can you shoot all of them with your gun from here without risk?"

"I told you before. I've never shot someone without a good reason. I have no reason to support the village. Besides, they refused to charge my scooter."

"I'm not surprised. Their power generator clearly isn't enough to support an entire settlement."

"If I had to come up with an excuse, I'd say that if I clean up all the guys on the slope, I'll get a bunch of ammo. That's not really all that valuable, though," Toshiru admitted.

Electric pump guns were developed for frontline soldiers in the Winter War to use any kind of metal as ammunition because the conflict had gone on for so long that traditional resources were scarce. For that reason, this particular sort of arms became synonymous with "weapons" from the post-war collapse through the expansion of Yokohama Station.

Haikunterke gazed at the village, and the visuals on the screen in her left hand changed to show the settlement. Now Toshiru could see the face of the young man lying dead in front of the gate.

I wonder if that's the guy who refused to let me charge my scooter when I asked, Toshiru thought. He couldn't clearly recall the man's face, however.

"Well, we should probably avoid them. Let's go around to the other side of the hill," Haikunterke suggested.

"Good idea."

Toshiru maneuvered the scooter on the narrow road and began riding away from the village. After a little while, they were around the other side of the slope. The sound of gunfire could be heard, along with a few human yelps of pain. Toshiru couldn't tell which side they were coming from, however.

Onward they went, until night arrived. Despite the rainy season having recently ended, the night was still cold, and riding on the scooter caused the chilly breeze to hug Toshiru's body.

He and Haikunterke stopped at a place far downriver from the village. There were no people nearby, only the incessant croaking of frogs.

"I've still got plenty of battery power. What about you? You've been running for a while," Toshiru said, putting down the scooter's stand. If needed, he could provide Haikunterke with a little power. A little.

"I'm fine, but I might have a problem if we continue like this for two or three more days. Can we stop at a charging station on the way?" requested the robot. She was sitting with her knees drawn up.

"I'm just tagging along with you. I'll follow whatever you need to do," Toshiru answered, using his device to display JR Fukuoka's military map. It showed the known locations of the Shikoku power stations.

Toshiru was unsure of his current location, but the nearest was probably about ten kilometers away. That was a tough trip after nightfall on a scooter.

"You can see in the dark, right? I'll be fine on my own. You just go here by yourself and come back."

"Thank you, but I'm going to sleep for a bit," Haikunterke declared.

"Robots sleep, too?"

"Yes. I need to allow my supplemental memory to compile, reflect on its contents, and attach them to my main memory. It's a constant process, but I still need to turn off my external sensors to kick it into high focus now and then. It should only take about two hours."

"You really are built to be like a human. Isn't that inconvenient?"

"My sensors remain minimally functional and will react when someone approaches," Haikunterke explained. Then, she closed her eyes. In addition to the constant chorus of frogs, there was a quieter clicking sound, like metal gears turning. Toshiru thought it was all rather tasteful.

He loaded metal pieces into Mizuho, his pistol, by the light of the moon. Once it was ready to fire at a moment's notice, he proceeded to break down Sakura, the rifle, to inspect its interior.

Many of the guns produced by JR Fukuoka were never used outside of shooting practice before they got replaced by a newer model. It was a sign of Kyushu's governmental stability that they had few reasons to use them. In that sense, Toshiru's N700 had been put through a much more rigorous battery of tests than most.

In thanks for its hard work, he spent any downtime he had ensuring the weapon received proper upkeep. Once he had reassembled it, he performed the same process on the short gun.

Instead of the two hours Haikunterke had promised, she opened her eyes a bit over three hours later. The moon was high in the night sky, providing some meager light to the area. The frog songs had stopped at some point.

"Yo. For a machine, I guess you're not that mechanical after all," Toshiru told her.

"I had much to compile," Haikunterke replied. The coordination of her mouth movements and speech was even worse than usual shortly after waking. "I had barely anything to think about while I was taking shelter at that generator, but I have seen quite a lot in the past day. Therefore, the process took longer."

"Does your supplemental memory thing save everything you see and hear?"

"Yes. But there's so much that it takes too long to call up the necessary information, which is why I compile and condense it. Otherwise, I can't assess risk and make instantaneous choices when I need to."

"Meaning that your leg got hurt because you misjudged a danger?"

Haikunterke nodded. She was still sitting on the ground with her knees up. "It happens sometimes," she admitted unhappily. Perhaps she was sensitive to having her failures raised. "When I assess that there's no risk to my mission, I will help people. You'd probably just laugh at that idea."

"I'm not laughing," Toshiru responded, getting a mat off the scooter and laying it out on the ground. "I just think it's strange. It makes me wonder what your design philosophy was."

"Is it truly that unusual?" Haikunterke made a face that made her displeasure plain.

"Yeah. It's an illogical conception. It comes off like a tool that was built for one purpose being reused for something else. Due to budget reasons or something."

"I don't want to talk about this."

"Okay," Toshiru accepted.

"Practically speaking, our defense of the strait is going well. The enemy's tactics are evolving, but we've managed to adapt to them," said Toshiru.

He was resting back against the mat. It was around midnight, but because the moon was so bright and he'd gotten up late in the morning, he wasn't quite falling to sleep. If only he could simply turn off his waking functions like the mechanical girl. That would be very convenient.

"They immediately tore down the bridge at Shimonoseki and then dug out the tunnel right from the rock, from what I hear. I don't know how they did it; that was eighty years ago. Maybe they still had gravity weapons back then."

"I see," Haikunterke remarked quietly. "The strait is wider in Hokkaido, so it can't get a corridor across. But we were too late in destroying the tunnel, so the structural genetic field had already infected the inside. If they had been quicker to make that decision, we might not have needed to undertake the current defensive battle."

But then I might not have been born, she thought.

"It's probably a difference in what you were seeing. We had the example of the Great Seto Bridge, so we knew a fair amount about the station's replication ability."

"That's a very calm assessment," Haikunterke muttered. She felt that Hokkaido had a better understanding of the nature of the structural genetic field, though.

"So as long as we block the corridors and they shoot across the Straits, we're fine. As long as we deploy a certain amount of manpower, we can stop it in time. The enemy's tactics have progressed, too, but it's an unthinking station. There are limits to what it can come up with. Humans will win in the end," Toshiru stated, as dispassionately as if he had no stake in it.

Haikunterke replied, "What end?"

Toshiru realized he'd never really thought about that. He just naturally assumed that there would be some kind of conclusion to the situation. The same way the civilization that had been so advanced had crumbled into dust over the course of the Winter War.

"Well, anyway, to our company, it's important that there's an enemy to fight. Yokohama Station's waiting just a few kilometers across the water, and if it crosses the sea to our side, basically everyone on Kyushu will lose their home. It's that fear that makes our company's centralized power possible," he explained.

Haikunterke sat there, listening. The fact that she could be perfectly still with her knees up to her chest like that without moving underlined the idea that she was fundamentally different from a regular human being.

"An enemy that can be fought back but never defeated. What situation could be better for those in charge? Does the boss of your place think any differently?"

"I don't know. I just carry out my mission."

"Nice," Toshiru replied.

"So you didn't fight to defend Kyushu against the station?"

"According to my title, I did. Not that I had much personal interest in that part of it."

"You didn't care about your hometown being swallowed by Yokohama Station?"

"...That was beside the point for me. I don't think my hometown will ever be part of Yokohama Station, even in the future," Toshiru said. He didn't have any particular attachment to the place anyway.

"Why not?"

"It's not on Kyushu itself. It's on one of the smaller islands. Tanegashima. You know it?" Toshiru inquired.

Haikunterke thought for a few seconds, then got a distant look in her eyes. "Tanegashima. An island forty kilometers from the Osumi Peninsula of southern Kyushu. Surface area of four hundred and forty-five square kilometers. Under JR Fukuoka control. It is known as the first place where firearms came to Japan during the military government era. Due to its southern latitude and the relatively lighter gravity there, it was once home to Japan's largest space center. During the era of High Civilization, they shot many satellites and crewed spacecraft up from the island. As the Asian center of the Allies during the war, it was also used to launch many satellite weapons. For that same reason, however, it became a major target for attack," Haikunterke parroted, as though reading off a script.

"Yeah. More or less. There's nothing there now. If anything, being devoured by Yokohama Station might liven up the place a bit. Maybe the structural genetic field will absorb and recreate the space center facilities."

Haikunterke made another of her clearly disgusted faces.

"You don't like that idea?"

"No. I was built for the purpose of protecting my territory. I reject that way of thinking."

"Well, I guess you can't fight your design. I don't tell my scooter to fly, either," he said.

"If you have no interest in defense, why did you join JR?"

"Oh, that?" remarked Toshiru. He gazed up at the stars in the sky and rolled over on the mat so his back was to Haikunterke.

"I wanted to go to space," he muttered. "I decided to go into JR Fukuoka's engineering division so I could learn about tech, but all they taught me was how to make and use weapons. In fact, I found out that going into space requires a ton of fossil fuel—way more than you'll find anywhere in the world—so I gave up."

"What's out in space?"

"I don't know. I just know there aren't any people," Toshiru replied, and left it at that. So did Haikunterke. The frogs and cicadas were no longer singing, and the only sound left in the area was the flowing of the Yoshino River.

◆

They reached the Naruto Strait on the eastern coast of Shikoku the following afternoon.

"I can see the station. As I expected, it's already crossed Awaji Island and started to erode into Tokushima," observed Haikunterke, pointing toward the sea. The coast had a complex, three-dimensional profile, but among the canyon folds was the sight of something white and amorphous. Like a pancake on a griddle just before it's flipped, there were little holes all over its surface.

"Is that part of the station structure, too?" asked Toshiru. The part of Yokohama Station he'd seen across the Straits with JR Fukuoka had already been established for fifty years and resembled a completely developed construct.

"It's the outward tip of the station's expansion. It's not connected to the Great Seto Bridge, so it must have crossed on its own from Awaji Island. The exterior hasn't fully formed yet, but there are probably properly hollowed Inside spaces within. In a few months, it'll generate windows and pillars and features like that."

"It's disgusting," Toshiru remarked, tearing his gaze away from the station. "It's making my head hurt to look at it. Is it sending out some weird waves or something?"

"I'm getting a bit of a Suikanet signal," Haikunterke said. "So I'll be going back Inside from there."

"Cool. I enjoyed the last few days. I feel like I talked enough that I don't need to speak to anyone again for the rest of my life."

Haikunterke stared at Toshiru in silence, then walked in the direction of the station. It didn't look like she was moving very fast, but she was out of sight very soon.

So, thought Toshiru. The place he'd heard about from Okuma was supposed to be nearby. Because of the advance of the station structure, he couldn't tell the exact location. All he could do was pray it hadn't been buried yet.

Toshiru recalled when Okuma had told him about the locale. The other man had been eating sweet potatoes.

"It was built before the war. You wouldn't believe human beings could make something like that. The era of High Civilization was a true wonder. If you ever get the chance to visit Shikoku, you should go check it out."

Space was likely beyond Toshiru's grasp, but this was the next best thing. Toshiru checked that his scooter still had plenty of power and continued on his way.

There was a small hill made of concrete before Haikunterke's eyes. It was curved and liquid-looking, like cooled and hardened lava. This was what it looked like when Yokohama Station first reached a place and was still deciding what shape it would eventually take.

The surface of the station writhed in elaborate fashion along with the shape of the land. First, Haikunterke sought out an inconspicuous location. It was best if none of the people of Shikoku saw her using the structural genetic field canceler.

"Is anyone there?" Haikunterke asked. Hiding in the folds of the partially formed station structure were two children, a boy and a girl, and a woman who looked like their mother. All three were dressed in rags.

The mother looked frightened at first, but when she saw the stranger was a child, she was relieved.

"We're waiting here," she said.

"For what?"

"For an exit to form."

Haikunterke looked at the wall, and sure enough, the precursor structure to a Yokohama Station exit had taken form there. In another month, most likely, there would be a hole for an entrance, automated turnstiles in place, and a sign reading, YOKOHAMA STATION EXIT XX. The number would be six digits.

"My children are still five and three, so they can get Inside. If they can get a Suika somehow before they turn six, they can live safely in there," the mother said.

Haikunterke remembered seeing people like this in Kagawa, on the northern middle part of Shikoku. Children under six could come and go in the station without being caught by the turnstiles. Many parents used them to procure things from Inside. To the people who lived off the station's goods, small children were a valuable resource.

"I wouldn't, if I were you," Haikunterke stated flatly. "There's no way for children from outside to get a Suika. The automated turnstiles will be on them the moment they turn six. They'll hurl them into the nearest station hollow. Most hollows are completely empty, so they'll die very quickly after that."

The mother looked hurt and sad, but responded, "I'd still rather do it. It's much better than living here."

Haikunterke imagined that the mother must've been through something terrible and that she'd fled her with her children. The young boy and girl were staring at her. They probably thought she looked like another child their age.

"...If that's really how you feel, then go a bit farther north tomorrow. You might find an exit there," Haikunterke said before walking away from the fold of the station. The boy tried to run after her, but when he rounded one twist of the station, she was nowhere to be found.

To the north of the sheltered spot where she found the family, Haikunterke finally located an area with no people around and used the genetic field canceler to create a small hole in the station structure big enough for a person to crawl through. She was Inside.

It was the first time she'd ever seen the station's interior while it was still growing. There were filaments like spider thread all over, but they were metal wires. The ground was sticky under her feet. It was like cement that hadn't dried yet. Visuals and chemical composition analysis would be very valuable to send back to headquarters.

There were no automated turnstiles nearby. When the station generation was still incomplete, the area was probably excluded from their patrols.

It wasn't smart to stay around for too long. Haikunterke headed farther Inside, her feet sticking and splotching as she went. At some point, she was going to pass the Great Naruto Bridge and reach Awaji Island.

After an hour, she arrived at a place where the structure was plenty solid. There were automated turnstiles here and there but no humans. It was an ideal environment.

Haikunterke started up her communication terminal. The Suikanet signal was strong here. She'd be able to transmit quite a lot of data.

> **Suikanet Status: Establishing connection**…
> **Searching for appropriable route**…
> **Awaji - Kobe - Fukuchiyama - Maizuru - Tsuruga - Fukui - Kanazawa - Toyama - Itoigawa - Naoetsu - Nagaoka - Aizuwaka-matsu - Koriyama - Sendai - Morioka - Hirosaki - Routing settings complete.**
> **Exchanging encoding keys.**
> **Secure connection established.**

Before long, Haikunterke had a route for real-time communication. It also happened to match the path of her travels. She had been responsible for helping JR North Japan capture many nodes, after all.

> **Beginning direct communication.**

"JR North Japan, Engineering 2nd Division, this is Kaeriyama speaking."

"It's Haikunterke. I'm sorry for not contacting you for so long. I've just reached the Naruto Strait. I'm sending my locational data."

The robot girl heard Kaeriyama murmur an expression of relief. The signal was very clear, and the delay was short.

"Did you run into any trouble out there?"

"As we'd expected, things on Shikoku have worsened. I had a *bit* of trouble but nothing major. I will continue my mission Inside from here."

"Well, the good news is that you're safe. The bad news is that you can connect to Suikanet from where you are."

"Yes. There were no existing railroads on Awaji, so the structural genetic field was slow to spread there, but Yokohama Station has already crossed the Naruto Strait into Shikoku itself. I'll transmit my supplemental memory data from what I can access now."

> **Sending data**...

"Okay, I'm getting it."

The bar that displayed connection speed was at the highest level it had been since Haikunterke reached Shikoku. She'd be able to transfer quite a lot by tomorrow morning.

"Just as a situational update for you, we lost Nepshamai's signal while he was active in the Kanto region. Headquarters thinks he ran into some kind of danger."

"Could he have gone outside of Suikanet coverage, like I did? He was always the type to go off and do things on his own."

"His last signal was in Kamakura, fairly inland. He couldn't have gone completely out of network in a single instant."

"I could easily imagine that he forgot to charge his communications module," Haikunterke remarked. Kaeriyama snorted in response.

"You're always so hard on Shamai."

"He's much more social than I am, but he's missing a few screws here and there. He must have turned out like his origin."

"According to his last message, he found an interesting person and was working with him at the time. I don't know what it was that he found interesting, but the person is probably involved with whatever befell him. In any case, you should be aware that the people of Shikoku aren't the only danger. You may encounter hostiles in Yokohama Station, too. Don't take unnecessary risks. Use your best judgment in returning home."

"Shall I send all of my supplemental memory data to you now? Just in case I die at any point ahead. At this signal speed, I can complete the entire process in about two weeks."

"No. I want you back here, safe and sound."

"Yes, of course. Losing an agent is a big blow to the company's resources."

"Look…if all we wanted were more agents, we wouldn't need to go to the expense of building androids. We could just sail over to the far bank and steal a few kids with Suikas. We wouldn't even have to worry about being attacked by the station residents."

"So you mean, 'Come back safe and sound because your body is a valuable resource.'"

"Don't say it like that, Terke. Yes, your body was built to be sturdy for a long-term mission outside of Yokohama Station, but that's not what I'm saying. Yukie will be sad if you don't come back. And so will I."

"If my body isn't that important, then maybe I should send you everything, main memory device included. It'll be the same as if I'm back," Haikunterke proposed, knowing full well that this was technically impossible.

"You might be highly active, but you've got serious social issues. You're the exact opposite of Shamai."

"I take after my origin, too. Anyway, I'd like to have some compiling time, so I'll say good night. If there's any data I should synchronize, please have it sent to me."

> **Ending direct communication.**
> **Sending data. Please do not interrupt network connection. Estimated time remaining: 8 hours, 11 minutes…**

With the conversation over, Haikunterke curled up in her sitting position next to an automated turnstile and closed her eyes.

Her main sensors stopped functioning, and her system stopped writing to her supplemental memory, switching over to rumination mode. Its first step was to run the data from the communication with headquarters through her main memory unit.

"Look…if all we wanted were more agents, we wouldn't need to go to the expense of building androids. We could just sail over to the far bank and steal a few kids with Suikas. We wouldn't even have to worry about being attacked by the station residents," echoed Kaeriyama's voice. Crossing the Tsugaru Strait to kidnap children and raise them into agents wasn't just a figure of speech; they'd been doing that until about ten years ago. Everyone in the upper echelons of JR North Japan knew about it.

It was an inefficient program, and it didn't even bring them anything significant in return. Eventually, some sharp-eared journalist on Hokkaido caught wind of the story and published it. Overnight, it became the biggest scandal since the defensive battle against Yokohama Station had begun. Those in charge managed to write it off as the rogue initiative of the engineering division and dismissed the chief of the unit and several executives. That paved the way for Yukie to enter the picture.

Her pre-JR history was shrouded in mystery, but once in place, she guided the engineering division toward rapid, dramatic advances. It led to the birth of Corpocker androids like Haikunterke and new technological weapons like the structural genetic field canceler.

As her rumination speed increased, her active processing became a larger burden. Eventually, Haikunterke's consciousness faded, and she went into sleep mode.

Hiroto's vision was split between black and gray. Escalators covered the entire floor, and concrete formed the ceiling overhead. The endless number of black steps, some moving upward and some coming down, brought to mind the vitality of some giant, writhing organism.

The Akaishi Mountains were one of the three ranges that made up the Japanese Alps, located to the west of the many-layered city of Kofu. The complex, rippling slopes of the mountains were virtually blanketed in inclining, moving staircases, with the occasional mega-wall or pillar supporting a mammoth roof structure.

Sunlight peeked in here and there. Unlike Kofu, there was no structure blanketing the mountains. Keiha's trick of fudging the altitude coordinates would not work on the automated turnstiles here.

Hiroto had hoped to sit on one escalator step and ride it to the top, but that was quite obviously not an option. There were no lanes that proceeded all the way up the slopes. Ascending required a constant process of switching over.

Traps were not uncommon, where an ascending stairwell would lead directly into a descending one. In such cases, Hiroto either had to run up the down escalator or hop over the railing to the next lane to escape. And jumping across lanes when the belts were moving was not child's play.

"while on the escalator, please hold onto the moving belts and stay within the yellow line."

"Playing on the escalators, leaning over the edge, and
running against the flow of traffic is very dangerous.
Please refrain from these activities for the safety of
all visitors."

These two PA announcements repeated in every direction but with
no consistent timing, creating an unintelligible fog of words that permeated the station interior.

Hiroto used the device Keiha had given him to check his time and
present location. It would soon be afternoon, but he was only halfway
to the mountain ridge. That was significantly behind his initial sched-
ule. On top of that, the temperature seemed to be rising as it got closer
to noon. Solar heat was likely coming straight through because there
was only a single wall separating Hiroto from the outside.

Hiroto had left Kofu with Nepshamai's electronic sign after eight
o'clock in the morning.

"I scanned the structure and tried to search for a match on Suikanet," Keiha said as he woke up. "But I didn't find anything. At the very
least, this thing doesn't resemble any kind of computer used in Yokohama Station."

"So that's how advanced JR North Japan's tech is?"

"That would be the straightforward interpretation," Keiha admitted,
a far-off look in her eyes. She took a small rectangular object out of the
scanner and stuck it into the electronic screen. It seemed that her view
of the situation was very different.

"First of all, the most practical solution will be to find the body he
was in originally. His boot sequence may be in there," she explained.

Hiroto wondered what the Kamakura station employees were going to
do with Nepshamai's body after they'd hauled it away. Keiha requested
that he leave the dormant electronic sign with her, but he refused.

"I made him a promise. I'm going to give him the expired 18 Ticket
when I'm done with it," he said. Of course, that was impossible at present, but he figured that somewhere in the vast expanse of Yokohama
Station, he could find a solution.

Keiha looked disappointed, but she replied, "Take this device with you. It's got Suika certification on it, so you can at least connect to Suikanet and make use of it," and handed him a small box-shaped computer. It was about the size of the 18 Ticket. "It's got an account belonging to one of my dead friends on it. Normally when a Suika user dies, the information is sent to Suikanet, and their account is deactivated, but I did some things to prevent the transmission this time. My address is saved in there, too, so you can contact me if anything happens."

"You sure? It seems like this thing is pretty important to you."

"Yes. It's necessary for someone in your position, and I'd rather have it go to good use, strange as that is to say."

Hiroto took the device from her and left Kofu.

In the day that he spent interacting with Keiha, Hiroto learned two things. First, Keiha resisted using the words "Exit 42" or even typing them in on her keyboard. And second, that she strongly wanted Hiroto to get there anyway.

Hiroto's journey took him across the mountains, so he chose the relatively lower parts of the ridge that connected peak to peak to get over to the other side. It took him to what some might've called "the station's pass."

Yokohama Station's paths through the mountains were not nearly as clear and straight as those on flat land. Because travelers used varying routes over the many escalators on the slopes, encountering others along the way was rare. At the pass, though, where nearly all the meandering routes gathered, people tended to congregate and set up rest areas. A lobby had been generated in what little flat ground there was, and some vendors brought goods up there to sell. Hiroto couldn't buy anything without a Suika, but since drinking water was free, he topped off his bottle.

Nearly all of the people at the station pass were travelers. Like Hiroto, they were just trying to get over the mountains. A few, however, were proper climbers. They would be climbing the escalators farther up the slope in the hopes of reaching the peak.

"The peak? What's at the peak?" Hiroto asked. He wanted to know because his destination, Exit 42, was also somewhere labeled as a peak.

A thirty-something mountain-climber said, "You can see the blue sky."

The nearby mountaintop hadn't been enclosed within Yokohama Station. For a several kilometer stretch, it was open to the natural surroundings, with no roof overhead. If the weather was good, you could see nothing but blue sky above. In other words, it was a giant station hollow.

"When I was younger, I climbed Mt. Fuji, but it was boring; even the peak is Inside. But there are windows so you can see out. The real joy of mountaineering is getting to feel the outside air and gaze at the blue sky as you crack a beer. Have you ever seen the sky?"

"Yeah," replied Hiroto. "A lot."

The mountain-climber looked impressed. "Mt. Fuji's got such simple slopes; there are a lot of escalators that will just take you straight to the top. It's weak. And because some people calling themselves the Yokohama Station Tourism Board decided to label it a kind of sacred ground, it's brought out a bunch more tourists, and they're really wrecking the place. When I scaled Fuji, it hadn't reached four thousand meters yet. There weren't many climbers back then. It was nice and quiet," the thirty-something man recalled.

Hiroto ate one of his rations while the man talked.

"Where did you come from?" the climber asked.

"From Kofu. I'm passing through here, then over the Kiso Mountains, and on to Mt. Ontake," Hiroto explained. That was where the map said Exit 42 was.

"Hmmm. That's a pretty long trip. When did you leave?"

"This morning."

"This morning! And you got here in half a day? That's some stamina. Do you play sports?"

"A bit of sea-swimming."

In Ninety-Nine Steps, when there wasn't anything to do (which was most of the time), Hiroto would go swimming out into the sea alone. He'd never thought of it as a sport. It was more like a necessary life-skill and a good way for him to burn off some energy.

"Seesweming? That something in Kofu?" the climber inquired, puzzled.

After a bit of a break, Hiroto began descending toward the Ina Valley from the pass. It was more comfortable to walk down the descending escalators, which unfortunately allowed Hiroto to pick up too much speed. He lost his footing at one point, crashing and sending his bag flying onto another escalator lane. That was an ascending staircase, so recovering it cost him a lot of unnecessary time and energy.

There was less sunlight coming through the windows in the concrete ceiling now. As he got closer to Ina Valley, Hiroto began to grasp the particular patterns of escalator movement on the slope.

Eventually, the sun peering through the windows of the escalator highlands sank behind the concrete walls. It was his third night Inside. The screen of the 18 Ticket showed that he had two days and thirteen hours remaining.

He took as much sleep as possible while moving on escalators to buy a bit of extra travel time. He would nap for a half-hour or so on a descending escalator that continued straight down for several kilometers so it woke him up when he reached the end. At which point, he would search for another long one. He kept his belongings wrapped tight against his stomach with his arms for protection.

After midnight, Hiroto had made it into the Ina Valley. The directional signs hanging from the ceiling informed him that this was Yokohama Station, Nagano District, Komagane. In a larger thoroughfare that seemed like the city area, the stores and residences were shuttered, and no one was walking around. It was deathly quiet after the cacophony of endless safety announcements on the escalators. The lack of sound had a presence of its own in his ears. It left Hiroto feeling unsettled.

Unlike Kofu's spacious basin, the Ina Valley was a narrow strip of land running north and south between the Akaishi and Kiso Mountains. There was little open space, and Yokohama Station had built itself up on the sides of the valley in steps. For that reason, each layer was constructed around solar intake, and the residents all lived in sync with the sun's rhythm. When it got dark, they all went right to sleep.

It was a different kind of night Inside, one Hiroto hadn't seen in the Kanto plains or Kofu.

In any case, Hiroto wasn't planning to stick around. His interrupted sleep on the descending escalators had left him feeling exhausted. He headed straight for the Kiso Mountains on the western side of the valley. He'd been descending for so long that just walking on the flat ground felt strange.

The next day passed almost precisely the same way. Hiroto climbed the escalators, crossed at the station pass, then descended into the valley beyond.

If there was any difference, it was that there were far fewer people here than in the Akaishi Mountains yesterday and that Yokohama Station covered less of it. Patches of natural ground and sky poked through in places as Hiroto marched onward. The sky looked contentious in his first view of it in days. Several times, he wound up traveling over rainy ground.

Keiha's device showed Hiroto that he'd come very far from Ninety-Nine Steps. He'd been walking ceaselessly across escalators this whole time, but the thrill of visiting a place he'd never been to before helped assuage his fatigue.

Kiso Valley rested on the western side of the Kiso Mountains. It had a very peculiar shape when seen from a distance. It was even narrower than Ina Valley, but rather than nestling itself on the valley floor, Yokohama Station had grown massive connecting hallways that went straight across from slope to slope, like the sticky tendrils of natto.

In one of the hallways leading toward Kiso Valley, automatic doors suddenly closed from either wall to block Hiroto's path. They were glass barricades with a thick metal frame, adorned with stickers that read, Do not lean belongings against platform doors, and Rushing to pack cars is dangerous.

He spun around on reflex, but it was too late; another door was behind him. Hiroto was trapped inside a ten-meter span of hallway. Then, a man who looked about thirty years old came around a corner on the other side of the door ahead of him.

He was small and wore camouflage patterns that had been cobbled together from different sources. It was the first time Hiroto had seen anyone Inside who looked so shabby. It was the kind of thing people in Ninety-Nine Steps would wear.

"Hey, we got someone!" the man shouted back toward the side corridor.

"How many?"

"Just one."

"Any weapons?"

"Nope. Just a small bag."

Another man appeared. He was about fifty and had bulging eyes. Unlike the other person, he was garbed in an entirely blue uniform of waterproof fabric. What required waterproofing Inside?

The elder of the pair had a long gun in his hands. It was the kind that'd been used to shoot Nepshamai in Kamakura—what they called an electric pump gun.

"Just one isn't going to do us any good," said the blue uniform.

"What do you want me to say? He just wandered in here alone. There's got to be something we can do with him, like use him as bait to summon more of them," said the camo. The blue uniform with the gun stared at Hiroto appraisingly.

"Hang on. I'm just a traveler. I came from the east, and I'm only passing through," explained Hiroto.

"Passing through? Where to?"

"To a place called Exit 42," he said. Camo and Blue looked at each other.

"This guy's a Sabo. And look how far he's gotten," snarled Camo. It was like some kind of pestilence had been brought upon them.

"Nah, it ain't a Sabo. He's alone and doesn't have anything red."

"Probably hidin' it. I'll go ask the mayor. You keep an eye on him here," said Camo, vanishing around the corner. He looked like he wanted to stay as far away as possible from Hiroto. Only the blue uniform with the gun was left.

"Hey, I'm not Sabo or whatever you're talking about. Whatever it is you think, you're mistaken. Let me out of here," insisted Hiroto, banging on the transparent door. It wasn't glass, in fact, but some other clear, solid material.

"I know that. Where'd you come from?"

"From Kofu. I crossed two mountains to get here."

"Kofu? Which Kofu?"

"It's a big city to the east of here."

"And you crossed the mountains?" demanded Blue, whose already large eyes were bulging out even further. "If you crossed the mountains, you must have a hideout."

"Hideout?"

Hiroto consulted his memory. There were a few places with livable areas on the vast escalator highlands along the way, to be sure. But in Yokohama Station, where rooms grew all on their own, it was difficult to say from appearance alone if they existed because there were people there or just from some quirk of the station.

"What kind of hideout?" he asked.

"For the bandits."

"Is that the Sabo you were talking about? Bandits?"

"The hell you talkin' about? Why would Sabo be bandits?" scoffed Blue, giving Hiroto a pitying gaze.

They weren't seeing eye to eye. On the other hand, it was a wonder that Hiroto, who grew up on the cape outside along the sea, could hold a conversation with these people from the central mountains of Yokohama Station at all.

The blue uniform man refused to say anything after that, so Hiroto decided to go to sleep. If he wanted to, he could use the genetic field canceler to escape, but he wasn't inclined to waste the batteries. Getting through the valley was probably going to be a hassle even if he did escape.

It was Hiroto's first time sleeping in captivity since being stuck in the holding cell in Yokosuka his first night Inside. That was only three days ago, but it felt like the distant past at this point.

Crossing the two mountain ranges should have left him exhausted, but he found it hard to fall asleep in the brightly lit hallway. He could hear the men saying things like, "He's asleep," "Let's get it over with now, while we have the chance." Each time, Hiroto had to force his eyes open to prove he was still awake.

The guards changed shifts every few hours, giving them the chance to rest, but Hiroto had to stay alert the whole time, sapping his mental strength.

"At any rate, you're lucky. You came alone," stated the fourth escort as the dawn approached. He was a friendly looking thirty-something wearing an old, tattered suit. By this point, Hiroto had figured out that the residents here just wore whatever they had, regardless of its original purpose.

He'd thought of Inside as a rich, abundant place, where things were provided in endless supply, but that wasn't quite the case. This area had to be like Ninety-Nine Steps, where the only things the denizens got were whatever was discarded from elsewhere.

"At first, we'd catch a bunch of 'em at once, then toss in enough food for one person and plenty of guns. Once they'd killed each other off, we'd let the holy turnstiles take the survivor away," said the man in the suit. Compared to Camo and Blue, he was much more conversational.

"Listen, this is all just a big mistake. I'm on a journey from the far east, and I have to get to a place called Exit 42 by tomorrow. Let me out of here. What are you guys fighting against, anyway?" Hiroto pressed.

The man in the suit looked like he wasn't sure whether to believe this or not. "Hmm, well, you don't seem to be one of the bandits. I've never seen anyone as huge as you before," he admitted. Then, at last, he began to explain.

A group of mountain bandits nearby often came to attack the village, stealing goods and people. There was no violence allowed Inside, of course, but through lots of experience, these ruffians knew how to pillage without attracting the attention of the automated turnstiles.

One of those tricks was not to inflict direct harm. If you set up a trap in a hallway, for example, then maintained a certain distance from it, the turnstiles wouldn't be alarmed if a victim sprung the thing and got hurt.

The villagers had been thinking up defensive countermeasures, and this door-capturing trap was one of them.

"They took my wife away five years ago," the man explained.

The bandits would take their kidnapped victims outside the station to hold them captive. The automated turnstiles wouldn't do anything if they couldn't see you. Conditions outside were harsh, and the hostages didn't survive long. The man in the suit had gone after his wife after discovering where she'd been taken, but he was too late.

"I remember the face of the one who took my wife. As soon as I see him, I'll shoot him with this," the man snarled, brandishing the long gun. "If the holy turnstiles are angry with me, that's a cost I'm willing to bear."

Learning about this new situation only made Hiroto worry about his remaining time. He was already on the morning of his fifth day, and Exit 42 would be close after he crossed the mountain ahead.

"In any case, let me out of here. If you want, I'll help you beat these—bandits?—in return."

"You can't. For one thing, if you're just a traveler, how could you possibly help us in a fight? If we let you out, you'll only get lost."

It was true. The village was a maze of crisscrossing passageways. Hiroto was an outsider, and he'd undoubtedly lose his way quickly. While he was bigger and more athletic than the majority of Insiders, the inability to commit violence left him without any particularly useful skills in a conflict.

So he'd have to do something else, although it wasn't his strongest suit. Hiroto thought up a plan and got to his feet.

"Oh, well. I didn't want to have to use this," he said. He then pulled out his structural genetic field canceler. The guard eyed it apprehensively. Hiroto switched it on and pointed it at the sidewall. A fist-sized chunk of concrete crumbled off its surface.

"This is, uh, a new weapon. It's powerful enough to easily destroy the station's wall, and the best part is, the automated turnstiles won't come after you. If I use this, I could wipe out your village. If you want to resolve this peacefully, open the door."

It was a bluff, of course. It sounded like such an obvious lie that Hiroto nearly chuckled while saying it.

The man in the suit, however, was having trouble grasping the situation. He looked back and forth between Hiroto's little tube and the broken wall, still clutching his gun. To people living Inside, seeing the station wall crumble had to be as unimaginable as seeing an object on the floor float into the air.

He was almost there; just one more push. Hiroto pointed the canceler at the transparent part of the door. When he kicked it, the circle where he'd shone the device broke out and fell into the hallway beyond.

Next, he pointed the canceler toward the man, who shrieked and got to his feet, pointed his gun at Hiroto, and fired. *Bam, pam*, two loud shots. The screws he'd used as bullets dug into the window between them, putting large cracks in the surface. Even fortified by the structural genetic field, the thin, transparent material could not hold up against the powerful pump gun.

"Aaahahhh!" wailed Hiroto's captor, falling to the floor. "H-help! He *is* a Sabo! Someone come quick!"

Footsteps sounded from farther down the hallway. They didn't belong to human beings, however, but a pair of automated turnstiles. They surrounded the man with the gun.

"ʏou have destroyed station property. ʏour suika account is rendered null and void. ʏou will now be escorted out of ʏokohama station," came a woman's voice. The turnstiles grabbed the person in the suit. One of them picked him up and zoomed away. Around the corner, Hiroto could hear the man screaming and someone else shouting something repeatedly, probably the unfortunate's name.

The other turnstile glanced at Hiroto, then at his bag. "1B ticket detected. Thank you for visiting ʏokohama station," it stated, then sat down on the spot and entered a resting state. The gun had been left on the ground.

With that, all was silent.

This seems pretty bad, Hiroto decided.

He'd tricked someone from Inside into getting exiled. Or did this count as the other man's mistake? In any case, Hiroto had intended to escape through intimidation.

There was no time to dwell on it, though. He shone the genetic field canceler at the door, kicked the glass through, and exited. The automated turnstile remained inactive and did not react as Hiroto walked past it.

Hiroto briefly considered picking up the rifle but decided to let it be.

Even here, where the corridors stretched over the valley like a gigantic spiderweb, Keiha's device continued to update its map with accurate information. Despite the early morning hour, many of the villagers were up and about.

It was a small settlement, so the outsider stuck out. Hiroto avoided the center of the town and took a roundabout path to the other side of the valley to continue in the direction of Exit 42.

Following the route laid out on the chart of the surrounding area, Hiroto stopped to peer around a corner and saw only a single automated turnstile. Once he was past that, he'd be out of the village and on the slope leading toward Exit 42. There was no one around. Hiroto started walking.

"Who's there?" called a child's voice coming from the automated turnstile. It wasn't the turnstile that'd spoken, however. There was a boy, about ten years old, sitting behind it.

"Who are you? A bad guy?" asked the kid. He was wearing what looked like an adult-sized T-shirt cut down to fit him. It was extremely baggy.

"No. I'm not a bad guy. I'm just a traveler passing through."

At the foot of the automated turnstile was a cup full of water and a small piece of thick, light blue paper. Hiroto crouched to take a closer look and saw it bore location names and numbers written in dense, small writing. It seemed to be some kind of charm.

"What are you doing?" Hiroto inquired.

"What do you mean? I'm praying."

"Praying?"

"A bad guy took my mom away, so I'm praying to the holy turnstile to beat up the bad guy and give my mom back," the boy explained. His face looked familiar. It slightly resembled the man in the suit who'd been hauled off by the turnstiles earlier.

"Are you a station staffer?" the child questioned.

"Staffer?"

"The mayor said that he asked the staffers in Matsumoto to get rid of all the bad guys."

Like Kofu, Matsumoto was a basin city that Yokohama Station had turned into a many-layered metropolis. Going by the map on Keiha's device, it was huge and probably had a robust staffing organization. It was far away, however.

"There aren't any staffers here?"

"There used to be. But then the bad guys came, and now they're gone. But if I listen to what the grown-ups say and be a good boy, Daddy says the holy turnstile will kick all the bad guys out of Yokohama Station."

Hiroto looked up at the turnstile's face. Its body was quite faded, and its joints were losing paint. It was quite old; he couldn't tell if it would even move. There wasn't a speck of dust on the body, but that was clearly because the villagers were tending to it, not because it was operational.

These people had been living Inside for ages. Why did they believe in the righteousness of the automated turnstiles so fervently? One of their own had just been tossed out of the station by the things.

It was just a machine. A robot that mechanically followed its own rules. Whatever it did, it wasn't going to answer their prayers.

Hiroto thought he should say as much out loud, but after looking at the boy and the turnstile some more, he said, "Hey...these bandits. Where's the bad guys' hideout? Is it close?"

"Are you gonna beat the bad guys?" the child asked.

"Yeah. I'll get rid of 'em."

The raiders had initially lived in the Matsumoto area. They attacked travelers trying to cross through the station pass, but as the staffer faction in Matsumoto grew stronger, they'd been chased out to this more remote valley.

They had one hideout Inside and one outside. The group moved between the two as needed. From what Hiroto learned, they were currently outside.

The Inside spot was located in a long passageway that crossed the mountains from east to west for several kilometers without supports. Only the structural genetic field made this possible.

Hiroto took out his genetic field canceler. He'd gotten quite used to breaking down concrete with it, but this task would require much more precision than anything he'd done prior.

First, he shone the canceler at the passageway floor—the full width of it, and one meter long.

"What are you doing?" asked the boy, who was watching from the end of the corridor.

"This is dangerous, so keep your distance. Stay right there."

After a bit more application, the ground grew brittle and ceased to function as a support. It was only the walls and ceiling propping up the hallway, a fact that could be detected in the way the passage wobbled as you walked through it. Hiroto had chosen to erase a meter's worth in anticipation of the speed of the genetic field's recovery over the next few days. It was just a guess, though. He had no idea if it was enough.

After using the canceler so much, he'd run down its battery to below thirty percent.

"That should be good. Now tell the people of the village to stay away from here for a while. Don't come in, no matter what. Got that?"

"What will happen?"

"If it works, the next time they come to this hideout, the ground won't be able to support their weight, and it'll break."

"The hallway? Break?"

The boy clearly didn't understand what that meant. Hiroto didn't have a clear vision in his head of how this would work, either. He just knew that Nepshamai had told him about how Yokohama Station tried to send corridors over the Tsugaru Strait that eventually collapsed from their own weight.

"The point is, it'll snap. Then, the passage will fall down to the bottom of the valley. Yokohama Station might be tough, but from that height, it's bound to at least break some windows. It'll be the bandits' fault that they damaged the station, and the turnstiles will pounce on them and beat them up…or maybe the punishment is different if it's considered an accident. I don't know if it'll actually destroy anything, either. The point is, it's a gamble. Even if we don't win, though, we won't lose anything from it."

The child was clearly at a complete loss.

"Anyway, to reiterate, don't come near this hideout until the bad guys try to come back. Warn the other villagers as well. Can you do that?"

"Yeah. I can."

"See, if you're a good boy, the holy turnstiles will beat up the bad guys. I've got to get going now. Hang in there, kid," Hiroto said, and he left the child behind.

As he walked, his mind found a host of things to worry about. What if he hadn't shone the canceler enough? What if he'd done it too much, and the passage crumbled on its own? What if the chunk that collapsed landed on the part of Yokohama Station in the valley where people lived and they got hurt? Unfortunately, his concerns would change nothing at this point.

The last hill to climb before Exit 42 was narrow and cramped—quite unlike the mountain ranges that Hiroto had crossed already. There was virtually no choice of routes.

The peak, once known as Mt. Ontake, like Mt. Fuji, was covered with layers of escalators and roofing, pushing the apex higher than the mountain's natural tip. Hiroto's destination was near the peak, beneath the many stacked layers of Yokohama Station, buried out of human sight over the many years.

He'd slept a fair amount in the settlement and hoped to have enough stamina to finish his journey but found himself running short of breath. It was an unpleasant feeling the likes of which he'd never experienced before. His muscles weren't tired; he just couldn't get enough oxygen into his lungs, no matter how hard he worked them.

It was as if something inside was punishing him for what he'd just done. Hiroto had to stop walking, sat down on the escalator, and waited for it to carry him upward.

If the hallway collapsed as planned, all of those bandits were likely to die in the fall. He'd consigned a group of people he'd never met or seen before to death.

The structural genetic field canceler in his hand wasn't a lethal weapon by itself, but it had far more frightening powers. He'd used it to exile someone from the station and create a trap meant to plunge an unsuspecting group to their deaths in the valley below. Hiroto hadn't even been punished or pursued by the turnstiles for it. Here he was, still free to move about Inside.

Of course, the automated turnstiles were just machines following their fixed routines. However, it seemed to Hiroto like they were malicious agents that existed to discipline and torment him and others.

It was the first time he'd ever felt that way. When he'd lived in Ninety-Nine Steps, the automated turnstiles were just part of the background. They blocked him out and kept his world small, but they were only a part of the life Hiroto had been dealt, another piece of the station's outer wall.

The map on Keiha's device showed that the red dot marked Exit 42 was slowly growing closer. Like a machine resting on a factory assembly line, Hiroto trundled automatically toward his goal.

◆

It was much too strange to be called an exit.

A concrete wall continued to the vanishing point, with yellow braille blocks arranged in front of it. There wasn't a single poster on the wall, but it had been exposed to the light for so long that the surface was discolored. Hiroto couldn't see the entirety of it from where he stood, but according to the map on the device Keiha gave him, this wall surrounded a roughly three-kilometer circle of space. Inside of it was Exit 42. It was as if Yokohama Station itself had sealed off the area around it, hiding something unpleasant.

The PA voice warned, "ꜰᴏʀ ʏᴏᴜʀ ᴏᴡn ꜱaꜰeᴛy, pleaꜱe ꜱᴛay inꜱide ᴛhe yellᴏᴡ line." However, with things as they were, it was impossible to know which side was "inside" the line. In geometric terms, the space beyond the wall was the inside part of the line. On the other hand, he was already Inside on this side of the line.

Hiroto circled the wall, approaching the spot marked Exɪᴛ 42 on the map. Then, he shone the genetic field canceler at the wall to make a small hole. The remaining battery readout was down to sixteen percent. He probably had one good use left.

On the other side of the wall was an illuminated yellow sign with a bordered 42, the word Exɪᴛ, and an arrow pointing right.

Below that was the phrase, To JR Iɴᴛᴇɢʀᴀᴛᴇᴅ Iɴᴛᴇʟʟɪɢᴇɴᴄᴇ Dᴇᴠᴇʟᴏᴘᴍᴇɴᴛ Lᴀʙ.

"A lab…? Up on top of a mountain?" Hiroto muttered. He went through the hole, and the floor soon went from concrete to exposed earth. So it seemed there was a hollow outdoor space about a kilometer in radius covered up under Yokohama Station like a giant bubble. The ceiling was about ten meters tall overhead and had no lights. It was very dark, with the only illumination coming from the space between the walls and the ceiling. As Hiroto's eyes adjusted, he could see natural rocks everywhere on the ground around him.

The backlight of the 18 Ticket was his source of luminescence as he carefully made his way forward. Just as he was getting used to the low light, he arrived at a room.

It was less of a building and more a single enclosure placed directly on top of the ground. The door had been designed for use inside a structure, and there were corkboards and whiteboards on the wall. The place hadn't been meant to be exposed to the elements.

Overall, it gave the impression of a room that had been lifted from somewhere else and dumped into the mountains, then covered with walls and a ceiling to hide it. It reminded Hiroto of how the superconductive railway had been concealed. Nepshamai said the structural genetic field disliked superconductive material, and that was why it put up walls to wrap the tunnels.

Third Development Division, Ichinomiya Lab was written on a metal plate next to the door. Beneath it hung a plastic board with the word *Absent*.

Hiroto carefully opened the door to Ichinomiya Lab.

The lights were on inside. As he squinted against the sudden brightness, the first thing he noticed was a giant server rack. A number of thin computers were inserted into it, with wires running out of them in a spaghetti tangle.

With a sonorous *booong*, the server machines booted. Red and green lights flickered rapidly, and exhaust fans spun up. Opening the door must have activated a sensor and restored power to the room.

The scene reminded Hiroto of Keiha's place in Kofu, though there were some differences. Upon a closer examination, the computers were covered in choking dust, and a mysterious, slimy substance spread across the floor. The machines must have lain dormant for quite a long time.

In the center of the room stood a large pillar about a meter across with four display monitors affixed to it in vertical portrait mode.

On the back wall was a steel set of shelves. Inside a glass compartment resting on one of the rungs was a set of book spines written in old-fashioned letters with titles like:

Distributed Intelligence Society, April '84 Bulletin
Theory and Practice of Network Intelligence
Developments in Modern Information Science
JR Timetable, March '84
The Collected Dostoyevsky
Machiavelli's The Prince, A New Translation

A screen displayed a spinning start-up logo, which eventually changed to read, "synchronizing data." Sometime later, there was a voice.

"Is someone there?"

It was coming from the room's speakers. A man wearing a suit seated at a desk appeared on the four monitors installed on the central pillar. He looked just like a newscaster in a studio. Surprisingly, Hiroto recognized him.

"…Professor?"

"Oh, you know me?" the man asked.

"No. You look like him, but you're much younger than the professor I know. And your voice is different."

"Ah. Well, this appearance is based on when he was duplicated. The voice you hear is being automatically translated to contemporary pronunciation according to what was just downloaded. It might seem unnatural, but I have not been awake in a while. You'll have to be patient for all the updates to permeate my system."

The man on the screens yawned. "I have been asleep here for quite a while. For some reason, my power supply was cut off, so I had to shut down to avoid wasting my battery store. What year is it by the Gregorian calendar?"

"Gregoria-what?"

"Hmm. It would seem it's been quite a long time, then. Ah, well. I must say, you seem to be rather exhausted. Aren't you thirsty? There should be a stock of food and water in the adjacent room. You may help yourself," the man stated. There were no other rooms.

"Hey, who are you? Where are you talking to me from? I came here because the professor said I would find all the answers here. What are you, a relative of his or something?"

"Not so fast with the questions. My parallel processing ability is limited," the man replied. A cup of tea appeared on the screen, and he took a sip. "Allow me to answer in order. As for the question of where I am, I'm speaking to you from here. From the server rack behind you."

He pointed over Hiroto's back. The fans of the stacked computers whirred and buzzed. The exhaust had a peculiar smell that suggested old age.

"You're an artificial intelligence?"

"In a broad sense, yes. But the question of what 'artificial' means is rather tricky. You were born of human parents, for example. Does that make you artificial or natural? You're undoubtedly man-made. Your mind was cultivated by speaking with others and learning from them. Does that make your intelligence artificial?"

These odd questions reminded Hiroto of the professor. The

difference was that the words were much more straightforward than those of the man he knew.

"I've gotten off-topic—next, the question of my identity. I am the entity in charge of maintaining the JR Integrated Intelligence. Or I should say, I was. The professor you speak of is most likely my origin. He was the lead developer on the JR Integrated Intelligence."

"Lead developer...? Wait a minute. I thought the integrated intelligence was created hundreds of years ago, right?" said Hiroto, recalling what Keiha told him.

"Hundreds? Oh dear, it's been a very long time, then. What has our lab been doing? At any rate, it might have taken time, but it seems it's been a success. Just a moment, please. I'd like to pull up the present conditions of... Hmm? Something's wrong."

The man on the screen swiveled his head around, searching for something.

"I should see Tokyo Bay just to the east of here...but I'm missing locational data. Have the GPS satellites stopped working? Atmospheric pressure is too low. Are we at a high altitude? Where are we?"

A small map promptly appeared in the lower right corner of the screen. It was a map of Japan. All of Honshu and the northeast edge of Shikoku were covered in black. A red blip indicated the lab's current position.

"What is this? All of Honshu is now Yokohama Station?" the AI professor queried, eyes wide. "I'd heard it was theoretically possible... and now it's true? Ha...ha-ha-ha. It's like a bad joke."

He covered his eyes with a hand and grimaced with mirth. Hiroto didn't understand what made it funny.

"Regardless of how far the station has expanded, the outcome will be the same. Listen, I'm sure you have many questions for me, but I need to sum up the situation for *you* first. We're going to erase Yokohama Station off the face of the earth. And I need your help to do it."

On the 117th floor of Kofu, in the back room of a place called the Trinket Shop, was a computer with possibly the highest processing capability in the entire city. Keiha had scrounged together all the resources she could find into this cluster.

The machine's electrical consumption far exceeded the cost any person could pay, but Keiha had fiddled with the power utility's meter to eliminate the excess. The station's power utility basically existed only to ensure that energy moved along from the matter furnaces in the depths of Yokohama Station, and there was no professional pride among the people who worked there. They would never discover what Keiha had done.

Her monster of a computer was running a circuit simulator that had been passed around on Suikanet for ages. She would physically scan a machine to input its circuit structure as information, then feed virtual power through the virtual circuit data. It would run a ghost of the circuit and display the output on the monitor.

> **Booting Kitaka OS 4.2**...
> **Loading complete.**
> **Multiple hardware not recognized. Serious error may have occurred to body.**

After several messages passed, a command prompt appeared on the screen. Keiha leaned over to her mic and spoke into it.

"Hello. I'm Keiha Nijo. Can you understand what's happening?"

When she turned off the mic, the system sent the voice data into the circuits, the computer's cooling system ran faster, and white exhaust poured out of the machine. After three minutes of silence, letters appeared on the monitor.

> **I understand your speech. I do not recognize myself.**

"Your name is Nepshamai. You're an agent sent from JR North Japan."

More time passed with no answer. It was concerning that the cooling system's nitrogen was filling the room, since the stuff was only vented from the chamber in small bursts. Managing exhaust vapors in the middle of the stratified Yokohama Station without drawing attention was one of the trickier aspects of Keiha's work.

One time, Keiha had even blacked out from a lack of oxygen. She'd only survived because one of the local electronics handlers had spotted her. Living on a higher floor would have afforded her better conditions, but being among the wealthier citizens would draw attention from the station staffers. Keiha's ICoCar System fooled the automated turnstiles, so it was the staffers who frightened her the most.

> **I understand JR North Japan. I do not recognize my individual. Concern for major error in main memory device.**

"Is there anything you do remember? Do you recall the token you used to connect to the communication port with JR North Japan in Hokkaido?"

A few moments went by with no response. Keiha refreshed her tea while waiting for the machine to reply.

> **Token existed in main memory device. Cannot be recalled due to major error in repair. Confirming problem cause currently.**

Keiha's shoulders slumped. She'd hoped to extract enough of his data to make contact with JR North Japan, but it wasn't going to work out.

"I'm sorry. I couldn't understand the formatting of your main memory, so I scanned the entire physical structure. It's all simulated, so it's taking at least ten times as long to run. I'm just amazed we can have a conversation at all. Your system must be very robust. Do you have any information on the format of your main memory device?"

Keiha had to wait nearly twenty minutes for the answer. Maybe talking to it too much at once confused its circuits.

> **I have format no information from the start. It is possessed by the engineering division for classified.**

"Is there a way for you to contact the engineering division? I want to get in touch with your organization. I think it will help both of us."

> **In my knowledge you fragments exist. The engineering division however requires secret clear reason.**

Keiha realized that her scan of Nepshamai's language center was probably inadequate, but it would take too long to ask again. What's more, if she taxed it to the point that it shut down, it would be hours before she could get it running again. She needed to ask everything she could now, while she had the chance.

"If possible, I'd like for you to tell me as much as you know."

> **As much as I know not recognized. Suggesting a specified request.**

"Okay, how about this. Who is Yukie, your creator?"

> **Yukie is the developer of the Corpocker series which is us.**

"I know that. What I'm asking is how she was able to gain such advanced tech. My guess is that she extracted data from a surviving JR Integrated Intelligence unit in Hokkaido while looking for information to use against Yokohama Station. Then, she deciphered the system language. It's the only way I can think of that someone could create AI as advanced as you, not to mention the genetic field canceler. Am I right?"

> **In regard to Yukie, by the company I can say it is forbidden.**

"So that subject is classified. Have you ever met Yukie directly before?"

> **Directly meaning is undefined. Memory exists within main memory device of data existing within supplemental memory device. Supplemental memory device not recognized.**

"All right. Next question: Do you remember the person you were traveling with for the last few days? It was a guy called Hiroto Mishima."

> **There is no information regarding name. The person is 18 Ticket.**

"Yes, that's him."

Keiha brought up a map on another screen. It displayed the location of the machine she'd given Hiroto as a blue dot. He'd crossed the Kiso Valley and was approaching the red blip that marked Exit 42.

"He's heading here now," Keiha said, pointing at the spot. "Do you know anything about this place?"

> **In regard to Exit 42, by the company I can say it is forbidden.**

"...What does that mean? Did JR North Japan forbid you android agents from talking about the place?"

Keiha took a deep breath, then made an effort to speak slower.

"I want to work with your organization. If my guess is correct, something deadly to Yokohama Station is dormant there. My goal is to get it, and it should be yours, too. Sharing information will be of mutual benefit."

She waited for minutes and minutes, but there was no response. Either it didn't understand what she was saying or was keeping mum. Keiha didn't understand enough about how this intelligence worked to tell the difference.

Keiha's laptop beeped. There was an alert on the screen.

"Looks like he's made it there," Keiha muttered. The location of Hiroto's device overlapped with Exit 42 on the map. It had the ability to transmit both locational and voice data.

Keiha could hear someone at Exit 42 talking. It was not Hiroto's voice; it sounded more like a man in the prime of his life. Unfortunately, because Hiroto was so far removed from any of Keiha's captured Suikanet nodes, she did not have immediate communication with him. Given the physical distance, there would be about an hour's delay in reaching him.

◆

"This all began with a mistake by JR Integrated Intelligence," admitted the man on the screen, who called himself the maintenance entity of JR Integrated Intelligence. He talked about the long, long Winter War, the birth of the integrated intelligence based on the railway network, and how, despite the human government in charge, it was the integrated intelligence that did the ultimate decision-making for the country.

Still, Japan had continued to collapse. The JR Integrated Intelligence was far more intelligent than any human being, but it was still just a brain. It had no powerful means of defense. Satellite weapons steadily destroyed the train stations that were its individual units.

The various JR companies, like advisors to a king, attempted to defend and repair. However, there were too many spread out all across the country to maintain, and the war showed no signs of letting up.

This state of affairs lasted for decades. At some point, the integrated intelligence came to a decision. It concluded that human reconstruction could not maintain it, and the AI resolved to implement an autonomous rehabilitation system in its units.

"This gave birth to the intelligence network's self-repair system, using memory and replication of physical structure, and a quantum field to propagate it. Nowadays, they call it the structural genetic field."

Yokohama Station was chosen as the test case for this new function. The place had been in a constant state of development ever since it'd first been built. The simple initial structural genetic field would take in the memory of the many years of renovation and renew it as an autonomous entity capable of rebuilding itself. The genetic field would then be transferred to other units, rendering the integrated intelligence immortal as a whole. That was the plan.

"I suppose it's the nature of a ruler to seek immortality eventually. In the distant past, the first emperor to unify all of vast China sought an elixir of immortality and ingested mercury, which ironically shortened his life. Even a creation as smart as the JR Integrated Intelligence was not immune from this fixation on life."

But that was a mistake. Immortal life to a biological creature—cells that repeatedly replicate without growing old and dying—is nothing more than cancer. Once injected with the seed of the structural genetic field, Yokohama Station exhibited the memory of its many additions to its fullest extent. It did not stop at repairing damaged sections. It grew along the neighboring train lines until it had covered all of Japan's railways, and eventually, the land itself. Like a malignant growth devouring its biological host, Yokohama Station ate up the country it called home.

Yokohama Station swallowed up the other stations that were fellow units of the intelligence. At the point that the growing network's complexity made it impossible to maintain conscious thought, the integrated intelligence simply stopped acting rationally.

Yokohama Station continued to expand, covering the entire island of Honshu, until the present day.

"The integrated intelligence's immortality project had plenty of dissent within the lab itself. It was wartime, though, and the AI always held the deciding vote. By that point, the Japanese government was nothing more than a spokesperson for the computerized mind. So our lab prepared a countermeasure, in case it went out of control...but I couldn't have guessed that it would come around so very late."

"Countermeasure?" inquired Hiroto.

"Yes. The integrated intelligence was planning to remove the genetic field from the station interior once its test using Yokohama Station was complete. This lab still contains the means to do that. Look on the other side of this support."

Hiroto walked around to the back side of the pillar and saw a yellow box about the size of his 18 Ticket. There was a red button in the middle, with a sticker that said EMERGENCY STOP.

"That's an antiphase genetic field oscillator. If activated while in contact with Yokohama Station, it will fluctuate and deploy a genetic field with the reverse structural genetic field phase. Ultimately, the antiphase genetic field will permeate every corner of Yokohama Station, and all of the structural genetic field will be eliminated. In other words, Yokohama Station will die."

Hiroto understood this as a gigantic version of the structural genetic field canceler.

"No one expected the place to get this large, so it's hard to guess exactly how much time purging it will take. If we extrapolate from the data performed on a lab-sized scale, the station should be entirely gone in the span of a few years to a few decades."

"If you've got that, why didn't you use it before now?" Hiroto asked.

"That is exactly the reason I want your help. You see, the developer of the JR Integrated Intelligence implemented a major taboo in the system."

"Taboo?"

"A taboo against self-destruction. It was made so that no unit within it could actively destroy another one. Yokohama Station may have consumed everything, but this still holds true."

The maintenance entity was a partition of the integrated intelligence, so it was essentially a sibling of Yokohama Station, which was one of the intelligence's units. Because their parent forbade the brothers to fight, the maintenance entity could not activate the system that would destroy the cancerous growth.

"So you were waiting for a human being to come along and press the button for you?"

"That's not all. No one with a Suika can press the switch, either. The Suika is an organ that identifies humans as part of Yokohama Station's structure, allowing them to escape its immune system that purges everything foreign. There's a force that cracks down on humans without a Suika trying to sneak Inside, isn't there? And if someone with a Suika tries to destroy part of Yokohama Station or commits violence against another person, the immune system removes them, too."

Hiroto recognized that the younger professor was talking about the automated turnstiles.

"This device was originally installed outside of Yokohama Station, but it seems the entire lab was swallowed up before it could be deployed. No wonder it took so long for a response. That's why I had to wait for someone like you to come along—someone without a Suika who could reach this place and activate the antiphase genetic field oscillator."

"You needed me to come here?"

"That's right. I don't know how it happened, but because you used a temporary pass and were able to reach this far inland, it's solved our paradox. A human being without a Suika can press the button. You've saved the nation. I am deeply indebted to you. I shall report directly to the prime minister."

Hiroto didn't know what a nation or a prime minister was. He keenly felt that he'd been given some very crucial role to play, though.

"The station will disappear?" Hiroto inquired. "I never considered that outcome."

He'd never seen its existence as something that blocked his possibilities or limited his life. No matter where you were in Ninety-Nine Steps, the ocean was on one side and Yokohama Station was on the other. That was where they lived and how they supported themselves.

Those two things were Hiroto's givens, his environment, facts that had been set in stone since he was born.

One push of this button could undo all of that.

"Do you really want me to decide that?" Hiroto asked.

"I do. If you do not press that switch, it will never activate. Or, to be more explicit, the device will not initiate if pressed by the volition of anything related to the integrated intelligence, myself included. You must move your body of your own will and physically depress the button."

"My own will," repeated Hiroto. He realized then that the corners of his mouth were raised. Either his facial muscles were fatigued, or he was subconsciously grinning from the folly of it all, but he couldn't tell which.

"It's true that I've felt like the world Inside is wrong somehow. Not that I can really explain why. But I'm just a traveler. I've only been here for five days. Getting the 18 Ticket, getting the canceler, and coming this far was all just a series of coincidences."

Breathing was getting more challenging again. It was like all the air in the room was being sucked up by the crowd of computers behind him.

"Maybe you don't realize it because you're stuck here in the middle of the mountains, but there are tons and tons of people living in Yokohama Station. They've been living there for way over a century. What right do I have to steal the lives they've built for themselves? What does that make me?"

"What you are does not concern me," the maintenance entity retorted coldly. "But there is one thing I can say. You used the word 'right,' but that does not apply here. I am not asking you to decide the fate of Yokohama Station. If you do not press that button, I will have to wait for my next visitor. That might be tomorrow, or it might be a hundred years from now. Either way, the end will come eventually. That much is certain. Columbus did not have the right to determine the fate of the Native Americans. Their destiny was already decided at the point that two civilizations differed in strength."

The face on the screen was frigid. Hiroto didn't know what Columbus was, but he got the impression that it was supposed to be a significant moment in human history.

"Allow me to make an analogy: You have a pile of sand sitting on top of a table, and you are dropping the grains from above, one at a time," began the calm, relaxing voice from the monitor. The man looked like a father patiently teaching his child how to do their homework.

The maintenance entity used his hands to mimic the outline of the sand pile, and an actual heap appeared on the screen. At first, it was small, the size of a rice ball, but as the stuff sprinkled down, it got bigger and bigger.

"Initially, it is just a little mound, but in time, it will become an enormous mountain."

The pile grew until it engulfed the desk, concealing the man behind it.

"However, the process will never end. Eventually, there will be a collapse. One of those grains of sand will cause the mountain to topple."

An avalanche rolled over the right side of the little sediment mountain, spilling a great deal off the desk.

"Why does the sand mound collapse? It's simple. Because this desk cannot support an infinitely growing mountain. Eventually, something will give way. It is not some special granule with great power and will that does it. As long as the pile cannot exist infinitely, there will inevitably be an ordinary bit of sand that causes it to collapse. It is that simple. You do not need to be a special person. You don't need to be the hero who saves the world or the demon that destroys the station. I just want your help as a single grain coming down onto the pile," the man stated.

"I don't really understand what you're saying," Hiroto admitted. "But I've lived my whole life on a tiny cape called Ninety-Nine Steps. It's like a little blank margin between worlds. I just want to know what everything beyond is like so I can bring about a little change to the world *I* know and move it forward just a small amount. That's what brought me here."

After a brief silence, Hiroto's hand moved over the button, as smoothly as water flowing downhill, and pressed it.

Bzzz, bzzz.

Bzzzzzz.

A sound like thrumming insects' wings filled the entire room, to the point that it even shook a little. The bug noise slowly began fusing with Hiroto's breathing and heartbeat. He sat down at the foot of the table beneath the button.

6. Turnstile Organ

Even in Kofu, Keiha observed the brief warping of communication through Suikanet. She picked it up as a kind of static, rippling outward in circular fashion, like the surface of a pond after a rock is thrown into it.

Keiha kept the Suikanet nodes she had control over in communication with each other, giving her a constant window into the network's state as a whole. The number of securable points was less than one percent of what they'd had at the Dodger Alliance's apex, forming a narrow line from Kyoto to Kofu. That also happened to be the year-long trail she'd followed while on the run.

It was difficult to capture more nodes. Keiha didn't have a functioning Suika, and all the computational resources she could use went toward the ICoCar System that protected her. Her trusted companions were gone. The best she could do now was to collect information on this narrow line, interfere a little with the automated turnstiles, and observe the state of the network.

So she could tell that for a few seconds, a slight wave of noise had spread across Suikanet like that ripple from a stone in a still pond. Once the surge had crossed through the station's entirety, everything seemed to go back to normal.

Exit 42 had been the center of that fluctuation.

"He activated it," Keiha said into a mic. It was connected to her massive supercomputer cluster where the virtual replica of Nepshamai's main memory device slumbered.

"I don't know why your company was keeping this place a secret, but he made it there. I win this round."

There was no response. Keiha realized that the energy readings of the physical simulator were much higher than they'd been initially. Either it was a lack of precision in the scan, or the structure itself was unstable.

The device Keiha had given Hiroto possessed the ability to transmit locational data. He'd made it to Exit 42, and within an hour, the ripple had happened. Several hours had passed since then, but Hiroto had yet to move from that spot.

"Well done. When Yokohama Station, the final unit of the integrated intelligence, is eliminated at last, I will be automatically deleted as its maintenance entity. It has been a very long job, indeed," said the display overhead. "I am rather surprised, however. To think that so many people have been implanted with Suikas... I had figured it stood to reason that once their land was stolen, they would fight to steal it back."

"...What does that mean?" Hiroto asked, sitting on the ground. The man did not respond. Hiroto looked up and saw that the monitor had gone dark. The fans on the server farm were still. A few moments later, the lights went out, too.

Everything was dark and quiet.

It wasn't cold, however. The temperature remained the same as everywhere else Inside. Curiously, Hiroto couldn't stop trembling, though. It was like his body was expelling all of its heat in an attempt to burn out and be as motionless as everything else.

The entity had said that the antiphase genetic field would take years, possibly decades. At the very least, it wasn't likely that the building would start to crumble around Hiroto, trapping him.

Even so, Hiroto couldn't move. He felt as if taking action now would cause him to think about things he shouldn't.

A high-pitched beeping sounded. Hiroto had never heard it before.

Some machine in the room is working again, he thought. It wasn't the servers behind him. After a while, he realized the noise was coming from inside his bag. It was Keiha's device. On the display were the words, *Incoming Voice Call.*

"This is just a short-term route, so I can't talk for long. Get out of there now," instructed a distorted voice.

"Keiha?"

"Yes. You've been there for eight hours now. Why aren't you leaving? Did something capture you?"

"Eight hours?"

Hiroto looked at the clock readout on the device. It was ten at night. Talking to the AI and pressing the button couldn't have taken more than thirty minutes, though.

Hiroto took a slow, deep breath, and answered, "The entire station will collapse, according to the facility they have here. I pressed the button."

"I know. Your voice data was transmitted back to me."

"Hey, did you know about all of this? About what was here and..."

There was silence.

"Not everything," Keiha admitted. "But I had a hunch that place housed something significant—perhaps fatal—to Yokohama Station."

"Why didn't you say so?"

"I didn't think you'd do it if I explained it all to you in Kofu. At that point, I don't think you could've brought the station to ruin. My gamble was that you'd come around to the idea after three more days Inside."

It got quiet again.

"You're messed up."

"I told you, I'm more selfish than anyone else. Everything I do is in service of my own goals."

"Well, what I've learned after the last five days is that I'm not a person who can achieve his goals through great willpower like you. I just do what I'm asked, and now I can't even move—"

"Stop whining, get up, and get out of there!" Keiha shouted. It startled Hiroto so much that he nearly dropped the gadget. "Let me tell you, at this moment, you're the only companion I have, so I need you to leave. That was part of my plan, and you're still my responsibility."

A lull washed over the room.

Hiroto got to his feet, picked up the bag, and began to walk.

He slipped through Exit 42 and back Inside. There was nothing different about the station from before, just an endless, flat concrete wall. Interestingly, the gray of that barricade no longer seemed the same symbol of permanence that had loomed over the people of Ninety-Nine Steps his entire life.

Having been burdened with the impossibly heavy choice of destroying the station, Hiroto was now visited by an unstoppable deluge of frustrated misery.

I came so far from home and only got spun around and manipulated by other people. I'm not in charge of my own life. My one notable feature was not having a Suika. I got these jobs because people gave me an 18 Ticket and a structural genetic field canceler. Without them, I'm nothing at all.

"You don't need to be the hero or the demon. I just want your help as a single grain of sand," the maintenance entity had said. The words echoed through Hiroto's mind. Now they seemed very insulting to him. Yes, he was just a single speck on a pile, with no special abilities. That was why he'd left Ninety-Nine Steps. He'd hoped to become something.

"Can you still hear me? Like I said before, if you make your way south, you'll reach an area where I've got control of Suikanet nodes. Head there for now. I'll get the automated turnstiles as far out of the way as I can," Keiha instructed through the device. "This short-term route is closing, so I'll end this call now. I'll contact you again when you're closer to your destination."

◆

It was a very garbled connection, but even from Kofu, Keiha was able to make out the sound of Hiroto getting up to move.

She exhaled with relief. The 18 Ticket would expire at nine o'clock tomorrow, so he still had eleven hours—plenty of time to escape.

Since the fall of the Dodger Alliance, Keiha had spent four years continually losing. This was the first time she felt like she'd won something in ages.

She faced the mic and said, "If you forbade any comments about that place, that would suggest that you didn't want the end of this station to happen yet. I thought we might work together toward a common goal. Too bad."

The mic sent the words into the virtual copy of Nepshamai's main memory device. It had stopped answering her yesterday, likely because of a poor-quality scan.

Keiha had expected as much, however. In fact, it seemed like a miracle that she could have a meaningful conversation with the thing at all. She concluded that the original contents of the device must have really liked talking.

"But I've won this time. We activated the device. Its own preservation systems will undo the integrated intelligence's mistake."

The computer cluster squealed and spun. Keiha had not been speaking into the mic to get an answer but because she wanted someone to hear what she had to say.

> **Yukie is different.**

"…?"

> **Yukie is, JR Integrated Intelligence created structural genetic field. Based on purpose, entirely plan. In this way she thinks.**

"What are you trying to say? That the JR Integrated Intelligence intentionally created the expansion of Yokohama Station so the world would be this way?"

> **Yes. Integrated intelligence is ruler, and needed, during chaos of war, Yokohama Station, rule by automated turnstiles. Yukie thinks.**

Keiha's pulse quickened. It had been years since she felt righteous anger toward something. The last time had been when her companions were captured by the automated turnstiles while fleeing to Kofu.

"Your master might be brilliant." Keiha scowled. "But I will never accept that answer."

As Keiha had said, there were no automated turnstiles on the southern slope leaving Exit 42. It was a fairly open area by Inside standards, and it was rare for there to be no turnstiles around at all. There were almost no people, either—perhaps because it was the middle of the night. The only others Hiroto saw were a pair of men in station employee uniforms coming up the slope, much farther down.

Escalators grew in Yokohama Station along any incline of a certain size. However, the escalator itself could only have one angle. Thus, when the ground's angle was milder, the automated stairwell had to be broken up with frequent landings to fine-tune the slope. Hiroto was making his way down one such set of escalators. At intermittent points, there were flat spaces a few meters long before the moving steps resumed. It allowed Hiroto to switch escalator lanes whenever he wanted.

Each time the rising staffers reached a platform, they altered their lane to intercept Hiroto. They were coming after him. When he got a closer look at them, he noticed how shockingly similar they appeared. Their heights and faces were the same. The two seemed to be androgynous, and it was difficult to discern their ages.

The majority of staffers Hiroto had seen wore dark blue uniforms with hats. Much like the automated turnstiles, there were subtle differences depending on the region. The defining feature here was a red hanging cloth near the waist, like a handkerchief.

At the bottom of Hiroto's escalator was a circular landing. A large pillar in the middle blocked his view, but it looked like the stairs fanned out in an array behind it. He could see the two staffers beyond. They were pointing at him and talking about something. They'd probably ask him why he was out alone in the mountains late at night like this. Upon closer examination, he saw that one of them was not pointing with a finger but a metal object in his hand.

No sooner had Hiroto identified this detail than a high-pitched, silly sounding *pomp!* echoed across the lanes of escalators.

Hiroto immediately felt the strength go out of his right leg. He lost his balance, tumbled down a few steps, and landed loudly on his backside. He didn't know what had just happened. There was a powerful sensation of heat emanating from his right knee on down. One of his pant legs was dyed a deep shade of red. That was when he realized he'd been shot, and stabbing pain commenced.

"Aaah…"

As Hiroto swooned in sudden agony, the escalator brought him to the bottom and rolled him onto the landing. The staffers approached and stood over Hiroto. Even up close, it was almost impossible to tell them apart. Their uniforms were identical, too. The only difference was that one had a pistol.

"Don't move, please. If you try to run, it won't be your leg I shoot next," threatened the one with the weapon. It was probably a type of electric pump gun, although less powerful than the rifle that had shot Nepshamai in Kamakura. The two ignored Hiroto's gasps and moans as the blood poured out of his leg.

"Well, I've fulfilled my job. That's it for me. You take care of the rest," stated the shooter, handing the pistol to the other man.

"You didn't need to shoot him yourself, did you? We could have used one of the people we captured," replied the other person. The voice was identical.

"That would be irresponsible. As protectors of the station's stability, we must be responsible for our actions."

"That's a wonderful mindset. However, are you sure this was the right man?"

"Yes. We confirmed it moments ago. There was an impromptu vibration through Suikanet, then this man appeared. He has no Suika. That's certainly enough evidence."

"Sounds logical."

The staffer who handed over the gun looked around. "Hmm, I don't see any turnstiles coming. I wonder what that means."

"That the disaster has already reached this far?"

"That would be very bad."

"We need to confirm."

The man pointed the gun at the pillar in the middle of the landing and fired it. *Pomp.* The bullet struck the post and shattered into pieces. The shards of metal made it clear that the projectile had been one of the brass buttons from their uniforms. There wasn't a scratch on the pillar.

"Doesn't seem to be a problem. Perhaps something is delaying the automated turnstiles."

"It's possible that our long years of upholding righteous and responsible causes has earned us special privileges from Yokohama Station."

"Yes, very possible."

"In that case, you ought to carry this pistol."

"No. I have already entrusted this job to you. I cannot take it back, even if there is a delay in the station's response."

"On the other hand…"

The two continued foisting the gun off on each other. At this point, it was getting impossible for Hiroto to tell which of them had shot him.

"What the hell is wrong with you?" Hiroto shouted at the pair. They looked surprised, as though only now remembering he was there.

"Oops, we shouldn't be standing around conversing. What shall we do with him?"

"We'll take him with us. I did not shoot him as a form of punishment, you see. They might need him higher up. That's why I aimed for the leg."

"I see, I see. As time passes, the situation only gets worse. I shall take him to Exit 42," one of them stated. He then offered Hiroto a hand, still entirely devoid of expression. "Can you stand? It would help us if you could walk on your own."

Hiroto didn't know what was going on except that these two were clearly his enemy. He should have figured that out earlier, but he'd never considered the possibility that he had real enemies Inside in the first place.

He grabbed the staffer's outstretched hand, then yanked it closer. The man grunted and lost his balance, falling over and dropping the pistol in his other hand. Hiroto quickly grabbed for the gun, but it wasn't loaded. The other assailant tried to rip it out of his hands, so Hiroto hurled it as far as he could instead. The pistol curved through the air and landed several escalator lanes away, where it began to ride upward.

Hiroto quickly scooped up his bag from the floor, then practically toppled down the escalator on the opposite side of the pillar. The two uniformed people were left on the landing.

"He resisted us," remarked the standing staffer, reaching out to pull up his fallen partner.

The other welcomed his help and wondered, "Why did he resist us? We're only acting in the proper interest of all."

"I don't know. I'll retrieve the gun. You follow him," decided one of the two, heading up the escalator. The other went down.

Hiroto fled as best he could, but with his leg shot, he could barely walk. He'd only gotten past a few landings when the man caught up to him at an easy walking pace.

"I wouldn't resist if I were you. If you attack me here, you'll be taken out by the automated turnstiles, and that will not fulfill our righteous purpose."

"Hang on. Who are you people? You're not station employees?"

The man gave him a look that said he couldn't fathom the meaning of the question. "Let's go back up. Your unnecessary actions have taken us farther from Exit 42. The situation will worsen to the point of costing us time," he insisted, grabbing Hiroto's arm. Someone approached from behind the speaker. Hiroto assumed it was the other staffer—but it was a turnstile.

The automated turnstile told the man holding Hiroto's arm, "you have committed an act of violence inside the station, which is not allowed. your suika credential has been revoked. you will now be escorted out of yokohama station."

In his usual expressionless way, the curious person replied, "Yes, that is correct. I was acting on my purpose and my responsibilities, so there is no problem."

The automated turnstile bound him with metallic wire and turned to Hiroto. "A notice to you, visitor. Your 18 ticket will soon expire. After it expires, you will be removed from the station. Please be aware of this and act accordingly."

Then, the machine escorted the staffer away, walking in single file back up the escalator. Once they were out of sight, the only sounds were the movements of the steps and the repeating announcements of, "Please hold onto the moving belts," and "Leaning over the edge and running against the flow of traffic is very dangerous."

Hiroto was left trembling for a little while. He tore part of his jacket to make a bandage that he used to stop the bleeding in his leg, then resumed his descent to where Keiha had told him to go.

Only an hour remained on the 18 Ticket.

Hiroto checked his location. Once the 18 Ticket expired, automated turnstiles would appear and chuck him out of the station's nearest exit. If he happened to get caught here, that meant he'd be tossed into a spot the size of a lobby three kilometers west of here, where he'd be trapped forever. It would mean game over.

"My system keeps the automated turnstiles away as best as possible, but it's only buying you time. Hurry," Keiha urged through the device.

Keiha had a pretty solid grasp on the behavioral algorithms of the turnstiles. They acted very simply within Yokohama Station. They spread out as evenly as possible Inside, and when intruders or Suika violators appeared, all turnstiles within a certain radius rushed to that spot. While the density was tighter in cities, the general pattern was the same.

The control program for the automated turnstiles was not something designed by a specific programmer but by a routine that had evolved through the structural genetic field as Suikanet required. Therefore, it could not rise above a certain level of complexity.

Keiha's disruption system used the Suikanet nodes under her control to send falsified information to the net that multiple turnstiles were already present at certain coordinates (in this case, Hiroto's location). The real turnstiles would move away from Hiroto to avoid surpassing the maximum necessary density.

However, this was predicated upon Hiroto's not being a target for elimination already. Once the 18 Ticket expired, Keiha's meddling would only provide a slight delay before the automated turnstiles appeared. The capture of the staffer earlier was evidence of that. Naturally, because Keiha's Suika was no longer valid, she couldn't use this system to help herself.

Hiroto could barely feel the pain in his leg anymore, but he was getting a bit woozy from blood loss. There was still a ways to go until he reached Keiha's destination. He didn't think he was going to make it. Hiroto let the escalator carry him downward and dreamed with his eyes open.

It hadn't been long after the professor had arrived to Ninety-Nine Steps. His mind was still sharp, but his speech was nearly unintelligible.

"Professor, you came from somewhere far away, right? Where? Inside? Shikoku or Kyushu?" Hiroto had asked, showing him a map. The professor had pointed at a spot on the map and seemed to be indicating something. It was a little bit north of Ninety-Nine Steps.

"That's not that far from here. Is the weird way you talk what people sound like there?"

A few years later, the professor had learned how people like Hiroto spoke, but his head had gone fuzzy in the meantime. Frequently, he would say things like, "I was in a place called the Lab, and it was always cold."

At the time, Hiroto had thought that it was probably chilly because it was in the mountains. He'd seen a movie scene with men exploring a snowy peak on one of the films that circulated on Suikanet.

Thinking back on that now, though, he understood that Yokohama Station regulated the temperature, even at the tops of mountains.

A beeping brought Hiroto back to the present. He'd fallen asleep sitting on the escalator. He looked inside his bag and saw a message on the screen of the 18 Ticket: *This ticket's valid period has expired. Thank you for your patronage.* A sudden chill ran through him.

Hiroto had reached the bottom of the slope down from Exit 42. He now stood before a flat corridor. Keiha's destination was still ahead. There didn't appear to be any automated turnstiles around for the moment. Hiroto put the 18 Ticket back into his bag and fished out the communication device.

"Keiha, it's me. The time's up. I don't think I'll make it."

"Oh. The closest automated turnstiles are about a kilometer away. I can buy you about ten minutes. Just keep moving."

"Got it."

After a few minutes of walking, Hiroto made it out of the twisting, narrow hallways of the mountainous area and entered a level, wide, straight passage. The signs said, To Kiso and To Nakatsugawa. Following the information on Keiha's device, Hiroto headed for Nakatsugawa.

After a few hundred meters, two automated turnstiles appeared. They were approaching, their speakers in announcement mode.

"your 18 Ticket period has expired. you will now be removed from the station. we appreciate your cooperation."

Two more of the machines appeared from the other direction, leading toward Kiso.

"There are no plans to reissue 18 Tickets. For more details, please contact a JR Group company," they announced. Hiroto was trapped.

"Well, that narrows it down. Just keep going toward Nakatsugawa. Every step closer helps," Keiha instructed. Hiroto obeyed. He was hoping he would surprise them and just slip past, but that didn't happen. The two turnstiles ahead of him blocked his path with mechanical reaction speed.

After one hundred and twenty hours and eleven minutes since going Inside at Ninety-Nine Steps, Hiroto had finally been caught by four automated turnstiles.

"ᵞou will now be apprehended."

One of the turnstiles extended a wire and deftly spun it around Hiroto's body, then grabbed him with both arms. To his surprise, it wasn't painful at all. After the difficulty of walking, he even found it pleasant. The other three turnstiles took positions in a triangle around the one holding him.

"Hiroto, can you hear me?" asked Keiha's voice from the device clutched in his right hand. He'd already cranked the volume as high as it would go.

"Yeah, but I can't see the screen."

"Not a problem. Which way are they going?"

"Toward Nakatsugawa."

Hiroto heard a faint sigh of relief from Keiha's end. "We just made it, then. If they're going that route, then you'll be taken to a small station hollow in Nakatsugawa. Along the way, you'll pass through my safe zone. When I give the signal, you attack with all your strength. Can you do that?"

"My hands are free. I can manage."

"I'll give you a ten-second countdown before it's time."

"Got it."

The automated turnstiles continued marching, utterly oblivious to the conversation the humans were having. They couldn't actually understand speech in the first place, so they had no interest at all in what he was holding.

At that moment, Keiha was monitoring Hiroto's path and distance to the destination from her store in Kofu. The corridor ran from northeast to southwest, and the line to the destination crossed that corridor at a thirty-degree angle. She had a margin of error of maybe ten meters. There were times when Suikanet's locational readings were terribly off, but Keiha had no choice other than to trust that they were correct this time.

"Almost there. Are you ready?"

"Yeah."

"...Ten seconds to go. Nine. Eight."

Hiroto put a finger against the power switch of the structural genetic field canceler. The output setting was already at max. Sixteen percent of its battery charge remained. He was going to use the rest of it in one go.

"Three, two, one, zero."

At the end of the countdown, Hiroto aimed the canceler at the foot of the automated turnstile. The device shone as brightly as if the sun itself were pouring into the corridor connecting the Kiso and Nakatsugawa regions. He could see the reflected light melting the walls and ceiling around them, too. The concrete floor had already disintegrated, along with the structure one story below, leaving a giant hole the full width of the passageway.

The entire phalanx of turnstiles fell in, and Hiroto went with them. There were four tremendous metallic crashes around him. Despite dropping from a height of two stories, Hiroto felt no pain. The turnstile holding him used its joint shocks to absorb the impact of his fall.

There was a familiar and distinctly damp mustiness to the place in which Hiroto now found himself.

"The superconductive railway... It comes out this far?"

It was the tunnel Hiroto had used to get into Kofu with Nepshamai. They'd been built long before the expansion of Yokohama Station, during the era of High Civilization before the Winter War. The track was still in this massive tunnel because the superconductive material repelled Yokohama Station's expansion.

"Yes. You're now outside of Yokohama Station. The automated turnstiles shouldn't chase after you there. If you head to the west, you can pass through Nagoya and exit into Ise Bay," said Keiha, her relieved voice resonating against the tunnel walls.

Of the four turnstiles that had fallen into the tunnel, three had spun their limbs to brace for impact and landed without damage. The one holding Hiroto had broken its arms and neck, exposing the cables beneath them. Parts of it were twitching, like a fish stranded on land.

Presumably, to preserve its prisoner, the turnstile hadn't been able to enter the appropriate defensive position. Hiroto extricated himself from the wires extending from the machine's broken arms, feeling a bit sorry for it.

The other three turnstiles swung their heads and arms around in apparent search for something.

"Locational data incorrect. Turnstile functions cannot be executed."

"Locational data incorrect. Turnstile functions cannot be executed."

"Locational data incorrect. Turnstile functions cannot be executed."

They spoke slightly out of sync. The reverberation in the tunnel gave their words an odd echo.

"Ending turnstile program. Returning to normal mode."

The three of them toppled forward and rested their arms against the ground. It was almost like they were prostrating themselves. Their face displays hung down to the floor such that they resembled four-legged tables.

"Beginning normal mode initialization. This process may take up to several minutes. Please wait for the process to complete."

After that, the limbs of the three functioning turnstiles were still. Instead, there was a sound of metal clicking and scraping within their bodies. It looked like they were rearranging their internal mechanisms.

"Wait, Keiha, can you hear that? They're acting strange."

"...I can hear it. I've got a terrible feeling about this. Get away from there."

Hiroto wanted to start running, but his legs refused to obey. He was only moving at the speed of a brisk walk.

The automated turnstiles existed to remove intruders and Suika violators from Yokohama Station. One could only wonder what happened to them when they left its confines. Hiroto had lived outside the station his whole life, and he'd never once considered such a thing. He only knew that turnstiles were found Inside.

A few minutes after Hiroto hurried off, the automated turnstiles began moving again.

"Establishing connection to tactical node... Tactical node not found."

"Waiting for signal from satellite... signal not received. Searching for outdoor route... Route to outdoors not found."

·"Orders from higher function not detected. Transitioning to self-defense mode."

"Unit within group has been destroyed. Hostile units likely nearby."

"Requesting backup. Requesting backup from nearby units."

The three automated turnstiles began skittering in Hiroto's direction, still on all fours.

Keiha's ominous feeling stemmed from an idea that had been rattling around in her head for a while. There were production plants for the automated turnstiles all over Yokohama Station. Such complex facilities could not have been Yokohama Station's own doing. As happened with other buildings, Yokohama Station had absorbed an existing place that people once built, then replicated it within the structural genetic field.

So why did the automated turnstiles exist before the entity they seemingly existed to guard? The answer was that they'd initially been meant for some other purpose, and Suikanet then overwrote that with its own programming. This transformed the robots into a system for maintaining order Inside. It was the only possible explanation for the automated turnstiles. The structural genetic field only evolved on the spot in response to stimuli. It didn't have the planning or precision to develop such intricate mechanisms.

What had the automated turnstiles originally been for, then? While many machines had been developed during the Winter War, most weren't fully autonomous or mobile. Plus, the four-limbed, humanoid design of the robots was clearly not intended for the flat floors of Yokohama Station. It was a structure better suited for uneven terrains— like a battlefield.

With that in mind, Keiha said into the mic, "This is counter-evidence against you...or Yukie."

Keiha's voice was fed from the instrument to the virtual replica of Nepshamai's main memory device. "If the JR Integrated Intelligence created Yokohama Station of its own will, then it must have created the automated turnstile system, too. That being the case, it would have constructed a much more advanced and robust interface. The fact that Yokohama Station repurposed human-made robots for itself is proof that the station expanded against the intention of the integrated intelligence."

As one who'd spent a long time fiddling with the automated turn-stile system, that was something she could assert with confidence.

She had faith in her own technical skills, but that was only by con-temporary standards. She assumed that she would be several levels below someone of equivalent expertise from the Winter War or the Internet age before it. If she could handle the robots that patrolled Inside, they couldn't be that advanced. At the very least, they hadn't been built by something superior to humanity.

The saboteur from JR North Japan waited a few seconds.

> **There is necessity. Please the start-up process do. Send communication.**

"...?"

At first, Keiha thought the response had been an answer to her state-ment, but she soon sensed that it was something else. The replicated intelligence had a task in mind.

"Start-up process?"

> **Wiring is AAT compatible. Please hurry is necessary. Unstable signal.**

"AAT compatible wiring?"

There was only one thing she could think of that related to AAT compatible wiring. It was the mechanism Nepshamai had used to control the superconductive railway and get to Kofu. It would have been a memory just before he ran out of power, so it was stored intact in his short-term memory bank.

> **Start-up process, please send. Hurryryryryryry**

"Wait a minute, what's the matter?"

Unfortunately, that was the end of the text on the monitor. No further reply came. The computer itself was functioning, but the recreation of Nepshamai's main memory device on it no longer grasped what she was saying as legible vocabulary.

The scan Keiha had made of Nepshamai's memory hadn't been accurate enough. Processing and numerical errors had built up to the point that it was no longer a functioning intelligence.

She could recreate it using the data at the point of replication, but continuing to use such vast computational resources beyond this point risked Keiha's own safety. Most of the computers in this shop were meant to be running the ICoCar System that kept the automated turnstiles in Kofu at a safe distance.

Keiha decided to stop the simulator.

"Human figure detected."

"Warning. Stop, or I will fire."

Hiroto ignored the automated turnstiles behind him and kept running. The tunnel was dark and had no lights.

The three robots in pursuit had their arms on the ground to run on four legs. He had never seen them move like that before. Yet, for some reason, it seemed like a more natural state for them.

There was a gunshot, and something sped into the wall nearby. Hiroto glanced over his shoulder and saw the three turnstiles facing him. One had produced a small tube protruding from a panel on its torso. It was pointing in Hiroto's direction. The turnstile was equipped with an internal gun. The other two had nothing, though. Their panel portions were open, too, but Hiroto could only see exposed machinery.

"offensive device not detected. engaging in direct capture," the two weaponless turnstiles declared.

The other one fired a few more times, then stated, "inadequate illumination for identification. target location cannot be identified. using infrared system. infrared detection system not loaded."

It promptly fired another round. This shot carved a hole into the right side of the tunnel. It wasn't even close to Hiroto. It really seemed like the machines couldn't see him now.

Hiroto hadn't noticed before, but the turnstiles were actually moving rather slowly. Their bodies were encased in heavy metal armor, so a human running at full speed could break away from them fairly quickly. Within Yokohama Station, they used their sheer numbers to surround and capture targets. Against only a handful of the robots, a human being stood a fighting chance.

A battle of stamina was a different matter. Hiroto had already been shot in the leg and couldn't run—and the automated turnstiles could move as long as they wanted without getting tired. Hiroto didn't know what they used for energy, but they had to be capable of running for a pretty long time if they were built for battle.

Finally, Hiroto's strength gave out, and he collapsed onto the metal plate beneath him. The chill of its surface settled into his body. The one turnstile continued firing every few seconds, making little holes in the concrete of the walls and floor. It was incredibly inaccurate. As the machines drew closer to him, he could sense the shots were getting nearer, though.

Am I about to die? Hiroto wondered.

He'd certainly done enough to deserve it. He'd led multiple people to their deaths, and he'd pressed the button that would erase the whole of

Yokohama Station. Over the next several years, the anti-something field would permeate everything Inside and steal the homes and livelihoods of the people who lived there.

To the Insiders, it was an utter natural disaster. In that sense, Hiroto deserved to die here, down in a tunnel where no one would ever find him.

If there was one thing he wished, it had to do with Nepshamai's electric sign, still resting inside his bag. Hiroto wished he could do something for him. Perhaps he should have left the device with Keiha back in Kofu.

Unbelievable. I'm more concerned about one machine than I am about all the people living in the station. I'm totally inadequate as a human being and totally inadequate in a pinch.

Hiroto felt like he was about to burst into laughter. He looked up and saw that one of the three turnstiles was close enough that it was visible, even in the dark tunnel.

"ᴡᴀʀɴɪɴɢ. sᴛᴏᴘ. ᴏʀ ɪ ᴡɪʟʟ sʜᴏᴏᴛ," commanded the automaton, pointing its gun at Hiroto.

"I already stopped, you dumb bucket of junk," Hiroto spat, still sitting on the ground.

"ᴡᴀʀɴɪɴɢ. sᴛᴏᴘ. ᴏʀ ɪ ᴡɪʟʟ sʜᴏᴏᴛ," it repeated in precisely the same tone.

"Oh, go to hell."

No sooner had the word "hell" left Hiroto's mouth than a tremendous, high-pitched *bang* filled the tunnel. He felt like it had ruptured his eardrums.

The front half of the automated turnstile blew off and clattered to the ground several meters away. Sparks and smoke sputtered from its exposed mechanisms.

It exploded?

Hiroto looked back and saw another figure. For an instant, he thought another turnstile had come from the other side of the tunnel, but it was a human.

He was riding a little scooter with a long gun strapped sideways to it.

Whoever it was was small but about Hiroto's age. His weapon was trained on the automated turnstiles.

"Who the hell are you?" the armed man asked Hiroto.

"Who the hell are you?" Toshiru Kubo demanded, removing his earplugs. He always made sure to wear them when firing his weapon at maximum output, especially in an enclosed tunnel like this.

"Did…did you just save me?" inquired Hiroto, reeling from the ringing in his ears. "I'm just a traveler. I came here from a cape far to the east. I got Inside with an 18 Ticket, but the time on it ran out, and I made it down to this tunnel trying to escape."

"I didn't ask all of that. Who the hell are you? Human, machine, some kind of ghost?"

"Human," Hiroto replied. "I'm…human."

Hearing that, the man with the gun seemed to lose interest and turned to face his half-destroyed victim. There were exposed circuits and mechanical bits in the portions where the machine's facade had been torn away.

"Is this an automated turnstile, too? The one I saw at the strait looked very different," Toshiru muttered. An infrared scope popped out of the robot's shattered body. The device was meant for acquiring targets in the dark, but the lens was pointed inward toward itself and wasn't even connected to the circuitry. It was affixed in a completely impotent manner.

The little appendage was a vestige of a feature with which the turnstiles had once been equipped. In the same way that biological creatures living in a cave evolved until they lost their eyesight, the long process of growth in Yokohama Station had robbed the turnstiles of equipment they no longer needed. Now all that remained were superfluous traces of what once had been.

"Eugh, what is that? It's disgusting," Toshiru grunted, pulling the scope free as gingerly as though touching something contaminated.

He quickly collected some of the small bits of metal that had flown loose from the damage, then went back to his scooter, put in his earplugs, loaded the metal into the gun, and took aim at the two other approaching turnstiles.

"You can shoot these machines."

Bang, bang.

With two more loud bursts, the remaining robots practically exploded. Even against moving targets, this person on a scooter accurately struck the turnstiles' exposed panels. They were less armored there, so a precision shot could take them down in one go.

With his ears ringing again, Hiroto recognized that the man was using the same kind of electric pump gun that had destroyed Nepshamai in Kamakura. The destructive power and precision of this weapon seemed on a different scale entirely, however.

Toshiru stripped the first turnstile of its circuits with a disgusted look as he searched for parts he could use.

"Well, I don't know who you are…but you saved me. Thanks," said Hiroto, bowing his head. Toshiru couldn't hear him because of the earplugs but understood the gesture of gratitude.

"Ahh, so this is what it means to save people. Aha," he muttered without looking at Hiroto. It reminded him of Haikunterke. She'd once said something about him not understanding what she meant.

"Yeah, I still don't get it. What's the point?"

Three days earlier, Toshiru Kubo had found the entrance to the superconductive railway in Tokushima. It had been planned to travel from Osaka through Kobe, then it would cross Awaji Island to Shikoku, but the Winter War had brought the project to a halt. All that was left was an exposed tunnel entrance sticking out of a hill in the middle of the woods.

The shaft inside was finished, and it still had power, which made it a very comfortable place for Toshiru to ride his electric scooter.

There were no plants for sustenance around, so he had to scrape off moss to break down into a solution with his catalytic bottle. If Toshiru ignored that part, it was probably the most pleasant place he'd ever been in his life. Nobody was here, and it just kept going forever.

It seemed a bit like outer space, and that was where he truly wanted to be.

Unfortunately, a human and three automated turnstiles had appeared and soured his mood.

When JR Fukuoka defended the strait and shot down the extending corridors, they would occasionally recover automated turnstiles in the process. The military division would send them to engineering for an examination of their internal workings. Every time, Toshiru would think, *I wish I could meet the person who designed this grotesque thing. Actually, I'd rather not.*

Of course, there was no creator to speak of. Perhaps there had been one, long ago, but the structural genetic field's spontaneous mutations had slowly leached out the original reason and logic of the construction over time.

There is a phrase called the uncanny valley. It states that as a robot's appearance becomes more humanlike, it is considered more likable by human test subjects. Just before that facade becomes indistinguishable from an actual human, people's comfort levels drop precipitously.

Toshiru never liked others to begin with, so he didn't have to worry about a robotic uncanny valley. He did feel a similar sensation regarding mechanical designs. That was why he found the automated turnstiles so creepy.

It was about the last thing he wanted to see in a tunnel like this.

If only he'd met something fun, like that mechanical girl, instead.

"Hey, you," Toshiru called to Hiroto. His face was turned in Hiroto's direction, but his eyes were looking elsewhere. "I saved you, so give me something in return. Preferably something to eat."

"Uh, okay. Give me a moment."

Hiroto opened his bag. He'd brought plenty of meals for himself. Plus, he'd eaten out a few times, so he still had a few rations left.

Just then, a device in the bag fell out onto the ground. It was

Nepshamai's electronic scrolling sign. It rolled over the sloping tunnel toward Toshiru's feet. He picked it up.

"Sorry. Give that back. I know that guy." Hiroto felt like it was a strange request, even as he said it. Toshiru ignored him, however, and peered curiously at the electronic sign. He opened the front case and saw Nepshamai's main memory device inside. Next to it was the small fox insignia of JR North Japan.

"Hey, what does this mean?" Toshiru demanded. "Can you hear me? Did you get completely destroyed this time; not just the leg? Hey! Man, you're a wreck."

The electronic sign didn't respond. Its power was gone.

"Hey, what happened to the body?" Toshiru asked Hiroto.

"Got shot by a station employee. They took the body away," he replied.

For the first time, Toshiru actually looked Hiroto in the face. "Where?"

"Kamakura."

Toshiru pulled a map up on his device to confirm the location of Kamakura. When he saw that it was over in the Kanto region, he made a bitter face.

"Dammit, that's far… Oh, well. Guess I can do another rescue. Is this place Inside? That'll be a pain, but I bet I can make it work."

"Can you do it?" Hiroto asked. Toshiru put the electronic sign in the seat pocket of the scooter and said nothing.

"If you can help, take this, too. It goes with that," Hiroto continued, putting the dead genetic field canceler in Toshiru's hand. "Oh, and this. I was supposed to hand it over when it expired." He surrendered the 18 Ticket.

Toshiru took them both without a word and stared closely at the objects. He seemed to find them more interesting than the man who'd given them to him.

Then, Toshiru put the tube and the little box into the pocket along with the electronic sign. He started up the scooter's motor and promptly took off in the direction from which Hiroto had come.

Within moments, the scooter was out of sight, and all was quiet.

All that was left in the tunnel with Hiroto was the trio of fallen turnstiles.

He wasn't entirely sure what had just happened, but it seemed like an improvement. There was little for Hiroto to do now but trust the man. Despite having known him for less than three minutes, Hiroto felt like the guy with the gun was dependable.

There was another light from the far end of the tunnel. It felt like something was approaching from the distance.

"orders from higher function not detected. Transitioning to self-defense mode."

"unit within group has been destroyed. Enemy units likely nearby."

It was the familiar synthesized female voice: automated turnstiles. The four who'd fallen during Hiroto's escape were destroyed, but more were on the way.

The only thing left in Hiroto's bag was Keiha's device, which coldly read, *Out of network*. The tunnel was going deep underground, out of the range of the station's Suikanet signal.

Below that was a notification that said, *One new message*. Based on the time stamp, it had been sent just after Hiroto tumbled into the shaft.

> **Superconductive railway start-up sequence program**
> **Acquire an AAT-format cable (see image) and connect this device to rail car, then start attached program. KN**

That was the entire message. It was succinct, but Hiroto understood.

Somewhere in this tunnel should be another vehicle like the one he and Nepshamai had taken to Kofu. If he hooked this device to the car, it would run like that one. Keiha had sent over the program to do it, anticipating this situation. She was very thorough.

That left the cable as the only obstacle. If Hiroto was going to find a working line in a shaft like this, it could only come from one of the turnstiles on the ground around him.

Hiroto rushed over to one of the halves of the split turnstile. In the darkness of the tunnel, it was hard to make out anything as small as the connector format Keiha had indicated. He reached into the open face panel and pulled out a number of things that looked like cables, jamming the bunch into his bag.

The five days Hiroto had spent Inside had been full of new experiences from moment to moment, but the sheer bizarreness of rifling through the guts of an automated turnstile made him dizzy. He was searching through something that represented the boundary of possibilities, hoping to find the means to survive.

There was a pile of black cables in Hiroto's bag now. It reminded him of Keiha's set of drawers back in Kofu. *One* of them had to be what he needed. Next, he had to look for a train car. Hiroto started running.

The newer automated turnstiles were still far off, but they were definitely advancing Hiroto's way. In a sense, they were coming to avenge their fallen family. Perhaps they meant to kill him at all costs.

Hiroto could sense the hostility of the station thick on his skin. He wanted to live.

Toshiru rode along on the scooter until the tunnel started to brighten a little. There was a huge hole in the ceiling, letting light in up ahead.

"What is that? Was it an explosion?"

He looked up but didn't see the familiar blue sky, only some guidance signs that read, To Nakatsugawa and To Kiso.

Ahh, so this is directly below Yokohama Station.

It was the first time in Toshiru's life that he'd seen the Inside world.

At least it wasn't as unpleasant as the newly formed structure in Tokushima. Something was different about the completed interior. Perhaps it was because the actual station structure traced its lineage back to proper, logical design principles created by human beings.

What was the giant hole, then? It would take massive firepower to punch an aperture this big in Yokohama Station, with its structural genetic field. Perhaps some group Inside had the same kind of muscle that JR Fukuoka did. The military division would pale if they heard that.

Many automated turnstiles were milling around at the edge of the hole. It was like their movement algorithms wanted them to move forward. With the corridor blocked, though, they just shifted around in place.

To get to Kamakura, Toshiru would have to get Inside at some point. Could he manage to climb up and get in here?

Unfortunately, the hallways were narrow, and there were many layers. A scooter wasn't ideal for mobility. What's more, Toshiru couldn't think of a way to lift a hundred-kilo machine up there. Having a smaller, two-legged body was more convenient Inside. That was very logical design.

He looked down and saw an automated turnstile with its arms and neck broken. There was a metal wire tangled around its limbs. The thing was still, but it was making a hushed sound. Toshiru listened intently to make it out.

"Requesting backup. Requesting backup from nearby units," it muttered.

Just then, two automated turnstiles from the upper level fell into the superconductive railway tunnel. They landed with heavy thuds.

"Locational data incorrect. Turnstile functions cannot be executed."

"Locational data incorrect. Turnstile functions cannot be executed."

"Ending turnstile program. Returning to normal mode."

"Ending turnstile program. Returning to normal mode."

"Beginning normal mode initialization. This process may take up to several minutes. Please wait for the process to complete."

The turnstiles flopped forward, dropping their head displays down and assuming a shape like a four-legged table.

"That's not good," said Toshiru. He looked up; more automated turnstiles were gathering. Apparently, the broken robot was calling more of its kind from Inside. As each of them descended into the superconductive railway tunnel, they transitioned into "normal mode."

"I don't know what that is, but it's not good. Gotta avoid them," Toshiru declared, and he sped off on the scooter. He couldn't push it that hard in the darkness, but thirty kilometers an hour was enough to shake off the turnstiles.

To get to Kamakura, he'd have to get Inside somewhere. Maybe he could track down a cybernetic engineer and ask for a Suika implant. It was the first time in his life he'd ever wanted one.

Sadly, he had nothing to trade for it. He couldn't hand over the long gun, and he doubted the scooter would be worth anything Inside. Maybe there was a way to steal the body back without actually going Inside.

"In any case, I'll do whatever it takes to rescue you, Haikunterke."

Toshiru then realized that he'd forgotten to take the food from that weird guy back there. Not that it was a big loss.

At that moment, Haikunterke was in Wakayama. In the three days since she'd split with Toshiru in Tokushima, she'd crossed Awaji Island to Kobe, then around Osaka Bay and south down the Kii Peninsula.

"Can you read me, Haikunterke?"

It was the voice of her case officer, Kaeriyama, coming to her through Suikanet from JR North Japan's headquarters. It wasn't a physical voice from vibrations in the air but digital data directly input into Haikunterke's main memory device. She nearly answered before remembering that it wasn't a real-time two-way communication but a packet of voice data he'd sent her in one big chunk.

"Something strange happened midday yesterday, and I wanted to make you aware. We observed a very brief and unprecedented kind of noise wave that spread across the entire station. Initially, we thought it was an earthquake, but the physical sensors didn't pick up anything. It might be the precursor to something major. Be careful. We'll keep an eye on automated turnstile activity from here as best we can, but so far, there hasn't been anything out of line. No problems with immune memory, either. Still, make sure you have a route identified to get to the sea as quickly as possible. That's all."

The signal time put that message at about three hours ago. JR North Japan did not have adequate Suikanet node control in the Kii Peninsula to conduct proper conversations. Capturing those nodes was her mission, in fact.

"This is Haikunterke. I'm in Wakayama now. I haven't seen any obvious signs of an anomaly here. My voice and other sensors aren't picking up anything, either. I'll be as careful as possible and continue securing nodes along the Pacific coast. Over," she reported back. This, too, was not spoken aloud but was instead sent as data to her communication module and uploaded through Suikanet.

Reporting back to headquarters was nice because Haikunterke didn't have to move her mouth. She preferred it that way. Talking with humans meant she had to match her mouth movements to the vocalizations, something she'd always had trouble with. The harder she tried to unify them, the less coordinated they became.

It was a wonder that Shamai could speak as effortlessly as he did. She called up her memory of the way he verbalized from her supplemental memory banks and saw that his mouth was slightly off as well. He didn't care, though, so you wouldn't notice unless you were paying close attention. That irritated Haikunterke.

She'd done quite a lot of moving around since heading Inside three days ago, but her leg mobility was still holding up. That former member of JR Fukuoka was quite the engineer.

The metal clanking against the floor clattered through the tunnel. The pursuing turnstiles were a ways behind Hiroto. His throat was dry.

He pored through his bag as he walked, pulling out his water. The bottle was dented. When he opened it up, it hissed as it sucked in the tunnel air.

The last time he'd opened up the bottle was just before leaving Exit 42. He'd come all this way without drinking anything.

"Oh," he murmured, recalling his unnatural difficulty breathing there. "It was the difference in air pressure. The air's just thinner up in the mountains."

He took a swig of water and chuckled to himself.

A long time ago, either the professor or someone else from the village had told him, "The air pressure is weak on the peak of Mr. Fuji, so it's harder to breathe and easier to boil water." To think that a day would come when Hiroto made use of that knowledge. Even under the multilayered structure of Yokohama Station, where neither sunlight nor rain reached and temperature fluctuation was slight, air pressure was the one thing that faithfully obeyed the laws of nature.

Hiroto looked down at the metal plate under his feet. He thought that the tunnel flooring had just switched from concrete to metal, but what if this was the same sort of train car he and Nepshamai had used to travel to Kofu?

If so, it was much longer than the tatami mat–sized one from Kofu. Perhaps it was for transporting larger cargo. Hiroto opened the cover in the front and saw a familiar grouping of ports.

Hiroto went through his bundle of cables one by one, looking for something that matched the shape of the intakes. The sound of the four-legged turnstiles approaching and shooting was getting louder, but for some reason, Hiroto didn't care. He knew he was going to escape alive.

After flipping around the last cable to its opposite end, he finally managed to connect Keiha's device. Upon starting up the computer program, a bunch of white letters scrolled past on the black screen, the metal plate rose by a centimeter and then began to accelerate forward.

The wind pressure against Hiroto's face was incredible; the air roared in his ears. The edge of the plate dug into his fingers where he gripped it. The gunfire of the turnstiles behind him got more and more distant.

A few dozen minutes later, the metal plate began sending up a spray of water. At first, Hiroto thought it was because of some kind of buildup, but then his perspective changed. The tunnel itself was descending into the water. The scent was very familiar to Hiroto. For the first time in five days, he was smelling the ocean.

◆

During the Winter War, Nagoya had suffered constant gravity attacks, until the entire city sunk about twenty meters. One of the three greatest cities of Japan was now nearly eight stories below Ise Bay.

Ironically, it was this disaster that had left Nagoya as a recognizable relic. The seawater prevented the structural genetic field from absorbing it whole.

Tokyo and Osaka's structures had all been incorporated into the structural genetic field, turned into Yokohama Station, and changed in ways that their designers had never intended. Nagoya was the one major city on Honshu that still remained as it was.

The areas along Ise Bay were bustling with people seeking anything useful from the ancient settlement. Few paid any heed to the ruined buildings sticking hundreds of meters out of the sea. It seemed impossible that humans could've erected such things. The residents of Yokohama Station naturally assumed that anything there had just grown on its own.

Tourists only gazed out at the city from Inside and never tried to sail to it on boats. For one thing, residents of the station hated going outside, and there was the danger of the ruined buildings collapsing. So when Hiroto surfaced along the barnacled ninth-story wall of the ancient ruin, it was a pair of non-Suika brothers out in the bay who spotted him.

"Hey, you there! You alive?" they shouted from a distance, waking Hiroto up. He could hear their boat motor. He turned and saw two men approaching him.

"Let's not, brother. He must be an exile. Nothing good ever comes of dealing with Insiders."

"Don't be stupid. You ever seen an Insider with skin that dark? He musta washed up from some other part of the sea."

"I ain't heard about any strangers passing through the strait. C'mon, let's not."

"Maybe he's a spy comin' up from Owase. Those folks been pushing their luck more and more these days. In any case, we gotta check it out."

While the younger brother was reluctant, the elder had the overriding vote, so their vessel moved in on the ocean-weathered building.

The Nagoya Navy (as they called themselves) were a collective of non-Suika holders who sailed around the Ise Bay. They took residence on the isolated little islands around the bay and on the tip of the Chita Peninsula. They were similar to the people of Ninety-Nine Steps in that they lived off the junked goods that came out of Yokohama Station, but they had a population thirty times the size. They'd developed an advanced distributed-work system where food, tools, and information devices to be repaired or augmented were delivered to different regions.

The brothers first took Hiroto to the navy's main base on the island of Kamishima to meet their boss. He was a large, well-muscled man close to fifty. Hiroto had never seen a fisher with that kind of size and physique in Ninety-Nine Steps, much less Inside.

The chief refused to believe that Hiroto had used an 18 Ticket to travel through the station. The things he'd acquired Inside—the electric sign, 18 Ticket, and genetic field canceler—had all gone to the man on the scooter. Keiha's device had become underwater scrap matter, along with the superconductive railway car.

That reminded Hiroto that Keiha had said no records of the superconductive railway remained on Suikanet, so it was mysterious that she had somehow prepared the program to start up the car. Keiha was mysterious in general, though. She probably had some special knowledge that was beyond his understanding.

In the end, the Nagoya Navy didn't believe that Hiroto had journeyed for several days through the Inside. However, when he told them he was from a cape settlement called Ninety-Nine Steps on the Miura Peninsula, the boss made him a promise that they'd take him back home.

"We've wanted to expand our activities to the east anyway. We've got some arrangements for trade with the Izu Peninsula, but we hardly ever venture past that point," he explained.

The person in charge of the Nagoya Navy was an ambitious man who dreamed of ruling over Yokohama Station's entire Pacific coastline. He'd already expanded his base of operations past the Kii Peninsula to the west. By helping this drifter out, he saw an opportunity to grow his power in an easterly direction, too.

Hiroto asked to stay in the area for a while first, however. He wanted to learn from them about cultivating sweet potatoes and pumpkins.

"But why? Your home is small, and you're well-supplied by what comes out of the station. We do some farming of our own, but it's not the most productive work," the boss said.

"Because we'll need it," Hiroto replied. "After a while, we won't be able to get stuff from Yokohama Station anymore."

"Why do you think that?"

"Because Yokohama Station is going away."

The boss stared at Hiroto like he was crazy. His followers looked at each other and said, "I think something's wrong with him."

"Must have been put through hell by the Insiders, I bet," they murmured. Still, Hiroto was allowed to remain with the Nagoya Navy.

Any attempts at farming in Ninety-Nine Steps were entirely experimental. There wasn't enough information for the people there to go on. You could learn a lot about industrial engineering from fishing on Suikanet, but nothing on agriculture was remotely helpful. All the food production Inside was grown using hydroponics under strict and precisely managed artificial lighting.

Once his leg healed, Hiroto helped with cultivating on the Atsumi Peninsula south of Chita. While the farm was small compared to the navy's scale, it was much more advanced than anything at Ninety-Nine Steps. It was almost a year later, in the spring, that Hiroto finally rode one of their ships going east.

He sent a letter informing of his return before the trip, so Maki was there to greet him at the cape just a bit before Ninety-Nine Steps.

"I thought you weren't coming back," she stated flatly, their first words shared in a year.

"I told you I'd return."

"It was supposed to be five days and turned into a year. I assumed you weren't coming."

"Sorry. I went through a whole bunch of stuff. I'll tell you about it later. How's the cape doing? Is the professor okay?"

"He died."

"He died? When?"

"A week after you left. He wasn't getting up and walking around, so I went to go check on him, and he'd just died in his sleep. I don't know what it was. Probably just old age."

"...Oh."

Pretty much everyone back home wanted to hear about Inside, so they held a public forum that night, where Hiroto told them the things he'd seen and heard in Yokohama Station during his five days there. Lastly, he gave them his warning: "Yokohama Station will be going away in the near future."

The villagers didn't know about the structural genetic field, so instead, Hiroto told them that he'd discovered the interior was weakening, getting old, and would soon crumble into bits. He swore to himself that he would never tell them that he was the one who'd pressed the button to set the whole thing in motion.

After that, he impressed upon the people of Ninety-Nine Steps the importance of producing their own food and explained the different crops he'd brought from the Nagoya Navy. They didn't believe that Yokohama Station would go away (such a concept was beyond them), but he got their approval to produce more food anyway. For one thing, there was little manual labor to go around for their colony and plenty of young people with nothing productive to do.

Hiroto went to see Yosuke in the flower field, too. When he saw Hiroto coming up the down-only escalators, he said, "Oh, you're still alive?" Hiroto thought his friend looked even fatter than he'd been a year before. "If you go in the station, you should come back out the same way," Yosuke complained, pointing at the automated turnstiles lined up at the entrance. They sat there silently in the exact same position as when Hiroto entered a year ago with the 18 Ticket.

"Is there anything different about Suikanet? Any extra instability?" Hiroto asked.

Yosuke replied, "It's as unstable as ever. Sometimes you get in, then you disconnect."

Without Suika credentials, all people like Yosuke could do was collect data packets passing through Suikanet and reassemble them. It wasn't possible to send anything from this side.

Hiroto often wondered about Keiha. Was she still in Kofu? Was there any way to send word that he'd made it back home safely?

The professor had been cremated, then scattered to sea. Ninety-Nine Steps had no burial custom. They kept one photograph of him for the town hall's album. It was taken when he first came to Ninety-Nine Steps, and in it, he looked much younger than the professor Hiroto knew. It was the face of the maintenance entity for the JR Integrated Intelligence in Exit 42.

A young married couple and their infant child were now living in the professor's old house. The cape was perpetually short on land, and memories of the professor were already being washed away. Unlike Yokohama Station, which preserved centuries-old things and continued expanding, the natural ground did not keep its records for long.

A few days after Hiroto's return to the cape, the concrete-covered White Fuji turned escalator black overnight. It was a sign that the long rainy season was over and summer had arrived. The mountain was probably taller than the last time Hiroto had seen it.

There was no telling how many more times this transition would occur. For now, the only thing to do was prepare for the loss of Yokohama Station.

EPILOGUE

The structural-genetic-field-resistant polymer covering JR Fukuoka's Straits base had long surpassed the designer's intended lifespan. The parts where it was broken and cracked expanded from sunlight, making it look like the entire base was in the shade of a leafy tree.

There were two reasons they hadn't put up the budget for polymer replacement. One, the necessity of keeping up the strait's defense was falling year after year, and two, a critical project was in motion that was consuming all the money.

"Here's the state of the tumor right now," said Okuma from the intelligence division, pointing to a tabletop map in a meeting room in the base. The rank badge he wore on his chest showed that he had far outpaced anyone else who'd entered the company at the same time he had. It was also a sign of how the power balance inside the company had shifted over the last five years in favor of the intelligence division—particularly Okuma's branch, Suikanet monitoring, which had grown much more important.

"It is expanding in a roughly concentric fashion. The broadening speed is not uniform, so I can't be entirely positive, but it should reach the sea somewhere between a month to half a year."

The map showed the island of Honshu covered in a network of lines representing the communication status of Suikanet. There was a black hole centered around the Kiso Mountains.

"So Suikanet will soon be split between east and west?" inquired

Kawakami, who was now general commander of the military division.

"Yes. In fact, they can barely communicate between east and west already. You're lucky if half of the data you send makes it across, it seems."

"I see. Then we'll be putting this into use soon," Kawakami replied, displaying a digital cover page for something titled *Project Yatagarasu* and showing it to Okuma. It was named after a mythological crow who led an ancient king from Kyushu to attack the center of Japan and establish the first Japanese government.

"The company president has issued a decree. As soon as the split has been confirmed complete, we will begin an invasion of Yokohama Station."

"Ahh, so we're going in at last?"

"According to the quaternary survey team's reports, the interior of the tumor is already split between several warring factions. It was leadership's decision not to get involved until the chaos has settled down somewhat. The approval has finally come down."

Yokohama Station's "tumor" was the nickname for an anomaly that had arisen in the center of Honshu five years prior, characterized by disrupted Suikanet coverage, loss of populace control by the automated turnstiles, and some crumbling of structures. While its cause remained unknown, it had been steadily spreading. At present, the entire Chubu region of central Japan was covered by the tumor.

Short-term, localized disasters in Yokohama Station caused by earthquakes and eruptions had been observed before, but everyone trusted that any damaged area would be rebuilt after the destruction. However, in all the recorded history of Yokohama Station, nothing had ever happened that lasted this long and spread so far.

Because the automated turnstiles had stopped performing Suika verification, JR Fukuoka sent some survey teams into the tumor. Their reports made it clear that things within were just as chaotic and dangerous as on Shikoku. Even though violence had been thoroughly under control in Yokohama Station, numerous armed factions arose like garden bugs from an overturned stone as soon as the turnstiles stopped policing things.

Now, a few years after the initial chaos, the Chubu region was currently controlled by a few different powers. There were the station staffers who'd been steadily stockpiling black-market weapons; bandits who'd made their home in the mountains; and non-Suika holders who'd appeared from the sea.

"You don't think we've waited too long, to where they all band together and form a force that can fight back against us, do you?"

"Not a problem. At best, they're outfitted with outdated guns. We've been fighting Yokohama Station for decades. We have real firepower."

Okuma and Kawakami knew that many of the weapons circulating Inside had been brought there by JR Fukuoka deserters. The best anyone in the station had was likely just some anti-personnel gun used for maintaining peace and order on Kyushu, however. The real military power—armaments that could destroy Yokohama Station and its structural genetic field—were kept under strict supervision where no disgruntled rank-and-file soldier could reach them.

"I see. So if anyone actually represents a potential threat to us, it would be the people in the north," remarked Okuma, pointing at the top of the map.

"Yes. That's another reason to wait for the net to split. In terms of information technology, JR North Japan is beyond even us. With Suikanet still whole, they could very likely have eyes on everything we're doing."

Okuma knew that better than anyone. JR North Japan had probably succeeded at deciphering the station's description language. If they could read even a part of the JR Integrated Intelligence's knowledge, there was no predicting what kind of actions they could take in the future.

"What's the possibility that they become a threat?"

"Completely unknown. Of course, there's a chance we could work together to plant a unified JR flag in the middle of Yokohama Station. We were originally one national enterprise, after all. But there are almost no historical examples of organizations that fused back together equally after being separated for a long time. That's all I can say at the moment," Kawakami explained.

Okuma sighed and reached into a paper bag for some sugar-coated noodles, then washed them down with tea. The polymer's chemical smell had softened in the last few years, but it was still baffling to Kawakami that the other man could constantly be eating in such a dirty and unappetizing place.

"We intend to dispatch many members of the intelligence division in our invasion of the station. You've been suggested as a possible leader. What do you think?" Kawakami inquired.

"Why, that would be quite an honor. I'll admit that I'm very curious to see the nature of this thing up close," said Okuma, pointing at the tumor with his teaspoon. "But I'm afraid I must decline. I enjoy using my mind more than my body. If you ever figure out the reason why, I'd love to hear it."

When the Suikanet communications aberration started, the first possible explanation JR Fukuoka postulated was intentional sabotage by Insiders. They knew about a group called the Dodger Alliance, which had at one time been in total control of Suikanet around Kyoto and had even managed to rein in the automated turnstiles to a degree.

Their control of the network had abruptly ended at one point, however, and the group's fate was unknown. JR Fukuoka concluded that a faction seeking to control Suikanet would not choose to destroy it, so that theory fell out of favor.

Next, naturally, they presumed it was an attack by JR North Japan. According to reports, they'd already put a means of eliminating the structural genetic field into practical use, so the north might have orchestrated some kind of attack in the center of Yokohama Station. JR North Japan had previously only ever shown an interest in defending the Seikan Tunnel to Hokkaido. For them to be deemed the culprit, there would have to be signs of JR North Japan military presence in the growing tumor. There was no such evidence.

Many other theories abounded, but in the end, they all fell apart because of a lack of motive to destroy Yokohama Station itself. Ultimately, JR Fukuoka was left to conclude that the tumor had not been the result of intentional action but was instead the product of an accident or perhaps just natural degradation.

Okuma had his own ideas, of course. Toshiru Kubo from the engineering division had vanished five years ago, and the tumor first manifested several months after that. Toshiru had said he was going to Shikoku, but there was no trace of him beyond that point. Maybe he'd had something to do with it.

Toshiru was the type of man who would've done such a thing without blinking. Okuma could imagine him returning and, without meeting Okuma's eyes, admitting, "It was disgusting, so I went and destroyed the station."

"Well, you're not going to move up any further staying here. Yokohama Station's only going to keep shrinking. There's no telling how much longer the net across the strait will continue to function. Your expertise is in analyzing Suikanet. You're going to be very bored soon," Kawakami warned.

Okuma just snorted. "The intelligence division doesn't have the final say on anything, so I'm not interested in small-time advancement. No matter what kind of success we achieve, the higher-ups will attribute it to the military in the end. They're all warfare nerds, that's why. Besides, I have something else to do."

Okuma glanced at the southeast portion of the map—to the outline of the Eurasian continent's eastern coastline. Kawakami knew that many of the younger members of JR Fukuoka were interested in the "mainland" and that Okuma was gaining their support.

JR Fukuoka company rules forbade overseas travel. Last year, a few in the military division had devised an unauthorized plan to cross the ocean. The scheme had been outed, and those responsible had suffered the consequences. There were still several so-called "Continentalist" factions lurking beneath the surface, however.

The end of Yokohama Station was coming. When that first became clear, most people in JR Fukuoka proposed taking over Honshu. A minority argued the opposite, that this was an opportunity to seek new fortunes across the sea.

A researcher in the engineering division called Yokohama Station a "human cultivation apparatus." Thanks to its controlled matter and energy loop, it supported a population density that was probably higher than anywhere else on Earth. It was a standard that could not be met elsewhere now that fossil fuels had been depleted.

Once Yokohama Station collapsed entirely, the islands of Japan would be unable to support the population. Many of them would die as conditions worsened, but some of those overflowing masses would be making their way overseas.

The east Eurasian coast was left largely uninhabitable during the Winter War. However, there wasn't enough reliable data to know how much the soil had recovered in the centuries since. Rumors said that a great migration across the continent from farther inland had already begun. If the inhabitants of the Japanese islands were going to emigrate, they would need to act quickly and seize the initiative. JR Fukuoka officially disavowed the interest in the continent, though, seeing it as an abandonment of its duty to protect civilians from the corruption of Yokohama Station.

Institutional fatigue. That was how Okuma described the attitude of the company's upper echelon. They'd been fighting Yokohama Station for so long, their organization had been streamlined for a single purpose and had become incapable of seeing things from any other perspective. If Yokohama Station ever truly fell, JR Fukuoka would lose its entire reason for existing.

"People grow old and die, and so will Yokohama Station. The same can be said of our faction. But my point is, while you're alive, you ought to do the work of setting up the transition to the next generation," Okuma stated.

He dug into the bag of sugary treats and found they were all gone. Okuma excused himself and left the base. Dusk had arrived outside. The white concrete of Yokohama Station across the strait glowed red in the light of the setting sun. Even as its opponent, Okuma had to admire the glory of it.

There'd hardly been any attempts to fire over hallways in the last few years. The aging that had begun with the tumor seemed to affect the structure's outer edges as well. Even the concrete metabolism was slowing down; there were visible stains of decline here and there.

Yokohama Station's visual degradation matched the state of JR Fukuoka's own base, where the structural-genetic-field-resistant polymer was cracking and falling apart. Both sides had grown to resemble each other over the course of their long battle.

Perhaps they'll die out together, Okuma thought. In the meantime, the sun slowly sank over toward the horizon and the continent beyond it.

WINTER WAR

The name of a long and protracted war that took place between major nations at the end of the Gregorian era. It was typified by satellite weapon attacks on major cities, destroying many centers of power among the nations. The war moved human society from a citycentric network to a broader distribution across territory, where radio communication and unmanned drone transportation of goods became the norm. The Japanese government transitioned from being centered in the capital to a distributed model via the JR Integrated Intelligence. The war ended when the lack of fossil fuels made preserving satellite weaponry impossible. The name "Winter War" was coined by historians after the fact, due to a cooling of the planet that happened during this time. It has no relation to the war between the Soviet Union and Finland during the 20th century.

JR NORTH JAPAN & JR FUKUOKA

Companies that arose as a result of splitting government factions during the early periods of the Winter War. They were originally government-run businesses, but as the war lengthened, they gained increased autonomy from the nation, eventually transitioning into private businesses entrusted with government functions. The Japanese government ceased to exist during the Yokohama Station era, but these companies continued to govern in its stead. There were formerly more companies in various regions of Honshu, like JR Tohoku, JR Chubu, and JR Kinki. JR is an abbreviation for "Japan Ruler."

SUIKA

A certification method for humans active inside of Yokohama Station. A microchip embedded in the body generates a bio-hash that Suikanet reads to identify the individual. The chips are simple enough that people can manufacture them, but registering for the net requires a deposit of 500,000 milliyen. The process will also cost tens of thousands of milliyen to the cybernetics engineer. A Suika is required for any person at least six years old Inside, as well as for settling payments and gaining access to Suikanet. The name supposedly comes from the Japanese word for requesting another's identity.

CIRCUMSTANCES ABROAD

Because communications cables and the means of travel no longer exist, there is virtually no accurate information on the state of the world outside of Japan. The coastal areas of East Asia were rendered uninhabitable by the Winter War, so the Japanese islands are physically isolated. Because the workings of the structural genetic field were a JR Integrated Intelligence military secret, it is unlikely that any other self-replicating structures like Yokohama Station exist elsewhere. Because no other nations had rail networks as dense as Japan's, even if a similar structure should exist, its speed of growth would be significantly weaker.

:: CURRENCY

There is no physical currency Inside. All transactions are carried out through Suika. Because it is electronic money, there is no smallest denomination. It started out as "yen," but over a period of deflation, the current standard is "milliyen."

In areas outside of Yokohama Station, the JR companies in control issued their own currencies following the expansion of the station and fall of the Japanese government. These are abbreviated JRY as opposed to JPY and come in physical coins and bills. The currency was originally shared among JRs, similar to the euro, but with only Hokkaido and Kyushu remaining, there is no longer any exchange between them.

There are also functioning networks outside of the station, similar to the Internet, but some smaller islands do not have network capabilities. For this reason, physical currency is essential.

:: TRANSPORTATION

There is only one station and therefore no actual railway. Because the passageways Inside are tight and feature many elevation changes, there are no wheeled vehicles like automobiles or bicycles. The primary form of transportation is on foot, with the aid of moving walkways and escalators. Because power is plentiful, there are some standing-type electric two-wheeled vehicles, but they are too expensive to be widely used. Because of these limitations on movement, the economic discrepancies from area to area are large. There are rumors that a mad engineer tinkered with automated turnstiles to repurpose them as vehicles. Though, if true, no one would want to risk coming into contact with tampered station equipment.

:: SUIKANET

The network system contained inside of Yokohama Station. Suika credentials are required to use as a general rule, but some terminals offer anonymous use to anyone.

Terminals themselves are often built by people, but the underlying network is generated naturally by the structural genetic field and therefore extremely unstable by the standards of the Internet. Sent data is collected in localized Suikanet nodes as information that may be recreated in distant nodes via a majority rule process. This means that real-time communication over long distances is for the most part impossible, and so most conversations take place over electronic mail that takes time to deliver, much like physical mail.

Because a number of nodes are actually under the control of individuals or groups, however, it is possible to have low-latency communication like phone conversations along those routes. If enough nodes are controlled, the information in those communications

AFTERWORD

Since the birth of Yokohama Station in 1915, it has never been without some kind of ongoing construction for over a hundred years. Some like to call it the "Sagrada Familia of Japan," destined never to be finished.

But think about that. What does "completion" mean for Yokohama Station? Is it complete when the renovation ends?

Generally speaking, completion means "to reach the final state." Gaudi drew up detailed designs for the Sagrada Familia, and it is considered incomplete because the construction work still pursues that design.

But Yokohama Station has not been under renovation for a hundred years in the aspiration of any sort of fixed final state. On the contrary, the way that it has continuously and flexibly changed and renovated itself in response to the shifting landscape of the city of Yokohama and of Japan's rail network is, in fact, the very model of a central, urban train station. Therefore, you should consider the state of always being under construction itself to be completion.

This is similar to behavior seen in the natural world. We human beings receive a constant supply of food and oxygen from the world around us and expel substances of our own, but it is not in the pursuit of a "complete" form of our humanity. We eat every day to maintain our bodies. That flux is the finished state of a human being.

Because of this dynamic system, our bodies maintain a constant temperature rather than allowing it to change with the outside air, fight off the never-ending assault of microorganisms with our immune systems, and repair physical wounds, to an extent. Paradoxically, we maintain our structure because we are continually changing. The end of this dynamism is the death of the organism.

Ilya Prigogine (1917–2003) described the overall preservation of order through the endless flow of matter and energy as a "dissipative structure." He received a Nobel Prize for his work on this theory in 1977. His point of view had a vast effect on scientific thought. This book is a work of science fiction predicated upon that tide of opinion.

I'd like to give a brief description of how this story came about. In early 2015, I posted a theory of Yokohama Station as a living organism on Twitter, which soon evolved into a science fiction outline of a replicating Yokohama Station that covered all of Japan.

At this point, it was mainly a parody of Tsutomu Nihei's science fiction manga *Blame!*, but thanks to the many responses to my tweets, I spent half a year fleshing it out into a long-form novel. Reading it now, I can see a strong influence from Makoto Shiina's *Ad Bird*, a story I loved in middle school.

Around this time, the Kadokawa publishing company created a user-driven novel submission site called Kakuyomu. To liven things up, I submitted to their first web novel contest (science fiction category) and received the grand prize, as well as a contract to publish it as a book. I'd heard that the first winner in a newly created literary contest was critical in terms of establishing the future direction of that contest. My response to that was, "Are you sure about this, Kadokawa?"

When I revisited the material to turn into a book, I realized there was too much content for a single volume, so I sectioned off the side-story material for a second publication. It will be significantly fleshed out, and should see the light of day in 2017.

There will also be a manga adaptation of this narrative drawn by Gonbe Shinkawa and published on the online manga site *Young Ace Up*. By the time you read this afterword, it'll probably already be up there. It's typical for the comic adaptation of a book to start only after the novel has become a hit, but what better genre to embody a time paradox than science fiction?

My point is that this book has been self-replicating beyond its author's intent for quite a while. It's entirely appropriate to the theme of the story.

I will also have an all-new publication in early 2017 from Seikaisha called *Gravity Alchemic*. It's a tale about a version of Earth that expands by three percent each year, leading to an overabundance of land. If you're sick of all the concrete in this book, perhaps that one will be a breath of fresh air.

Lastly, I would like to thank Tatsuyuki Tanaka for his evocative illustrations of this bizarre world, Gonbe Shinkawa for taking on the difficult work of designing the bipedal automated turnstiles, Dr. Endo from Yokohama City University for patiently lecturing the amateur author about the fundamental nature of a structural genetic field, Dr. Haruaki Tazaki from Gakushuin University for his early support (approximately twenty-six minutes after conception) of this book, Saito #2 for his useful critiques of android mental depictions based on personal experience, Benjamin the donkey for his life advice both deep and shallow, and everyone in the Kadokawa Books editorial department for giving me this opportunity.

On an auspicious November day Inside, 2016